OTHER THINGS BEING EQUAL

Emma Wolf

EDITED WITH AN INTRODUCTION BY

BARBARA CANTALUPO

Wayne State University Press

Detroit

Manufactured in the United States of America.
06 05 04 03 02   5 4 3 2 1

ISBN 0-8143-3022-3

A catalog record for this book is available from
The Library of Congress.

⊗ The paper used in this publication meets the minimum
requirements of the American National Standard for Information
Sciences—Permanence of Paper for Printed Library Materials, ANSI
Z39.48-1984.

071702 — 2585X14.

CONTENTS

ACKNOWLEDGMENTS

Researching Emma Wolf's biography was an adventure that began at the Judah Magnes Center in Berkeley in 1992, where I found an article by Richard Tornheim on the pioneers of Contra Costa County. This proved to be the vital piece of evidence that I needed to uncover the details of Emma Wolf's life. Ruth Rafael, head archivist at the Center, put me in contact with Dr. Tornheim, who answered my queries by phone and letter, confirming that the Simon Wolf whom Dr. Tornheim had written about in his essay was, in fact, Emma Wolf's father. I am especially grateful for Dr. Tornheim's work and for his introducing me to Donald Auslen of Marin County, Emma Wolf's great-nephew, who, in turn, led me to other relatives, including Richard Auslen, Barbara Goldman Aaron, and William Lowe, all of whom I thank for sharing their memories of their great-aunt. I especially thank Barbara Aaron for giving me access to Israel Zangwill's letters to Emma Wolf, which were carefully compiled by Barbara Aaron's father, Robert L. Goldman; these became an invaluable resource. As always with this kind of work, librarians are a critical asset, and I would like to thank Jane DiBonaventura, Judy Lichtman, Dennis Phillips, and Kathleen Romig of Penn State's Lehigh Valley Campus Library; Debra Heaphy and Barbara Land of Temple Emanu-El's Library, San Francisco; Ruth Rafael, head archivist at the Judah Magnes Center, Berkeley; and Sibylle Zemitis of the California State Library, Sacramento. I am especially grateful to Neil Baldwin, Charles Cantalupo, Meri-Jane Rochelson, Anne Rose, and Jonathan Sarna for taking the time to read and comment on my manuscript and for sharing their own work and expertise. For painstaking proofing assistance, I am indebted to Loretta Yenser, Robin Bloom, my husband, Charles, and my mother, Anna Dorosh. I thank the Pennsylvania State University for providing funding for this research, especially the Roy C. Buck Research Grant from the College of Liberal Arts and Faculty Research Grants from the Allentown Campus. And last, but not least, I thank Arthur Evans, director of Wayne State University Press, for believing in this project and patiently guiding me through the process of publication.

INTRODUCTION

BIOGRAPHY

Born in San Francisco on 15 June 1865 to Simon and Annette (Levy) Wolf, immigrants from Alsace,[1] Emma Wolf was the fourth of eleven children.[2] She grew up in the upper-middle-class San Francisco neighborhood of Pacific Heights where she and her family were members of Congregation Emanu-El.[3] Her father, considered "one of the most important Jewish pioneers of [Contra Costa] county,"[4] died suddenly when Emma was thirteen, and it seems no coincidence, as editor of the *American Jewess* Rosa Sonneschein noted, that it was then that Wolf began writing: "Her literary genius developed at a tender age, which she has cultivated continuously since her thirteenth year."[5] In *My Portion (An Autobiography)* (1925), Rebekah Bettelheim Kohut describes her high school classmate and close friend:

> Another fine influence in those days was my friendship with my classmate, Emma Wolf, later a brilliant authoress noted particularly for her story, *Other Things Being Equal*. She and I used to roam the sand hills together on botany excursions. . . . Saturday afternoons and Sundays we went over the hills of Saucelito and San Rafael, yellow poppies around us, carpets of maiden-hair ferns under our feet. . . . One of eight daughters, Emma Wolf, was handicapped from birth by a useless arm, but there was no defect in her mentality. Her memory was the most remarkable I have ever encountered. She could quote

with equal facility the texts of long poems or the fatality statistics of each of the world's great battles. . . . Those walks, indeed, did a great deal to stimulate our sense of beauty.

But what meant most of all to me, perhaps, in those impressionable days of adolescence, was the exchange of innermost thoughts with my classmate. I had begun to doubt the worthwhileness of all the sacrifices it seemed to me that my father and his family were making for Judaism. What was the use of it all, I questioned. Why make a stand for separate Jewish ideals? Why not choose the easier way and be like all the rest? The struggle was too hard, too bitter.

Emma Wolf was undergoing much the same inner conflict. It meant real suffering to both of us. The spiritual growing pains of adolescence are hard to bear. They cannot be laughed out of existence. . . . And as I meditated the thorny path which the Jew traveled, it seemed to me that if the Jew could assimilate with the Christian, many of his irksome trials would be eliminated, with no spiritual loss.[6]

Rebekah, ironically, went on to immerse herself in Judaism by marrying the prominent rabbi Alexander Kohut, a widowed Hungarian émigré with eight children. As his wife, she became intimately involved in the intellectual life of American Judaism. After his death in 1894, Kohut became more active in educational and service activities, and from 1894 to 1898 served as president of the New York section of the National Council of Jewish Women.[7]

Wolf's public life, on the other hand, was restricted by polio; she never married and led a relatively insular life, especially after being confined to a wheelchair. Wolf and her sisters were educated through normal school to become teachers; her sisters did become educators, but Wolf's polio kept her from putting her education to work in that way. Instead, she wrote, and, in doing so, extended her influence beyond the home. In Wolf's obituary in the 31 August 1932 *San Francisco Chronicle*, she is described as a literary figure whose home "was the mecca of a group who looked upon her as an uplifting, far-reaching influence." Rebekah Godchaux in a letter to the editor in the *San Francisco Chronicle* (31 August 1932) describes Wolf: "Emma Wolf—the frail, modest little woman, who, through illness, hardly ever left her room[,] . . . [a] writer, a poetess, a thinker, a philosopher[,] . . . [s]he gave each and every one the rare treasures of her heart and soul. She was able to adapt herself to all—from the simplest to the most eminent—who sought her company."

During the time that Wolf was writing, women's traditional roles were being actively questioned in the press and especially in the arena of women's clubs, a movement gaining momentum in the 1890s. Women's literary clubs, in particular, were popular throughout the country and provided a forum for the study and discussion of contemporary and classical literature. As Anne Gere points out, in the late nineteenth century, these clubs were a threat to the authority of the rising professional role of English studies in the academy—

> Higginson identified literature as a site of contest between the sexes and articulated the male English professors' fear that their field faced the threat of feminization. . . . [C]lubwomen in all social locations regularly included in their reading lists women writers, often living ones. . . . Such writers as Grace Aguilar, Emma Lazarus, and Emma Wolf appeared regularly on the reading lists of Jewish women's clubs. Even though these clubwomen embraced writers sanctioned by English professors, they extended the terms of literature to include women with whom they could identify.[8]

All that is known of Wolf's involvement in the club scene is her membership in the Philomath Club, San Francisco's only Jewish women's literary club, which was concerned not only with literary discussion but with social issues as well.[9] According to Josephine Cohn's article in the 17 April 1908 issue of *Emanu-El*, the Philomath Club was organized in March 1894; its formal purpose was "to encourage literary pursuits and to promote a higher ideal of life."[10] Cohn describes the merits of the club in the following way: "The Philomath Club has proven its worth and merited its high standing among women's clubs, since not only has it been a great social feature in the community, but it has stimulated among its members originality of thought and the power of expressing it."[11] Clubwork was an important aspect of women's push to gain recognition beyond their roles in the home. As Karen Blair notes, "[l]iterary clubwomen . . . utilized the domestic and moral traits attributed to the ideal lady to increase autonomy, assert sorority, win education, and seize influence beyond the home."[12]

Since none of Wolf's letters or diaries has been uncovered to date, it remains unclear if Wolf would have made the effort or had the stamina to participate publicly in the feminist cause. In addition, as Kuzmack points out, the women's movement in the United States had had a history of prejudice against Jews that was just beginning to wane in 1890: "By 1890, the newly named National American Woman Suffrage Association still faced persistent attempts to inject antireligious elements into the NAWSA platform. However, attitudes towards Jews were becoming less hostile; even though feminist groups remained Christian-centered."[13] In response, as Deborah Golumb observes, "even the organizers of the 1893 Congress of Jewish Women . . . 'identified themselves first as Jews and only second as females' ";[14] Kuzmack confirms this view and observes that "female Jewish club-women and social service volunteers were 'feminist in a larger sense' because they 'enhanced the self-worth of women and worked on their behalf.' "[15]

Even so, Wolf's fiction engages issues that concerned feminists of her time: the rest cure, universal suffrage, motherhood, and the role of the "new woman"; however, her consideration of these issues does not fit neatly into any ideology, and her work certainly could not be read as projecting a radical feminist viewpoint. This perspective may not have appealed to Wolf because she did not face the challenges of the workplace, marriage, or motherhood herself even though her sisters faced these demands. Emma was intimately involved with their concerns, and her fictional worlds reflect her imaginative projections of her sisters' dilemmas, as her inscription in a copy of *Fulfillment* reveals: "To my dearest sister Isabel—who helps me glimpse It—Emma Wolf, San Francisco, April, 1916." Another of Wolf's sisters, Alice, author of a novel, *A House of Cards* (Chicago: Stone & Kimball, 1896), married Colonel William MacDonald, a Christian, and this family circumstance may have had a direct influence on Wolf's depiction of interfaith marriage. Another family circumstance also had an influence on Wolf's writing: her mother, widowed with nine children[16] when her youngest was an infant, never remarried.

Emma must have been acutely aware that her family's position in the community was directly linked to their economic status. The constraints, benefits, and fears of economic vulnerability in the middle class emerge in Wolf's fiction. Her female characters' self-esteem is often tied to economic circumstances. In *Fulfillment*, Gwen marries impulsively because she is unwilling to be seen as "needing to work"; in doing so, she compromises both her self-respect and the respect of others. On the other hand, in *The Joy of Life*, Nellie's self-abnegation comes from having wealth: "we rich girls, who think ourselves the salt and pivot of the world, are only its ornaments . . . and don't amount to much, after all" (199). In *The Joy of Life* through the character of Barbara Gerrish, Wolf seems to come to the pragmatic conclusion that "poverty, or even gentility, is very piquant for an experiment, but for a permanent state, give me downright, all-powerful riches" (200). *Fulfillment*, Wolf's last novel, provides an alternative to that somewhat cynical conclusion; her female characters grow beyond the social expectations that demand that "ladies" not work, that "ladies" find fulfillment in marriage. Deb, the symbol of "law and order," with practical grace, engages completely with her role as social worker, going off to Chicago to learn from Jane Addams; Gwen comes to value the independence and self-respect that a vocation provides even though she never has to act on that realization because her marriage finally turns around and she finds fulfillment in it.

In 1895, Wolf was featured in the *American Jewess*,[17] and one of her poems and a short story were also published there. San

Francisco's *Mechanics' Institute Library Bulletin* for September-October 1901 paid tribute to their native San Franciscan with a full-page picture of Wolf "specially photographed for this publication" and a three-page article that provides an overview of her novels. It begins by quoting Israel Zangwill's 1897 review in the *Jewish Chronicle*—"the work of Miss Emma Wolf stands out luminous and arrestive"—and concludes with his belief that "those who care for sincerity, dignity and human insight in literature will appreciate her work and look forward with keen interest to the further development of her undoubted genius."[18] On 4 March 1910, the editor of *Emanu-El* described Wolf as "the well known California writer, whose works, by the way, are much appreciated in the Eastern States and in England."[19] Yet throughout her literary career, Wolf remained modest, as evidenced by her responses in an interview with Helen Piper in the 3 December 1930 issue of the *San Francisco Chronicle*: "A shut-in's adventures can't possibly be exciting. . . . One sits by one's window and watches the parade. There is time to think. There is time to enjoy much that others are too busy to see."[20]

This quality of quiet observation distinguishes Wolf's prose; her descriptions draw the reader into the comfort and security that intimacy and home can provide; the interiors of place and heart are described with a distant yet passionate reverence without the distraction of sentimentality. The setting for all of Wolf's novels is California, mainly San Francisco's upper-middle-class neighborhood, Pacific Heights. As a review of Wolf's work in the 2 April 1916 *San Francisco Chronicle* confirms: "San Francisco is writ large . . . the local color is faultless" (35). Wolf's fiction brings out the romantic grandeur of San Francisco—"the golden balls topping the old gray walls of the Temple Emanuel smile ancient benediction . . . up, up the steeps, past the Fairmont's granite pile laboring to completion, [he stood] for a second with indrawn breath on lordly Nob Hill to glimpse . . . the silvery waters rounding from Gate to harbor" (*The Knot* 26). Yet Wolf's fiction does not depend on local detail for its poignancy. Rather, Wolf's acute atmospheric rendering of the scenery surrounding her characters complements and reflects their inner perceptions, interpersonal engagements, and their struggles with social conventions.

WOLF'S VIEWS ON SOCIAL ISSUES

The only resource that exists to discover Wolf's views on such social issues as anti-Semitism, suffrage, divorce, or the rest cure is her fiction. Although Wolf's characters are faced with new choices for middle-class women in the last decade of the nineteenth century, her work does not present a feminist agenda. From this, it can be deduced that Wolf empathized with the dilemma of middle-class women who had to confront the implications and personal choices involved in the emerging role of the "new woman," but she did not have a political or ideological agenda to relay as did, for example, Charlotte Perkins Gilman, Wolf's contemporary. Unlike Gilman, who confronted the challenges of divorce and mothering on a painfully intimate level, Wolf did not experience the urgency of these demands.

In the early 1890s, Charlotte Perkins Gilman was a prominent figure in the San Francisco Bay area, and Wolf would likely have been aware of Gilman's political views and her controversial stands on the rest cure and divorce. Unlike Gilman's active commitment to radical social change through lectures and pamphleteering, Wolf's commitment to social issues was less public and not at all radical. Although her fiction shows a keen awareness of the struggles of contemporary life, especially for women, it presents what would be considered today as "conventional" resolutions, except, of course, in relation to her position on interfaith marriage.

Interfaith Marriage

Two of Wolf's novels, *Other Things Being Equal* and *Heirs of Yesterday* (1900) are set in San Francisco's middle-class Jewish community. Daniel Levy, cantor of San Francisco's Temple

Emanu-El and a prominent educator, describes the character of this community in a letter dated 20 June 1858: "Instead of social chaos . . . [you] would find a thousand Jewish families . . . linked by bonds of neighborliness and friendship . . . the influence of family feeling has restrained the former passionate fervor and led men back to the true path in which human society should move: . . . family life."[21] This environment, this class and these values were part of Wolf's legacy, and they found their way into her characters' lives as well. But as the century neared its end, social pressures challenging traditional roles, especially for women, and the reality of intermarriage often conflicted with the picture of traditional Jewish family life presented by Levy, and these conflicts became a prominent concern in Wolf's fiction.

Heirs of Yesterday and *Other Things Being Equal* directly engage the cultural separation between Christian and Jewish communities in the United States. They also depict the value of family cohesiveness and the important role women play in the family.[22] According to Kuzmack, these values were "vital to the Jewish family, which was perceived as the key to Jewish survival."[23] Wolf's work looks at the conflicts that surround these values, and even though her female characters often exhibit an independent sense of self, they always maintain their responsibility to family as most important even when the conflict between personal satisfaction and family obligations emerges. Though Wolf's fiction would not be considered radical in light of the feminist movement of her time, her first novel, *Other Things Being Equal*, published in 1892, did take a controversial stand on another social issue: interfaith marriage.

The main characters in *Other Things Being Equal* may have been modeled after Alice Wolf and William MacDonald; Emma would have been intimately aware of the implications of the courtship and eventual marriage of her sister Alice to a Protestant.[24] In Wolf's novel, Ruth falls in love with a Unitarian, making her dilemma and its resolution less traumatic than if she had fallen in love, for example, with a Catholic.[25] Nevertheless, to validate love above religious proscription in 1892 was a decisive risk,[26] especially when Wolf's fictional account effectively seduces the reader into empathizing with the intensity and emotional integrity of the main characters' relationship. Nevertheless, the novel's ending suggests that their struggle for acceptance has not been totally resolved and that the social complications associated with intermarriage would be imminent.

At the time Wolf wrote her novel the concern over intermarriage was growing.[27] In fact, in some parts of the United States, the incidence of intermarriage was seen as a threat to sustaining Jewish culture; yet in other parts of the country, intermarriage was so infrequent that it had negligible effect. As Anne Rose points out, "reasonable estimates of rates of interfaith marriages were nearly impossible to obtain" (50) in the nineteenth century. However, she notes, the heated debate regarding its implications had been documented as early as the 1840s.

> Sustained discussion of interfaith marriage in America began in the 1840s. It coincided with the growth of immigration, institutions, and channels of public expression among Catholics and Jews. . . . There was little agreement, most basically, on how commonplace mixed marriage was. The first sustained Jewish periodical, the *Occident*, reported in 1845 that "many of our people intermarry"; in 1866, it called the practice "epidemic." The editor of the *Israelite* judged the subject "useless" in 1880, however, because such couples were "exceedingly few." (49–50)

Although no consistent policy or practice regarding intermarriage between Jews and gentiles existed in the United States in the nineteenth century, the problem of intermarriage for Jews raised significant dilemmas because of matrilineal descent, not only on a theoretical level but on a very practical level, as well. As Paul Spickard explains, "Before Jewish law, children of Jewish mothers and Gentile fathers were Jews; offspring of the inverse combination were Gentiles. This rule of the womb dates from Talmudic times, though the reasons for its existence are obscure."[28]

Rose discusses an 1890 essay in the *Israelite*—"Who Is a Jew?"—written by Bernhard Felsenthal, a Reform rabbi, as an example of a liberal view toward intermarriage: "despite rejection of mixed marriages by *halakhah*, the body of Jewish law, bonds contracted 'in accordance with the laws of the state' [Felsenthal concludes] should be accounted 'perfectly valid by Jewish rabbis and congregations' "(57). Isaac Mayer Wise, one of the most prominent Reform rabbis in the nineteenth century and editor of the *Israelite*, according to Rose,

> waffled over the years [regarding the implications of intermarriage]. Many queries around 1880 provoked him to say that "where the mother confers any right on her offspring, the father certainly does in preference to her, if he acknowledges fathership." Yet in 1899, at the end of his life, Wise argued so strongly for the talmudic basis of the maternal line, "irrespective of its father's race or faith," that he seemed by omission to reject patrilineal descent. (58)

The discussion of the impact of intermarriage on the Jewish community in the United States reached a formal public consensus in 1909 at the Central Conference of American Rabbis. Here the Reform movement passed the first resolution against interfaith marriage. "[T]heir attention focused more closely on the tension between duty and freedom. The assembly rejected a text specifying 'that a rabbi ought not to officiate at the marriage between a Jew or Jewess and a person professing a religion other than Judaism.' Respect for individual conscience led to softened wording: intermarriage should 'be discouraged by the American Rabbinate.' "[29] This may help explain why Wolf, in the foreword to the seventh edition of *Other Things Being Equal* in 1916, chose to explain her decision to write about intermarriage:

> In presenting this revised edition to a new generation, the author feels that the element of change has touched very lightly the romantic potentialities obtaining at the time of the original writing, and which still obtain. Christian youth still

chances upon Jewish youth, with the same difference of historic background, the same social barriers and prejudices—the same possibilities of mutual attraction. The humanest love knows no sect.

Anti-Semitism

Wolf's two novels that depict the middle-class San Francisco Jewish community look directly at the problem of anti-Semitism. They provide an intimate picture of the personal struggles that ground social and political perceptions and choices. In this regard, *Heirs of Yesterday* shows the reasons for as well as the pain and foolhardiness of denying one's heritage, while *Other Things Being Equal* provides an intimate look at the complications caused by cultural differences at the same time that it ultimately questions the force these differences can apply, "other things being equal."

The extent of anti-Semitism in nineteenth-century America has been a controversial issue for historians, according to Hasia Diner's *A Time of Gathering* (1992). She suggests that no consensus existed in the nineteenth century and none has been reached by contemporary scholars and historians.

American Jews heard contradictory voices around them and could not decide whether America really differed from other countries or if it represented a kind of promised land[;] . . . [s]cholars [too] have been split between those who emphasize the existence of a vibrant anti-Semitic culture in America and those who argued that anti-Semitism hovered only on the margins of society . . . some historians noted that in America, Jews encountered little overt hostility and they listed the leveling impact of the frontier[;] . . . [o]thers have pointed to scurrilous rhetoric in fiction and journalism, on the stage and in songs, rhetoric that could be heard from the pulpit and, occasionally, from the politician's stump.[30]

Nevertheless, Diner acknowledges quite clearly that "[a]nti-Semitism surely existed in nineteenth-century America . . . [p]robably no issue loomed larger than the inherent incompatibility between the notion of America as a religiously tolerant and diverse society, and a deep American commitment to evangelical Protestantism."[31]

Naomi Cohen situates this prejudice quite definitely in the last decade of the nineteenth century, precisely when Wolf's novel appeared.[32] Leonard Dinnerstein confirms this, as well: "During the 1890's anti-Semitic sentiments visible earlier crystallized, intensified, and evolved. . . . There was hardly a major city in the United States where [anti-Semitism] could not be found . . . yet San Francisco's Jewish population generally fared better in terms of acceptance than coreligionists elsewhere in the country."[33] The conclusion of the *Chicago Tribune*'s 1892 review of *Other Things Being Equal* implicitly reveals the reality of these social circumstances: "We welcome this book as a message of peace and good will. . . . Racial and national rivalries, jealousies, misunderstandings, prejudices—there is nothing more fatal than these to the peace and the progress of mankind" (30).

The Rest Cure

Wolf's novels point out the failings of cultural norms that would see women as weak, petty, and dependent; nevertheless, unlike Charlotte Perkins Gilman's "The Yellow Wallpaper," which presents the rest cure as an oppressive, destructive tool of patriarchy, *Other Things Being Equal* and *Fulfillment* portray the rest cure as an effective method of relieving emotional exhaustion. Because of the prominence of "The Yellow Wallpaper" in literary studies, when the rest cure is mentioned today, the common response is to identify it as a late nineteenth-century medical practice that oppressed women. Yet, according to Wolf's fictional representations, the rest cure could be seen as a way to provide a legitimate "time away" from social and familial obligations, giving the patient the chance to recoup her emotional and physical strength, often strained by overexertion or continuous stress over "presenting herself" to the public.

Susan Poirier's essay published in *Women's Studies* in 1983 corroborates this idea. She points out that many women in the late nineteenth century sought such treatment on their own and were relieved to get it: "the use of rest *per se* for overworked women is sensible, and sensitive compared to those physicians who could see nothing demanding or demoralizing about 'woman's work.' To many of those women for whom Mitchell prescribed rest, with whom he sympathized, and to whom he listened, Dr. Weir Mitchell must have been a balm and a reassurance. Former female patients flooded his mails with letters of praise and admiration."[34] The popularity of the rest cure in the late nineteenth century, thus, was not solely a result of husbands forcing their wives to "take the cure" in order to rid them of undesirable characteristics and restore the more "admirable" attributes of acquiescence and passivity. Poirier also points out that "there can be no doubt that Mitchell did help countless women and that, however sexist his theories, he moved medicine one step nearer to recognizing the power of one's psychological existence."[35]

Wolf's portrayal of the rest cure counters Charlotte Perkins Gilman's in "The Yellow Wallpaper," written in 1890 and first published in January 1892, ten months before *Other Things Being Equal* appeared in print. Gilman was living in the San Francisco Bay Area at the time, having moved to Oakland in September 1891, and was a prominent figure in the intellectual community. She began an active career of public lectures and, as Larry Ceplair points out, Gilman "met most of the literary and intellectual notables who lived in or visited the Bay Area."[36] Emma Wolf, therefore, must have been aware of Gilman's views. Wolf's novel offers an alternative to the Dr. Weir Mitchell figure of "The Yellow Wallpaper" with the character of Dr. Herbert Kemp and provides a benign, if not altogether positive, picture of the effects of the rest cure itself. Overall, the novel engages the discussion of women's changing roles (as does much of Wolf's fiction) while offering an alternative to the denunciation of the

rest cure, marriage, family, and home. Wolf's fiction neither de-
nies women's individual potential and strength nor suggests that
marriage and the domestic sphere are implicitly imprisoning.

OVERVIEW OF WOLF'S FICTION

Emma Wolf published five novels, a novella, poetry, and numerous short stories from 1892 to 1916. Because of polio and her
unassuming personality, Wolf did not pursue the literary lime-
light as she might have. Nevertheless, Wolf had an active and
successful publishing career, with her novels accepted by presti-
gious publishers of her time: A. C. McClurg, Henry Holt, and
Harper and Brothers.[37] Her novella, "The Knot," was the feature
story in the August 1909 issue of the *Smart Set,* a New York
journal that published F. Scott Fitzgerald, Frank Harris, Dorothy
Parker, W. Somerset Maugham, and Theodore Dreiser, among
others, and whose reviewer for many years was H. L. Mencken.
Nine of Wolf's short stories appeared in the *Smart Set* between
March 1892 and June 1911,[38] and one was published in the
American Jewess.
  These short stories could be considered an equivalent of "popular romance." The main characters are mostly women who
struggle with their desires—for a more romantic life than marriage to a "steady" man seems to provide ("The Conflict" and
"A Still Small Voice"), for a life independent of marriage ("The
Courting of Drusilla West" and "A Study in Suggestion"), for a
new marriage after divorce ("Tryst"). Others describe the deter-
mination of an "illegitimate" child to find his unknown father
("The End of the Story") and the feelings of abandonment that
divorce brings to children ("The Father of Her Children"). All
written from 1900 to 1920, they engage issues that "modern" life
opened up for scrutiny: divorce, adultery, the romantic life of the
artist, "the new woman." An exception to this characterization
is an earlier short story published in 1896 in the *American Jewess,*
"One-Eye, Two-Eye, Three-Eye." The tone of this parable-like

story borders on cynicism, treating the married state paradigma-
tically based on three different "types" of women and their
choices regarding marriage. Of the three sisters involved, represented by the names in the title, the third, "Three-eye" called
the "Cross One," ends up crying herself to sleep in her "maiden-
bed" even though throughout the story, her criticism of her two
sisters—one who married for convenience and money, the other
for love—appears apt and convincing.

Overall, Wolf's fiction embraces three major concerns: problems associated with Jewish American identity, implications of
conventional morality especially in relation to women's roles,
and the constraints of middle-class status especially for women.
All of these evolve from and revolve around the question of marriage. Complicating these themes is Wolf's perception of love,
"the mantle of Elijah" (from her poem, "Eschscholtzia")[39]—its
consuming intensity, its irrefutable force, its indiscriminate nature, its grace, and, most of all, the belief that it happens only
once in a lifetime. This last aspect transforms the lives of many
of her characters, leaving them victims of loneliness as a result
of unrequited love or, as in her last novel, showing them the
vanity of believing in such a sentimental ideal.

Constance, a dedicated "mother" to her five younger sisters in
Wolf's second novel, A Prodigal in Love (1894), forces her own
love underground to save her sister's moral standing in the community. Constance sacrifices her own hopes for happiness by in-
sisting that the man she loves (and who loves her) marry her
sister because of Eleanor's apparent impropriety, though none
had taken place. When the novel begins, Constance is twenty-
six, Eleanor, twenty-one. Six years earlier their father had killed
himself over what had appeared to be a sudden but severe economic loss, and their mother died of illness soon thereafter, leaving Constance in charge of the family. The plot centers on the
differences between the two oldest sisters—Eleanor, a fiery, impulsive, dark-haired, young woman and Constance, the pale,
blond, maternal sister, "built in the large, easy lines of the great
goddess—round, full bust, and curves of quiet strength" (11)—
and their love for Kenyon, a rich, aspiring novelist.

In Wolf's third novel, *The Joy of Life* (1896), the main character, Barbara Gerrish, a college-educated woman, rejects the love
of one man for the romantic memory of his dead brother. Unlike
Constance, who sees her primary role as maternal, Barbara Gerrish is, in many respects, a "new woman" though she says she
hates the term: "of all the tawdry, run-to heel phrases that strikes
me the most disagreeably" (121). Gerrish maintains that no
woman should be denied the right to vote based on her sex if she
were qualified to vote, yet she does not believe in universal suffrage: "there are as many women as capable of casting an intelligent vote as there are men incapable of doing so" (120). She
believes that motherhood and only certain kinds of work can go
hand in hand—"You can't be a mother and a President, but you
might be a mother and a school-director" (120)—while she acknowledges and supports women who are "desirous and capable
of extending their influence beyond their homes" (121).

   Heirs of Yesterday (1900), Wolf's fourth novel, returns to a Jewish family setting. The novel's main character, Jean, falls in love
with Philip May, who had gone east to Harvard and Europe for
his education and while there chooses to "pass" as a Christian.
When he returns home, he is faced with the many conflicts that
such deception unfolds; this becomes especially problematic
when Philip finds himself attracted to Jean, who, in turn, feels
an attraction to him. Jean, however, chooses to reject Philip's
overtures because of his decision to deny his Jewish heritage. The
conclusion of the novel brings the two together by chance, and
in this meeting, we see how Jean and Philip resolve this long-
standing conflict.

   Fulfillment: A California Novel (1916) is a love story based on
what the reviewer in the 16 April 1916 *San Francisco Chronicle*
describes as "a very old problem. A young girl gives her heart to
a . . . man, only to have the declaration of her love followed by
the confession that he is a married man and a father" (35). The
Overland Monthly describes *Fulfillment* as an "atmospheric novel.
Love is the main force in it, whether it be that of the sisters for
each other, the reckless passion of the radical dramatist, the long
devotion of the husband, or his mother's love that made him

what he was. Beauty, whether it be that of the heroine herself, or of her maternal love, or of her California surroundings, figures constantly" (5 May 1916, ix).

OTHER THINGS BEING EQUAL

The plot of Other Things Being Equal, revolves around Ruth Levice, who falls in love with Dr. Herbert Kemp, the physician called in by Ruth's father to administer the rest cure to his wife, who has suffered a spell of hysteria. Ruth is an atypical upper-middle-class, young Jewish woman whose educational and emotional upbringing had been primarily her father's task. Ruth's cousin, Mrs. Lewis, openly criticizes Ruth's introduction to the social scene at the too-late age of twenty-one, saying that "the very idea of it is contrary to nature," and criticizes Ruth for her open acceptance of Christians. Strongly influenced by her father's intellectually liberal views that run counter to the ones accepted by her cousins and, in their eyes, counter to those of the rest of the Jewish community, Ruth confronts her cousin's belief that Christians and Jews can never be social equals: " 'I have always been led to believe that every broad-minded man of whatever sect will recognize and honor the same quality in any other man. And why should I not move on an equality with my Christian friends? We have had the same schooling, speak the same language, read the same books, are surrounded by the same elements of home refinement.' " Her cousin, however, remains skeptical: " 'Their ways are not my ways; and what good can you expect from such association?' "

Wolf further challenges these boundaries by having Ruth fall in love with Dr. Kemp, a Unitarian, and not with the brotherly figure of her cousin Louis Arnold, a wry, contentious, yet conscientious and honorable man who loves her and asks for her hand in marriage. Ruth refuses Louis because she is in love with Kemp, and, out of respect for her father, refuses Kemp's proposal as well. Ruth silently suffers this loss because she chooses to honor her father's strong belief that intermarriage is wrong although she argues openly and, in her mind, convincingly, against his premises. Nevertheless, because she values her father's loving devotion and familial values, she concedes to his unwillingness to bless their proposed marriage.

In the development of Ruth and Herbert Kemp's relationship, Kemp's strong personality traits emerge and can be seen, not only as what attracts Ruth, but as those attributes necessary for successful administration of the rest cure. Ruth's father describes Dr. Kemp to Ruth as "a man of great dignity, inspiring confidence in every one," and warns her not to "lose your head when you talk to him." Nevertheless, upon first meeting Dr. Kemp, Ruth observes that "strength and gentleness spoke in every line [of his face]," and, in fact, is quite taken by Kemp's commanding presence, forceful persuasion, and directive demeanor. Wolf's portrayal of Kemp counters Gilman's portrayal of the doctor who treats his patient like a child; Kemp's respect for women's strength is distinctly voiced when he assures Mr. Levice that his wife "is not a child," even as Levice tries to protect her from accepting her own illness. Again, when Kemp turns over the responsibility of the daily administration of her mother's rest cure to Ruth, he affirms Ruth's ability to take on the authoritative role that such a task demands.

Wolf, possibly in response to Gilman's critique of this medical practice, uses cousin Louis to voice skepticism about the effects of the rest cure on a woman's self-image. Louis confronts Ruth with how easily his aunt "submit[ted] to this confining treatment" and cynically suggests that women seem to "delight" in "giving in to the magnetic power of a strong man." His sarcastic tone leads to an argument, during which Ruth corrects Louis and points out a subtle distinction: "it is the power, not the giving in that we delight in, counting it a necessary part of manliness."

This "necessary part of manliness," rather than needing to be squelched in order to allow women's independence, becomes desirable for a strong woman like Ruth, whose upbringing has confirmed her own intellectual and emotional strength rather than reinforcing traits stereotypically attributed to a "weak" woman like her mother, who is characterized by her father as "never [having] known anxiety or worry." Mr. Levice has raised a daughter who can handle anxiety and worry, who has the intellectual strength to grapple with difficult and demanding problems, and who has been taught the value of perseverance: "one of her earliest lessons was 'Whatever you do, do thoroughly.' " Ruth's father has also taught her, if inadvertently, to respect a powerful man, but not to become weak in relation to that power.

Ruth is dramatically unlike her mother, whose primary concerns are her appearance and social acceptance, bringing to mind Jane Austen's Elizabeth and Mrs. Bennet. Ruth enters into society, as she is expected to do, but is not overwhelmed by the demands of its daily performances; she is reserved and respectful but does not gauge her every word or movement on the approval of others, as does her mother. It is precisely these demands along with the overprotection of her husband and the leisure that wealth affords that lead to Esther's exhaustion and eventual bout of "hysteria." As Mary Wollstonecraft observed nearly a century earlier, when women have no "serious employment to silence their feelings; a round of little cares, or vain pursuits fritter away all strength of mind and organs[;] they become naturally only objects of sense . . . trifling employments have rendered woman a trifler."[40]

Although Esther Levice may fit Wollstonecraft's universal description of women made ignorant by social expectations, Ruth does not. Ruth is neither the product of such socialization nor a "new woman," but someone whose devotion to family does not prevent her from taking risks and whose respect for learning allows her a wider perspective than social conventions would condone. In contrast to Louis's relationship to Ruth, which suggests an egalitarian friendship but, which, in practice, puts Louis in the traditional role of "man as protector," Herbert Kemp's relationship to Ruth, though seeming to position him as Ruth's superior because of his professional role, in practice, gives her the opportunity for independent action and risk-taking relationships outside the home.

In an important event in the novel, Ruth risks social censure to support a young woman of "questionable character" who is referred to her by Dr. Kemp. Ruth's father sanctions his daughter's actions (even though Ruth chose to act independently, without consulting either her father or mother) and Ruth's decision to adhere to her beliefs. He chastises his family members for their destructive gossip about Ruth's activity. Later in the novel, when the issue of intermarriage tests similar social parameters, Mr. Levice's first response is to hold to conventional wisdom and reject Ruth's request for his approval of her engagement to Kemp. On his deathbed, however, Levice overturns this decision and concludes that "character and circumstance are not altogether of our own making . . . only God can weigh such circumstantial evidence, . . . final judgment is reserved for a higher court."

Prior to his epiphany, Mr. Levice had refused his blessing for their proposed marriage because he felt he must be "strong enough to uphold a vanishing restriction," but he finally realizes that his refusal to bless his daughter's engagement had been selfish and foolish: "I stood convicted; I was in the position of a blind fool who, with a beautiful picture before him, fastens his critical, condemning gaze upon a rusting nail in the wall behind,—a nail even now loosened, and which in another generation will be displaced." Whether that nail has become completely rusted and replaced is an unresolved question even a century later. Wolf's courage as a writer comes from presenting these dilemmas openly and resolving them in a radical fashion relatively early in the history of American Judaism.[41]

Other Things Being Equal presents a portrait of a young woman raised to assert her own beliefs and act on her own judgment, yet one who respects the wisdom of her elders and the bonds of Jewish family tradition. As Jonathan Sarna has suggested, Wolf's naming her main character Ruth seems to resonate with the biblical Ruth, whose devotion to her mother-in-law is exemplary. *The Jerusalem Bible* suggests that "the main purpose of the [Book of Ruth] is to show, 2:12, how trust in God is rewarded and how God's goodness is not constricted by frontiers. That a woman of Moab should be privileged to become the great-grandmother of

David gives a particular value to this narrative."[42] Most emphatically, Wolf's novel questions religious and social practices that artificially separate people who come to love each other despite their differences while, at the same time, she gives voice to what Kuzmack describes as "Jewish women [who] attempted to strike a balance between their desire for emancipation and reverence for Jewish tradition, their hope for acculturation and fear of anti-semitism."[43] Wolf's fiction incorporates a respect for domestic and moral values,[44] but these values do not become restrictions that limit her female characters but rather vehicles to procure for them the kind of happiness that Winifred Harper Cooley invokes in her 1904 collection of essays, The New Womanhood: "There is a growing need for intellectual experiences, for travel, for divers means of development, the gratification of which is more satisfying even to the intensely feminine nature than men might believe. Blessed is she who finds these pleasures, and the elements of all joy, in life with a congenial and soul-satisfying husband."[45]

Marriage to an intellectual equal is valued in Wolf's fiction more than the single life of the "new woman," whom she also portrays with sympathy in her other fiction while investigating the limits of such independence.[46] Wolf's theme in Other Things Being Equal speaks clearly: when two people are drawn together—"other things being equal"—neither religion nor social tradition should separate them. However, Wolf's struggle with the implications of assimilation and intermarriage are not resolved in this novel, and the social complications of intermarriage are intimated in its conclusion.

Wolf's vision engages these complications directly, not only in her novels of Jewish life, but in the problems her other female characters experience as well. As her writing matured, the resolutions to these problems became more enigmatic. In a letter to Wolf, the Anglo-Jewish writer Israel Zangwill expresses his fear that the inconclusive ending of Heirs of Yesterday could be a problem: "Your end seems to emulate Charlotte Brönte's Villette with an even greater uncertainty. I don't know if it is a good plan" (12 December 1900). But rather than being a weakness,

this ambiguity reveals a more incisive examination of the problems of "modernity" and its implications for women's roles. Wolf's sustaining belief that "love conquers all" seems to override even the most difficult convolutions, making way for the possibility of human happiness within the constraints of law.

RECEPTION AND INFLUENCE OF *OTHER THINGS BEING EQUAL*

Other Things Being Equal was Emma Wolf's first novel, published in 1892 when she was twenty-seven by Chicago's A. C. McClurg.[47] The novel was reissued six times—1893, 1894, 1895, 1898, 1901—and a revised version published in 1916—its popularity sustained by its controversial stand on intermarriage between Jews and gentiles during a time when the subject was undergoing a heated debate. The novel's intimate depiction of middle-class Jewish family life in the Pacific Heights area of San Francisco was also a draw.[48] The 1916 "revised" edition is the version presented here not only because it is Wolf's "final word" but because it reflects her matured writing style. Wolf's "Foreword" to this edition plainly states that she chose not to make significant changes in the content of the original novel; she maintains her position on intermarriage and the value of family bonds, especially respect for parental authority and wisdom:

> The humanest love knows no sect. Only in one respect has the face of youth altered—to wit, in the ignoring of the Fifth Commandment. . . . Today [we have] the dominance of the individualistic creed with its substituted 'Honor Thy Self'[;] . . . with the passing of that older order, has there not passed a beauty from the world? It is the story of that beauty which the author, in this revised edition, for a new generation, has not cared to revise.

Wolf did, however, make significant stylistic revisions. These revisions not only demonstrate her maturity as a writer but reflect a decision to enhance the main character's strength in relation to her male counterpart, possibly pointing to Wolf's

increasing interest in the issues of the women's movement during the twenty-four years between the novel's first publication and its final edition in 1916. This change might be attributed, partly, to her friendship with Rebekah Kohut, whose paper was read at the 1893 Jewish Women's Congress in Chicago,[49] a turning point in American Jewish feminism, and Wolf's epistolary relationship with Israel Zangwill. Though none of Wolf's notes or letters have been uncovered to date, the extant letters from Israel Zangwill to Emma Wolf[50] suggest an ongoing literary relationship between the two and imply shared interests and respect.[51] Wolf admired Zangwill's work and looked to him for advice;[52] she would have known of his public support of feminism and his wife's involvement in the British suffragette movement.[53]

Zangwill's *Children of the Ghetto*, coincidentally, was also published in 1892, and, according to Meri-Jane Rochelson, it "created a sensation on two continents and established its author as the preeminent literary voice of Anglo-Jewry."[54] Both Wolf's novel and Zangwill's attracted a large readership even though both reveal aspects of Jewish culture that would have made many Jewish readers uncomfortable: Wolf's support of intermarriage and Zangwill's depiction of "intracommunal conflicts that many in the contemporary Jewish community considered a private matter."[55] Zangwill's 1908 play *The Melting Pot* also confirms the mutuality of Wolf's and Zangwill's philosophical and personal viewpoints, especially since Zangwill himself chose an interfaith marriage in 1903.[56]

Zangwill began his correspondence with Wolf on 2 December 1896, in response to Wolf's sending him her second novel, *The Joy of Life*, which he liked and later reviewed in the *Jewish Chronicle*.[57] Zangwill's eventual marriage to Edith Ayrton, a Christian, may have further enhanced Zangwill's attraction to Wolf's work, especially *Other Things Being Equal*, which, in his first letter to Wolf, he says he had heard of: "I had already heard of you—but vaguely—through your previous book on the inter-marriage problem." In this same letter, he compliments Wolf's writing:

> I am very glad you did send me your book [*The Joy of Life*] for it enabled me to become aware of surely the most promising

ISRAEL ZANGWILL
(courtesy of Barbara Goldman Aaron)

Jewish writer of the younger generation. I am so accustomed
to getting bad books sent me that it was an added pleasure to
find a gift one could be sincerely grateful for. I have only read
half the book because it was snatched from me by my friend
Mr. Schecter (of whom you may have heard)[58] but both he
and his wife agree with me that your work is strong and finely
reticent. . . . Certainly you are the best product of American
Judaism since Emma Lazarus.

Zangwill confirmed this sentiment in his 5 February 1897 review in the London-based *Jewish Chronicle*:

The Jewesses of America are bestirring themselves nowadays. . . . They have already beaten us in poetry, for not even

Amy Levy's output outweighs the work of Emma Lazarus. . . .
The appearance of Emma Wolf turns the scale decidedly in
favour of the States. . . . For in Emma Wolf, of San Francisco,
a novelist has arisen whose career must henceforth be followed
with loving interest by all of us who care for letters . . . it
remains undeniable that for thoughtfulness, grasp of character, brief, incisive handling and clever dialogue, the work of
Miss Emma Wolf stands out luminous and arrestive amid the
thousand-and-one tales of our over-productive generation.[59]

In the United States, Wolf's novels received no negative reviews; all praised her work for its style and content. *Other Things
Being Equal* received acclaim from Boston's *Literary World:* "The
picture of Jewish life and feeling is very attractive; but the charm
of the book lies in the clever delineation of widely differing per-
sonalities. . . . The story is strong and well written, and holds the
reader's sympathetic interest from the first page to the last.[60] The
review in Philadelphia's *Public Ledger* was positive: "The struggle
between orthodox ideas of marriage within racial lines,[61] and the
charming love story which is so complicated, is as powerful an
incident as anything in modern novel-writing. This is a story
well worth Gentile reading, and every Hebrew will find not only
much that is true, but matter of pride in it."[62] Wolf's novel was
one of three reviewed in the weekly *Chicago Tribune* column,
"Today's Literature," of 15 October 1892; the reviewer considers
the novel "a sign of the times."

It has a serious and beautiful purpose: . . . a freer intercourse
and a better understanding between Jews and Christians. . . .
Racial and national rivalries, jealousies, misunderstandings,
prejudices—there is nothing more fatal than these to the
peace and the progress of mankind. Humanity must be a unit,
society must become a single harmonious organism, before the
pressure of the struggle for existence can be appreciably light-
ened . . . we welcome this book as a message of peace and good
will.

There is another aspect in which the book is remarkable. It

is the work of a woman. . . . It is much that a woman should have written a book with tendencies such as we have described; it is still more significant that the woman in question is a Jewess. Verily, the strongholds of custom and prejudice are crumbling fast! (13)

The novel was also favorably reviewed in the *American Jewess* and the *Boston Post*. Acknowledging that "no criticism would be complete without fault-finding,"[63] in his review Zangwill criticizes Wolf's *The Joy of Life* (his favorite work), but only on a minor point; other reviews, in the obligatory negative part of their appraisal, generally concur with the conclusion of the *Mechanics' Institute Library Bulletin*'s review: "There is nothing to be gained by asserting that these books prove Miss Emma Wolf to be one of the world's great novelists."[64]

Rudolf Glanz's *The Jewish Woman in America* groups Emma Wolf with writers like Annie Nathan Meyer and Mary Antin whose "fiction publications [were] outside of the Jewish press group" and briefly notes that Wolf's *Other Things Being Equal* treats intermarriage "in a more serious vein than [fiction] by men who only described what they saw superficially."[65] A review of *Heirs of Yesterday* on the first page of the 14 December 1900 *Jewish Messenger* reiterates this sentiment: "[Wolf] is to be expressly omitted from the category of Jewish novelists who exploit their religion and special class of people and call the result literature. . . . Her delicacy, spirituality, intellectuality are not restricted to Jewish subjects."

Louis Harap's chapter, "Early American Jewish Novels," in *The Image of the Jew in American Literature* notes the emergence of American Jewish novelists in the 1890s, especially in New York and San Francisco, and describes Emma Wolf as "a gentle, intelligent, dignified, strong-minded, but rather genteel young Jewish woman brought up in a middle-class Jewish family."[66] Harap begins this chapter by reviewing both of Wolf's novels that deal with Jewish characters and criticizes Wolf, who, he argues, like the main character, Ruth, in *Other Things Being Equal*, has "to some extent and quite unconsciously, become insensitive" to the effects of stereotyping; Harap makes this judgment by asserting that "it becomes clear that in the end [of the novel] . . . Ruth expresses the author's views."[67] Harap, however, modulates this criticism by stating that he believes "there is no doubt of [Ruth's] wholehearted acceptance of her Jewish identity,"[68] implying, thereby, that Wolf's Reform Judaism, "all things being equal," could be Jewish enough.[69] Harap acknowledges that *Heirs of Yesterday* makes "a frontal attack" on "the new, more intense quality of anti-Semitism in the United States."[70] He describes Wolf as a "competent, though minor writer," but when he introduces the work of Jewish writers of the Midwest he affirms her talent: "The 1890s yielded other novelists of American Jewish fiction less talented than Emma Wolf."[71]

Diane Lichtenstein in *Writing Their Nations: The Tradition of Nineteenth-Century American Jewish Women Writers* positions Wolf's work as integral to a tradition of American Jewish women writers. In an earlier article in *Studies in American Jewish Literature*, Lichtenstein uses Wolf's novels to contextualize Fannie Hurst's work, placing Wolf's stance in between what Lichtenstein describes as the fairy-tale idealism of her predecessor Rebekah Hyneman (1812–1875), who "wrote almost exclusively about Jewish subjects in her poetry and fiction of the 1850s and 1860s,"[72] and Hurst's 1920s realistic ambivalence. Although Lichtenstein argues that *Other Things Being Equal* presents a "modified fairy-tale ending" to the problem of intermarriage, she points out that Wolf's novels provide an astute picture of the problems of assimilation and "reveal how ideals of Jewish womanhood and questions about assimilation have changed from 1860 to 1960." Lichtenstein sees Wolf as assimilated into American culture and suggests that her novels argue that "Jews could live among non-Jewish Americans, and even marry them . . . if they did not try to 'pass' or deny their Jewish identities" and that assimilation through intermarriage is possible since "love resolves all differences."[73] Lichtenstein also notes that Wolf's work tackles problems associated with changes in the expectations of women's roles and suggests that Wolf's female characters seem able to maintain the traditional values of Jewish family life even as they untangle the emotional struggles of what it means to be a "new woman."

Anne Rose's *Beloved Strangers* (2001) begins a discussion of Wolf's novel by noting that "her novel was unprecedented in American fiction in rendering the sensuality that contested religious proscriptions" (70). Ruth, Rose argues, is portrayed as "a woman with liberal attitudes of uncertain limits and intelligence without outlet" (72) and is attracted to Kemp because he offers Ruth a life beyond the superficiality of upper-middle-class social rituals: "Ruth is attracted to Kemp because he gives her something to do. She visits his patients—a poor, crippled boy and a girl pregnant out of wedlock—to lend them moral support" (71). Wolf's portrayal of Ruth's cousin's perception that such "charity work" was not an appropriate "occupation" for young Jewish women, ironically, coincides with the beginning of Jewish women's benevolence activity, which, Rose points out, "took off in the 1890s. The National Council of Jewish Women began, for example, in 1893" (71). The Sisterhoods of Service, begun at Temple Emanu-El in New York City in 1887, expanded nationally so that in 1896 a Federation of Sisterhoods was established.[74] Wolf's novel, then, according to Rose, not only promotes the value of middle-class women's participation in socially conscious activities outside the home but shows that such activity was still considered by many as questionable or potentially dangerous to delicate sensibilities. Ruth's strong character and proactive decision making also reflect a change in attitude toward women as a whole within the Jewish community, reflected by the Central Conference of American Rabbis' 1892 decision to "recognize women's equality in the synagogue" (70). Overall, Rose concludes, "*Other Things Being Equal* was a commentary on the times" (71), exploring the many changes that Jewish middle-class women were confronting at the end of the century.

Such criticism demonstrates that *Other Things Being Equal*, though presenting what radical feminists, now and then, would consider a relatively conservative point of view, nonetheless pictures quite astutely the newfound social and personal complications that middle-class women at the end of the nineteenth century were forced to confront. Wolf's stand on interfaith marriage, then and now, challenges the collective belief of the American Jewish community. The novel's force lies in its unwillingness to adhere to ideological stands. In the late nineteenth and early twentieth centuries, Wolf's novel would not have been popular to either the developing American Jewish Orthodox movement or the American feminist movement because the characters and themes of her novel moderate the extreme demands of both. In Wolf's fiction, a woman does not have to give up marriage and home to be strong, independent, and unconventional, nor does she have to be destroyed by the rest cure; a Jew does not have to be Orthodox to maintain a strong affiliation with her heritage and her faith. As Rabbi Irving F. Reichert said in the funeral service for Wolf on 31 August 1932: "Emma Wolf was a militant Jewess because she knew the epic of her people. However little store she set on conventional dogmas and traditional cults, she penetrated to the heart of Judaism in its spiritual essence."[75]

NOTES

1. See Paula Hyman, *The Emancipation of the Jews of Alsace: Acculturation and Tradition in the Nineteenth Century* (New Haven: Yale University Press, 1991), for a historical overview of Jews in Alsace.
2. See Barbara Cantalupo, "Emma Wolf," in *Jewish American Women Writers*, ed. Ann Shapiro (Westport: Greenwood, 1994), 465–72, for Wolf's biography, the only published biography to date. Special thanks to William Tornheim, whose follow-up letter (18 July 1992) to my inquiry provided further details regarding the family of Simon Wolf whom Tornheim included in his essay "Pioneer Jews of Contra Costa," *Western States Jewish History* 16, no. 1 (Oct. 1983): 3–22. Without his lead, all biographical research on Wolf would have been frustrated. In this letter, he notes that Emma's brother Julius was president of the Grain Exchange in San Francisco, and when he died in 1923, the exchange closed for the day; Tornheim characterizes this closing as "a unique event in its history." I am also grateful to Richard Auslen, Donald Auslen, William Lowe, and, especially, Barbara Aaron, all relatives of Emma Wolf, whose interviews led to new knowledge of Wolf's life and work.
3. With the help of Debra Heaphy, librarian in 1992 at Congregation Emanu-El (1 Lake Street, San Francisco), it was ascertained that Emma Wolf and her family were members of Congregation Emanu-El, a Reform temple. Bernard Kaplan in the 4 March 1910 issue of *Emanu-El* notes that "Miss

Emma Wolf, the well known California writer . . . has fa-
vored us with a feeling of appreciation and estimate of the
late Daniel Levy . . . this distinguished author [Emma Wolf]
has made the late Daniel Levy the model of one of the
finest characters in one of her novels" (p. 2, col. 3). Barbara
Land, librarian at the Temple Emanu-El in 2000, noted
that only a member of the congregation could have given
such a tribute.

4. Tornheim, 5.

5. Rosa Sonneschein, "Emma Wolf," *American Jewess* 1, no. 6
(Sept. 1895): 294–95. Wolf's response to her work being
published at the early age of twelve is revealed in her 1930
interview with *San Francisco Chronicle*'s Helen Piper: "At
12, Miss Wolf saw her first story in print: 'There was no joy
in the experience. I cried bitterly over the affair,' she
mused. 'You see, I had a daring cousin, who thought the
tale was a work of art. He was prompted by the noble purpose of presenting me to the literary world. He stole my
manuscript and gave it to the little village paper. For weeks
I was too ashamed to face anyone. I imagined that all the
townsfolk were laughing at me and my little love story' "
(47).

6. Rebekah Kohut, *My Portion (An Autobiography)* (New York:
Thomas Seltzer, 1925), 60–62, 64. The question of assimilation was not only on the minds of these two young
women, but on the mind of twenty-two year old Gertrude
Stein, as the recently discovered Radcliffe College composition class paper of Gertrude Stein—"The Modern Jew
Who Has Given Up the Faith of His Fathers Can Reason-
ably and Consistently Believe in Isolation" [*PMLA* 116,
no. 2 (Mar. 2001): 416–28) reveals. Stein, however, seems
to have come to a clear conclusion in her youth, unlike
Rebekah Kohut whose adolescent doubt is clearly expressed. Ironically, in her later years, this doubt trans-
formed into Kohut's adamant public defense of Judaism
while Stein drifted from such identification and defense.

In Stein's 1896 composition, she defines the term "isolation" as "no inter-marriage with an alien. The Jew shall marry only the Jew" (423) and argues for an adherence to Jewish values: "every strong feeling every spiritual legacy to the modern Jew, from a race of sturdy independent forefathers cries aloud for continuance of isolation. . . . let the modern Jew accept this isolation as his birth-right. Let him not attempt to escape from it and thus to do violence to the noblest part of him" (427). If we deduce from Stein's position that many Jewish intellectuals embraced her views during this time, then, indeed, Wolf's 1892 novel would have been seen as quite radical in its conclusion.

7. Barbara Sicherman, et. al., eds, *Notable American Women: The Modern Period: A Biographical Dictionary* (Cambridge: Belknap Press of Harvard University Press, 1980), 404.

8. Anne Ruggles Gere. *Intimate Practices: Literacy and Cultural Work in U.S. Women's Clubs, 1880–1920* (Urbana: University of Illinois Press, 1997), 212, 218, 220.

9. Reference to Wolf's membership in the Philomath Club appears in the reprint of the entry on Wolf in *Who's Who in America* included in Helen Piper's interview with Wolf in the *San Francisco Chronicle*. The Philomath Club was not a part of Congregation Emanu-El, according to Barbara Land, Emanu-El librarian, but she points out that one of its founding members was Bettie Lowenberg, a member of the temple. Fred Rosenbaum, *Architects of Reform: Congregational and Community Leadership Emanu-El of San Francisco, 1849–1980* (Berkeley: Judah Magnes, 1980), 67.

Evidence that the club engaged social issues comes from a 26 November 1901 *San Francisco Call* article, "Ladies Debate Race Question: Mrs. Julius Kahn Ably Defends the Negro Woman: Favors Permitting Them to Join the Federation of Clubs": "The rooms of the Philomath Club were crowded yesterday afternoon with members and friends of the organization. It was the occasion of the much talked of debate on the mooted question 'Should the color line exist in women's clubs?' This subject has been under discussion for the last month. It was brought up by the Women's Era Club of Boston, composed of colored women, when they applied for admission to the General Federation of Women's Clubs" (11). This public position was a direct response to the exclusion of African American women from the General Federation of Women's Clubs, made official at their 1900 national convention. According to Anne Gere, this policy was upheld at subsequent meetings of the General Federation of Women's Clubs. The members of the Philomath Club may have identified with the problem of exclusion of their East coast African American sisters since many Jewish women continued to be denied access to federation clubs: "Although some Jewish women joined federation clubs, many white Protestant groups barred them, borrowing from the construction of Jews as nonwhite" (6).

10. Josephine Cohn, "Communal Life of San Francisco: Jewish Women in 1908," *Western States Jewish History* 20, no. 1 (Oct. 1987): 15–36; reprinted from the 17 April 1908 *Emanu-El*.

11. Ibid., 35.

12. See Barbara Welter, "The Cult of True Womanhood: 1820–1860" *American Quarterly* 18 (Summer 1966): 151–74, for a discussion of the "ideal lady" and "the new woman." In addition, Karen Blair, *The Clubwoman as Feminist: True Womanhood Redefined, 1868–1914* (New York: Holmes & Meier, 1980), summarizes the shifting definition of the "ideal lady" as follows: "In the upper classes, the ideal lady was leisured and ornamental, absorbed in learning the niceties that would render her amusing and enable her to beautify her home. Wealthy young women learned to dance, sing, embroider, make wax flowers, paint china, and play the harpsichord. . . . Unlike her wealthier counterpart, however, the middle-class lady was judged not only by her amusing charms. She was defined by her supposedly natural qualities of domesticity and morality. The lady's function of embellishing her family's environment was expanded

into being the moral guardian of the home" (1–2). Quote in text from Blair, 4.

13. Linda Kuzmack, *Woman's Cause: The Jewish Woman's Movement in England and the United States, 1881–1933* (Columbus: Ohio State University Press, 1990), 39.

14. Ibid., 3, quoting Deborah Grand Golumb, "The 1893 Congress of Jewish Women: Evolution or Revolution in American Jewish Women's History?" *American Jewish History* 70 (Sept. 1980): 55–56. By 1898, however, evidence of the erosion of prejudice against Jews in the women's movement appears in an article by Mrs. J. C. Croly, *The History of the Woman's Club Movement in America* (New York: H. G. Allen, 1898), 249–59. She points out that the Century Club of San Francisco (organized in 1888 with the goal " 'to secure the advantages arising from a free interchange of thought and from cooperation among women' ") elected Mrs. P. N. Lilienthal as treasurer (252).

15. Kuzmack, 2, quoting Paula Hyman, "The Volunteer Organizations: Vanguard or Rear Guard?" *Lillith* 5 (1978): 17.

16. Two of Wolf's siblings died young: one at age four, another at three weeks.

17. For a description in the *American Jewess* of Wolf's role in the San Francisco literary scene, see Rebecca Gradwohl, "The Jewess in San Francisco," *American Jewess* 4, no. 1 (Oct. 1896): 10–12. Also, see Ann Braude, "The Jewish Woman's Encounter with American Culture," in *Women and Religion in America, Vol. 1: The Nineteenth Century,* ed. Rosemary Ruether and Rosemary Keller (New York: Harper & Row, 1981), 171–74. For a history of the *American Jewess,* see Jack Porter, "Rosa Sonnenshein [sic] and *The American Jewess,* the First Independent English Language Jewish Women's Journal in the United States," *American Jewish History* 68, no. 1 (Sept. 178): 57–63.

18. *Mechanics' Institute Library Bulletin* 5, nos. 9–10 (Sept.-Oct. 1901): 1–3.

19. *Emanu-El* (4 Mar. 1910): 1.

20. Piper, 47.

21. Daniel Levy, "Letters About the Jews of California: 1855–1858," trans. Marlene Rainman, *Western States Jewish Historical Quarterly* 3, no. 2 (Jan. 1971): 86–112. See Jacob Rader Marcus, *To Count a People: American Jewish Population Data, 1585–1984* (New York: University Press of America, 1989, 28), noting the dramatic jump in Jewish population in San Francisco from approximately three thousand in 1855 to approximately sixteen thousand in 1874.

22. See Jonathan Sarna, *A Great Awakening* (New York: CIJE, 1995), 18–27.

23. Kuzmack, 4.

24. Another possible source may have been the example of Rabbi Isaac Mayer Wise's daughter, who chose to marry a Christian, despite her father's position in the community and his sanction against intermarriage. Rabbi Wise could have been the model for Mr. Levice, who, like Wise, reverses his initial disapproval of his daughter's marriage. See Paul Spickard, "Ishmael Returns: The Changing Status of Children of Jewish Intermarriage in the United States," in *Jewish Assimilation, Acculturation, and Accommodation: Past Traditions, Current Issues, and Future Prospects*, ed. Menachem Mor (New York: University Press of America, 1992). Spickard refers to a newspaper clipping "dated July 15 [1884?] in the Isaac M. Wise Papers, AJA: 'Not Wise-ly but Too Well: The Disobedient Daughter of Rabbi Wise Married to Christian but Reconciled to Her Father' " and notes that "[e]ven Rabbi Isaac M. Wise, the foremost leader of American Reform Judaism, could not keep his daughter Helen from marrying Irish Presbyterian James Molony" (201). The thesis that Wolf fashioned her main characters on Wise and his daughter, however, could be called into question, as Jonathan Sarna notes in a 21 November 2000 email to me, "[T]he marriage of Isaac M. Wise's daughter, Helen, to an Irish Presbyterian is not 'common knowledge.' It did gain momentary attention when it happened, but it was subsequently hushed up, and

to this day, no biography of Isaac M. Wise discloses the fact. By the way, the marriage was actually performed, as I recall, by a Unitarian minister (Wendt). Note, too, that Helen was reconciled to her father and the descendants were Jewish." Although this marriage was not "common knowledge," as Jonathan Sarna points out, it's quite possible that Rebekah Bettelheim Kohut knew of it. Kohut notes in her autobiography that Rabbi Isaac M. Wise stayed at her home during his 1875 visit to San Francisco and that he and her father remained friends over the years. Because of this friendship, Rebekah could have known of Helen Wise's marriage in 1884 (when she and Emma Wolf were nineteen) through her father and most likely would have shared this knowledge with her close friend Emma, especially since this interfaith marriage would have touched their mutual concerns over the choice of assimilation. Rebekah Kohut describes Rabbi Wise's visit to San Francisco: "He became not only our guest but my father's inseparable companion during his stay, and we children got to adore him. . . . The remarkable thing about the relation between Isaac M. Wise and my father was that they remained close friends in spite of the differences in their attitude towards Reform and Orthodox Judaism. . . . Reform cut deep into the heart of Jewish life, and not rarely caused enmity between brothers and friends. It is therefore noteworthy that the friendship persisted between my father and Dr. Wise, who was one of the extreme Reformers" (43, 44–45).

25. To further the Wise/Wolf connection, Alan Silverstein describes Rabbi Wise's affinity to Unitarians: "Rabbi Wise's first pulpit was in Albany, NY, nestled with the cultural ambiance of the Boston-based Unitarian church. Unitarianism was the most extreme version of tolerant, liberal Christianity within antebellum American culture. Its adherents were high-status and upper-class individuals who had cast aside ritual as well as Christian theological dogmas. They relied upon the ethical and social justice imperatives of biblical prophets for inspiration" (40–41). From

Alan Silverstein, *Alternatives to Assimilation: The Response of Reform Judaism to American Culture*, 1840–1930 (Hanover: University Press of New England for Brandeis University Press, 1994). Also, see Rudolf Glanz, *The Jewish Woman in America: Two Female Immigrant Generations*, 1820–1929 (New York: KTAV Publishing House, 1976), for a discussion of the place of Unitarianism in the late nineteenth century. Glanz points out that Emma Lazarus's sister, Josephine, had "the distinction of having been the only woman who ever created a religious controversy by a collection of essays: 'The spirit of Judaism'. . . . Emil Hirsch took exception to her partial identification of Judaism with Unitarianism: 'Miss Lazarus has not grasped the principles of Jewish Radicalism . . . the Radical cannot exchange the sound, soul-inspiring 'law' for this sweet sentimental hysteria dignified by the label 'love.' Unitarianism and Judaism are not identical'" (162). For a discussion of the public positions of Catholic, Jewish, and Protestant religions on intermarriage, see Anne Rose, *Interfaith Families in America* (Cambridge: Harvard University Press, 2001), 50–66.

26. See Jenn Weissman Joselit, *The Wonders of America* (New York: Hill & Wang, 1994), 43–54, for other instances of literary treatments of intermarriage; all examples given, however, were published after Wolf's *Other Things Being Equal*—Anzia Yezierska's *Salome of the Tenements* (1923), Marian Spitzer's *Who Would Be Free* (1924), Leah Morton's *I Am a Woman—And a Jew* (1926), and Fannie Hurst's *Appasionata* (1926). "Throughout the 1920s and 1930s, dozens of potboilers, many of them authored by Jewish women, offered readers tantalizing, juicy insights into the drama of intermarriage. From Marion [*sic*] Spitzer's *Who Would Be Free*, a ringing endorsement of mixed marriage, to Fannie Hurst's *Apassionata*, 'the story of the girl who preferred the love of religion' to that of a non-Jewish man, the make-believe of fiction enabled American Jews to contemplate what was simultaneously too painful and too fantastical to confront in real life" (47–48). Joselit also discusses the

1927 novel by Anne Nichols, *Abie's Irish Rose,* that was adapted for Broadway stage and "ran for over five and a half years, generated nineteen different touring companies, and earned its creator, Anne Nichols, herself a party to a mixed marriage, over five million dollars" (48).

27. See Joselit, 43–54. Also, see William Toll, "Intermarriage and the Urban West," in *Jews of the American West,* ed. Moses Richlin and John Livingston (Detroit: Wayne State University Press, 1991), 165–73.

28. Spickard, 193.

29. Rose, 59.

30. Hasia Diner, *A Time of Gathering: The Second Migration, 1820–1880* (Baltimore: Johns Hopkins University Press, 1992), 170. See, as well, Naomi Cohen, *Encounter with Emancipation: The German Jews in the United States, 1830–1914* (Philadelphia: JPS, 1984), 224–31, for an examination of American anti-Semitism in literary journals (such as the *North American Review* and *Century Magazine*) and popular media such as comic weeklies and daily newspapers.

31. Diner, 172.

32. See Naomi Cohen, "Anti-Semitism in the Gilded Age: The Jewish View," in *Essential Papers on Jewish-Christian Relations in the United States,* ed. Naomi Cohen (New York: New York University Press, 1990). Here Cohen notes that "[a]lthough no consensus has been reached on whether hostility toward Jews was an example of ethnic prejudice which was also felt by the Irish, Italians, and Germans, or whether it more closely resembled religious bigotry experienced by Catholics, most scholars agree that it was not significant until the last quarter or even last decade of the nineteenth century" (127).

33. Leonard Dinnerstein, *Anti-Semitism in America* (New York: Oxford University Press, 1994), 48, 51. See chapters 3 and 4 for a comprehensive discussion of anti-Semitism during the period that Wolf was writing and publishing.

34. Suzanne Poirier, "The Weir Mitchell Rest Cure: Doctor and Patients," *Women's Studies* 10, no. 1 (1983): 15–40; 21–22.

35. Ibid., 35–36.

36. Larry Ceplair, ed. *Charlotte Perkins Gilman: A Nonfiction Reader*. (New York: Columbia University Press, 1991), 39.

37. Israel Zangwill offered to write a letter to Judge Mayer Sulzberger of Philadelphia on Wolf's behalf suggesting that the Jewish Publication Society take a serious look at her novel *Heirs of Yesterday* which Zangwill especially liked, but the JPS board had earlier rejected her work, because " 'some of the characters [are] immoral and the Rabbi hero impossible' " (Jonathan Sarna, *JPS: The Americanization of Jewish Culture, 1888–1988* [Philadelphia: JPS, 1989], 80), and they did not choose to publish *Heirs*. Instead A. C. McClurg published the novel in 1900. Zangwill praises *Heirs of Yesterday* in a 12 December 1900 letter to Wolf: "I have read 'Heirs of Yesterday' with much pleasure, not only on account of its art but of its information. The exact place of the Jew in the 'Republic of human brotherhood' is a point that interests me exceedingly. Apparently it is just above the coloured folk. There is a great tragic-comic mine for you in the States, & you are sinking your shaft much deeper than in 'Other Things Being Equal'. . . . saw a good deal of Jewish life in the States during my visits. (It is a pity I wasn't able to get to San Francisco.) Its development seemed to me characterized by superficiality. I am hoping your book will be widely read by both Jews & Christians, as it cannot fail to stimulate both." Zangwill continually encouraged Wolf to have her work published in England and made an effort to help her publish *The Joy of Life* in Britain: "You will see from the enclosed that I have not yet been able to place your book this side. The reason given is perfectly valid, though publishers would perhaps not be so cautious, were it not for the congestion produced by the Jubilee. Everybody I have shown it to has liked it. I do not despair of its appearing here some day, especially if you pave the way to it by a new book published simultaneously

on both sides of the Atlantic as suggested by the publisher"
(Letter of 2 July 1897).

38. See William H. Nolte, *H. L. Mencken's Smart Set Criticism*
(Ithaca: Cornell University Press, 1968). See Burton Rascoe, "The History of *The Smart Set*," in *The Smart Set An-
thology*, ed. Burton Rascoe and Groff Conklin (New York:
Reynal & Hitchcock, 1934), viii–xliv.

39. From Zangwill's letters to Wolf, it is apparent that Wolf
wrote poetry as well as fiction, but to date, only this
poem—"Eschscholtzia (California Poppy)"—in the *American Jewess* has been located in print:
   "The golden cup lies broken. At my feet four petals—
satin of hue of gold. In my hand a naked stalk topped by a
rose-tinted throne holding the shriveled stamens.
   'The flower is dead,' they say.
   Yet the stamens had never breathed perfume.
   At my feet four petals—satin of hue of gold. Together
they were a life. Rich, vivid, beautiful. Beautiful—no more.
Yet a something.
   The sermon of the flower: To have shown fair—of face,
of form, of soul—it matters not; to have shown fair, some-
how, sometime to some one.
   Thence immortality—the mantle of Elijah.
   San Francisco, November 10, 1895." From *American
Jewess* 4 (Jan. 1896): 195.

40. Mary Wollstonecraft, *A Vindication of the Rights of Woman*,
in *A Mary Wollstonecraft Reader*, ed. Barbara Solomon and
Paul Berggren (New York: New American Library, 1983),
320, 322.

41. Wolf may have taken the metaphor of the "rusty nail" from
nineteenth-century Reform Rabbi David Einhorn: " 'Each
intermarriage drives a nail in the coffin of Judaism.' " (From
Sprickar, "Ishmael Returns.")

42. *The Jerusalem Bible* (New York: Doubleday, 1966), 271. Jonathan Sarna pointed out this correlation in an email to me
on 19 December 2000: "Ruth's name is not an accident,
and there are passages in the novel that suggest that Wolf

is playing with the well-known phrases of the biblical book."

43. Kuzmack, 5.

44. See Joselit, 9–19, for a historical overview of the value of the Jewish home. The values expressed in Wolf's novels are similar to those expressed in an introduction by Marion Harland to James C. Fernald's *The New Womanhood* (Boston: D. Lothrop, 1891), 9–16: "The attempt to abolish the ideal home and keep the ideal woman is a predestined failure [argues Fernald]. Reformers, flushed with continuous victories over tyrant customs that once shackled woman's higher powers, would do well to pause and weigh this significant sentence. The relation of woman to home is one of reciprocal obligation. Home makes her as truly as she makes home. . . . In the growing, and, in the main, healthy desire for independence felt by our girls, there is a danger of shutting themselves out into the wide world where there are no homes. A vast number of our working women are unnested birds, who mistake the flutter of excitement at their novel freedom for contentment with their lot" (11–12). The same could be said of the sentiments expressed in Esther Rusky, "Progress: Its Influence upon the Home," *American Jewess* 1 (5 August 1895): 224–28: "The new government clubs in which cultured American men and women are striving for municipal reform, have no higher ideal than just this one of Israel that makes home the pivotal point around which the education, training and culture of its sons and daughters should center" (228).

45. Winnifred Cooley, *The New Womanhood* (New York: Broadway, 1904), 13.

46. See Ella Bartlett, "The New Woman," *American Jewess* 1 (4 July 1895): 169–71, for a discussion of the term, and Pauline Wise, "Woman's Part in the Drama of Life," *American Jewess* 1 (2 May 1895): 63–70, for advice given to women regarding this issue.

47. Three of Wolf's novels were published by McClurg, a well-known and respected publishing house and retail bookstore

in Chicago. According to an article in *Publisher's Weekly*
146 (2 Sept. 1944): 814–19, "McClurg Has Completed Its
First Hundred Years," Alexander Caldwell McClurg of
Pittsburgh joined the firm in 1859. Under his direction,
George Millard established the rare and used books section
of the retail store that in 1889 became known as the
" 'Saints and Sinners Corner' so named by Eugene Field,
where the literary-minded of Chicago gathered to read and
engage in intellectual conversation" (816).

48. Another novel, written years later, that describes life in the
San Francisco middle-class, Jewish community during the
time Wolf was writing is *920 O'Farrell Street* (New York:
Doubleday, 1947) by Harriet Lane Levy (first published in
the *Menorah Journal*'s winter and spring issues of 1937).

49. Kuzmack, 33. "Learned papers were delivered by outstanding
Jewish women on clubwork, social service, religion, the
professions, arts, and business. Rebekah Kohut, author and
editor of the Jewish women's journal *Helpful Hints*, had remained home at the plea of her rabbi-scholar husband, Alexander. Her absence lent an especial poignancy to her
paper, read by another, which connected women's 'messi-
anic mission' to their duties for home, Judaism, and the
Jewish community."

50. Private collection of Barbara Goldman Aaron, great-niece of
Emma Wolf. Ten original letters from Zangwill to Wolf beginning in 1896 and running through 1900 are mounted in
a bound book; the collection was put together in 1934 by
Robert L. Goldman, nephew of Emma Wolf, and is enti-
tled: *A Correspondence: Israel Zangwill and Emma Wolf*. The
collection also includes a photograph of Israel Zangwill on
hard cardboard with the inscription to Wolf: "Yours in the
Dream, I. Zangwill."

51. Zangwill is known to have corresponded with many aspiring
young writers, including, for example, Mary Antin. See Ev-
elyn Salz, *Selected Letters of Mary Antin* (Syracuse: Syracuse
University Press, 2000), 1.

52. In a letter dated 14 May 1898, Zangwill responds to poems

Wolf must have sent to him: "I like your poems, one and all, though in all there are unequal lines. In 'Prayer' the last verse is best, the 'Beethoven's sestet is stronger than the octave though all is good. In 'Pisgah'—a title of Browning's ('Pisgah-Reefs')—I object only to 'There art no child / to sob so wild.' Sobbing breaks the reticent tragic dignity of the atmosphere. Two doggerel lines that occur to me give a *suggestion* of what's wanted[:] 'Bear then thy pain, / 'Tis not in vain—.' Moses himself did not break down. He seems to have said no word. Your poem is good and true. The trouble, though, is that Gzuel, if not Moses, does enjoy the Promised Land & waxes fat & kicks the next Dreamer."

53. See Zangwill's pamphlets "Talked Out!" (London: Women's Social & Political Union, 1907), "Votes for Women" (London: Women's Freedom League, 1909), and "One and One Are Two" (London: Woman's Freedom League, 1913). See, also, Meri-Jane Rochelson's introduction to Israel Zangwill's *Children of the Ghetto* (Detroit: Wayne State University Press, 1998), 15.

54. Rochelson, 11.

55. Ibid., 20.

56. See Rose, 124–42, for a discussion of the increasing acceptance of interfaith marriage in the early part of the twentieth century in the United States, and especially the U.S. response to Zangwill's *The Melting Pot*.

57. Israel Zangwill, "A New Jewish Novelist," *Jewish Chronicle*, New Series, 1, no. 453 (5 Feb. 1897): 19.

58. This, most probably, was Dr. Solomon Schechter, described by Rebekah Kohut in *My Portion* as a "Reader in Rabbinics at Cambridge. . . . Schechter was a different type from most of the Jewish scholars, more like a purely literary man. In fact, he was an omnivorous reader of current books, which he always managed to beg or borrow from friends" (139–40).

59. Zangwill, *Jewish Chronicle*, 19.

60. *Literary World* 24, no. 1 (14 Jan. 1893): 3.

61. See Eric Goldstein, " 'Different Blood Flows in Our Veins': Race and Jewish Self-Definition in Late Nineteenth Century America," *American Jewish History* 85, no. 1 (Mar. 1997): 29–55, for a discussion of Jews and "race."

62. *Public Ledger* (20 December 1892): 3.

63. Zangwill, *Jewish Chronicle*, 19.

64. *Mechanics' Institute Library Bulletin*, 3.

65. Rudolf Glanz, *The Jewish Woman in America: Two Female Immigrant Generations, 1820–1919* (New York: KTAV, 1976), 162–63.

66. Louis Harap, "Early American Jewish Novels," *The Image of the Jew in American Literature from the Early Republic to Mass Immigration* (Philadelphia: JPS, 1974), 472.

67. Ibid., 473.

68. Ibid., 474.

69. See Rebekah Kohut, *My Portion*, chap. 5, "Spiritual Trials," for a personal account of the "heated" conflict between the Orthodox movement and the Reformed movement in the late 1880s and early 1890s in the United States, esp. pp. 76–86.

70. Harap, 474.

71. Ibid., 472, 476.

72. Diane Lichtenstein, "Fanny Hurst and Her Nineteenth-Century Predecessors," *Studies in American Jewish Literature* 7, no. 1 (Winter 1988): 26–39.

73. Ibid., 27.

74. Sarna, 25.

75. Excerpt of obituary found inserted in the collection of letters from Israel Zangwill to Emma Wolf compiled by Robert Goldman.

BIBLIOGRAPHY

PRIMARY WORKS

Novels

Other Things Being Equal. Chicago: A. C. McClurg, 1892, 1893, 1894, 1895, 1898, 1901, and revised 1916.
A Prodigal in Love. New York: Harper & Bros., 1894.
The Joy of Life. Chicago: A. C. McClurg, 1896.
Heirs of Yesterday. Chicago: A. C. McClurg, 1900.
Fulfillment: A California Novel. New York: Henry Holt, 1916.

Novella

The Knot. Smart Set 28, no. 4 (Aug. 1909): 1–38.

Poetry

"Eschscholtzia. (California Poppy.)." *American Jewess* 2, no. 4 (Jan. 1896): 195.

Short Stories

"One-Eye, Two-Eye, Three-Eye." *American Jewess* 2, no. 6 (Mar. 1896): 279–90.
"A Study in Suggestion." *Smart Set* 6, no. 3 (Mar. 1902): 95–100.
"A Still Small Voice." *Smart Set* 8, no. 2 (Oct. 1902): 157–60.

"The Courting of Drusilla West." *Smart Set* 9, no. 2 (Feb. 1903): 69–81.
"The End of the Story." *Smart Set* 14, no. 4 (Dec, 1904): 137–46.
"Tryst." *Smart Set* 16, no. 3 (July 1905): 109–16.
"Farquhar's Masterpiece." *Smart Set* 18, no. 3 (Mar. 1906): 101–11.
"The Conflict." *Smart Set* 20, no. 3 (Nov. 1906): 1–45.
"Louis d'Or." *Smart Set* 22, no. 4 (Aug. 1907): 94–104.
"Father of Her Children." *Smart Set* 34, no. 2 (June 1911): 135–40.

Reviews of *Other Things Being Equal*

American Jewess 1, no. 6 (Sept. 1895): 294–95.
Chicago Tribune (15 Oct. 1892): 13.
Literary World (Boston) 24, no. 1 (14 Jan. 14 1893): 3.
Public Ledger (Philadelphia) (20 Dec. 1892): 3.
The Story of the Files: A Review of California Writers and Literature. Ed. Ella Sterling Cummins. San Francisco: World's Fair Commission, 1893. 356.

Selected Reviews of Other Works

Review of *The Joy of Life*
    Overland Monthly, Second Series, 29, no. 172 (Apr. 1897): 454.
Review of *Heirs of Yesterday*
    "Miss Wolf's New Story." *Jewish Messenger* 88, no. 24 (14 Dec. 1900): 1.
Reviews of *Fulfillment: A California Novel*
    Overland Monthly, Second Series, 67, no. 5 (May 1916): ix–x.
    Reely, Mary Katherine. *Book Review Digest: Reviews of 1916 Books*. Ed. Margaret Jackson. New York: H. W. Wilson, 1917: 598–99. (Cites reviews in *New York Times* [8 July 1916], *Boston Transcript* [17 June 1916], *Literary Digest* [8 July 1916], among others.)
    "San Francisco Setting of New Emotional Romance." *San Francisco Chronicle* 2 (Apr. 1916): 35.

Selected Secondary Works on Emma Wolf

Cantalupo, Barbara. "Emma Wolf." *Jewish American Women Writers: A Bio-Bibliographical and Critical Sourcebook.* Ed. Ann Shapiro. Westport: Greenwood Press, 1994. 465–72.

Glanz, Rudolf. *The Jewish Woman in America: Two Female Immigrant Generations, 1820–1929, Vol. 2.* New York: KTAV and National Council of Jewish Women, 1976. 163.

Gradwohl, Rebecca. "The Jewess in San Francisco." *American Jewess* 4, no. 1 (Oct. 1896): 10–12.

Harap, Louis. "Early American Jewish Novels." *The Image of the Jew in American Literature from the Early Republic to Mass Immigration.* Philadelphia: JPS, 1974. 472–76.

Lichtenstein, Diane. *Writing Their Nations: The Tradition of Nineteenth-Century American Jewish Women Writers.* Bloomington: Indiana University Press, 1992: 78–80, 84–85, 113–17.

Marcus, Jacob. *The American Jewish Woman, 1654–1980: A Documentary History.* New York: KTAV, 1981.

Mechanics' Institute Library Journal 5, nos. 9–10 (Sept.-Oct. 1901): 1–3.

Mighels, Ella Sterling (Clark). *Story of the Files: A Review of California Writers and Literature.* San Francisco: World's Fair Commission, 1893. 292–3, 320–22, 256.

Rose, Anne. *Interfaith Families in America.* Cambridge: Harvard University Press, 2001. 67, 70–73, 76.

Zangwill, Israel. "A New Jewish Novelist." *Jewish Chronicle* (London), New Series, 1, no. 453 (5 Feb. 1897): 19.

OTHER THINGS
BEING EQUAL

BY EMMA WOLF

*"And now abideth Faith, Hope, Love, these three;
but the greatest of these is Love."*

FOREWORD

In presenting this revised edition to a new generation, the author feels that the element of change has touched very lightly the romantic potentialities obtaining at the time of the original writing, and which still obtain. Christian youth still chances upon Jewish youth, with the same difference of historic background, the same social barriers and prejudices—the same possibilities of mutual attraction. The humanest love knows no sect. Only in one respect has the face of youth altered—to wit, in the ignoring of the Fifth Commandment. Twenty years ago that Commandment was, to the child, the paramount Commandment, beautiful in concept, but carrying in its results many a silent tragedy. Today the dominance of the individualistic creed with its substituted "Honor Thy Self" holds no such tears of renunciation, but, with the passing of that older order, has there not passed a beauty from the world? It is the story of that beauty which the author, in this revised edition, for a new generation, has not cared to revise.

EMMA WOLF.

San Francisco, 1916.

OTHER THINGS BEING EQUAL

CHAPTER I

A HUMMING BIRD dipped through the air and lit upon the palm tree just below the open window, the long, drowsy call of a crowing cock came from afar off; up through a hazy splendor the city lifted its jocund hills. It was a rarely beautiful summer afternoon in old San Francisco.

Ruth Levice sat near the window, lazily rocking. Peculiarly responsive to her environment, mercurially so to mood of day or hour, the soft, languorous air had, unconsciously to herself, borne her to dim, far scenes where life sped in eternal summer, vague indeed, but instinct with all the indefinable joy and romance of youth.

So removed was she in spirit from her surroundings that she heard with an obvious start a knock at the door. The knock was immediately followed by a smiling, plump young woman, sparkling of eye, rosy of cheek, glistening in jewels and silk.

"Here you are, Ruth," she exclaimed, and kissed her heartily; whereupon she sank into a chair and threw back her bonnet strings with an air of relief. "I came up here at once when the maid said your mother was out. Where is she?"

"Out calling. You look so warm, Jennie; let me fan you."

"Thanks. Oh, how refreshing! Sandalwood, isn't it? Where's your father?"

"He's writing in the library. Do you want to see him?"

"Oh, no, no! I must see you alone. I'm so glad Aunt Esther is out. Why aren't you with her, Ruth? You shouldn't let your mother go off alone."

The young girl laughed in merry surprise.

"Why, Jennie, you forgot that mamma has been used all her

life to going out without me; it's only within the last few months that we've been such close companions."

"I know," replied her visitor, leaning back with a grim expression of disapproval, "and I think it's the queerest arrangement I ever heard of. The idea of a father having the sole care of a daughter up to her twenty-first birthday, and then delivering her, like a piece of joint property, over to her mother! Oh, I know that, according to their lights, it didn't seem absurd, but the very idea of it is contrary to nature. Of course we all know that your father was peculiarly fitted to undertake your training and, in that way, your mother could more easily indulge in her love of society. But as it is, no wonder she's as jealous of your success in her realm as your father was in his; no wonder she overdoes things to make up for lost time. How do you like it, Ruth?"

"What?" softly inquired her cousin, slowly waving the dainty fan, while a smile lighted up the gravity of her face at this onslaught.

"Going out continually, night after night."

"Mamma likes it."

"*Cela va sans dire.* But, Ruth—stop fanning a minute, please—I want to know, candidly and seriously, would you mind giving it up?"

"Candidly and seriously, I would do so today forever."

"Ye-es; your father's daughter," said Mrs. Lewis, speaking more slowly, her bright eyes noting the perfect repose of the young girl's person. "And yet you are having some quiet little conquests—the golden apples of your mother's Hesperides. But to come to the point, do you realize that your mother is very ill?"

"Ill—my mother?" The sudden look of consternation shattering the soft tranquillity of her face must have fully repaid Mrs. Lewis if she was aiming at a sensation.

"There, sit down. Don't be alarmed; you know she's out and apparently well."

"What do you mean?"

"I mean that Aunt Esther is nervous and hysterical. The other day at our house she had such an attack of hysteria that I had to call in a neighboring doctor. She begged us not to mention it to either of you, and then insisted on going to a meeting of some sort. However, I thought it over and decided to let you know, because I consider it serious. I was afraid to alarm Uncle, so I thought of telling you."

"Thank you, Jennie; I shall speak to father about it." The young girl's tone was quite unagitated, but two pink spots on her usually colorless cheeks betrayed her emotion.

"That's right, dear. I hope you'll forgive me if I seem meddlesome, but Jo and I have noticed it for some time, and your father, by allowing this continual gayety, seems to have overlooked what we find so sadly apparent. Of course you have an engagement for tonight?"

"Yes; we're going to a reception at the Merrills'."

"Christians?" came the sharp challenge.

"The name speaks for itself."

"What *does* possess your parents to mix so much with Christians?"

"Fellow-feeling, I suppose. We all dance and talk alike; and as we don't hold services at receptions, wherein lies the difference?"

"There *is* a difference; and the Christians know it as well as we Jewish people. Not only do they know it, but they show it in countless ways; and the difference, they think, is all to their credit. For my part, I always feel as if they looked down on us, and I should like to prove to them how we differ on that point. I have enough courage to let them know I consider myself as good as the best of them."

"Is that why you wear diamonds on the street, Jennie?" asked Ruth, her serious tone implying no impudence but carrying a pointed reproach. In the declining years of the nineteenth century good taste had decreed a quieter, more conventionally unobtrusive fashion in woman's street attire than obtains in these resplendent days of luxury and caprice.

"Hardly. I wear them because I have them and like them. I see no harm in wearing what is becoming."

"But don't you think they attract attention on the street? One hates to be conspicuous. I think they are only in place at a gathering of friends of one's own social standing, where they don't proclaim one's moneyed value."

"Perhaps," replied Mrs. Lewis, her rosy face a little rosier than before. "I suppose you mean to say it's vulgar. Well, maybe so. But I scarcely think a little outward show of riches should make others feel they're superior because they don't care to make a display. Besides, to be less personal, I don't think any Christian would care to put himself out to meet a Jew of any description."

"Don't you think it would depend a great deal both on Jew and Christian? I've always been led to believe that a broad-minded man of whatever sect will recognize and honor the same quality in any other man. And why shouldn't I move on an equality with my Christian friends? We have had the same schooling, speak the same language, read the same books, are surrounded by the same elements of home refinement. Probably if they had not been congenial, my father would long ago have ceased to associate with them. I think the secret of it all is in the fact that it never occurred to us that the most fastidious could think we were anything but the most fastidious; and so we always met anyone we cared to meet on a level footing. I have a great many pleasant friends in the court of your Philistines."

"Possibly. But not having been brought up by your father, I think differently, and perhaps am as different as they think I am. Their ways are not my ways, and what good can you expect from such association?"

"Why, pleasant companionship. What more?"

"Not even that. But tell me, can't you dissuade Aunt Esther from going tonight? Tell your father, and let him judge if you'd better not."

"I really think mamma wouldn't care to go, she said as much to father; but, contrary to all precedent, he insists on our going tonight, and, what's more, intends to go with us, although Louis is going too. But if you think she's seriously run down, I'll tell him at once and—"

A blithe voice at the door interrupted her, calling:

"Open the door, Ruth; my hands are full."

She rose hastily and, with a signal of secrecy to her loquacious cousin, opened the door for her mother.

"Ah, Jennie! How are you, dear? But let's open this box— Nora just handed it to me—before we consider you." Mrs. Levice softly deposited a huge box upon Ruth's lace-enveloped bed.

She was still bonneted and gloved and, with a slight flush in her clear olive cheek, she looked anything but a subject for fears. From the crown of her dainty bonnet to the point of her boot she was the picture of exquisite well-being; tall, beautifully formed, carrying herself with proud graciousness, gowned in perfect, quiet elegance, she appeared more as an older sister than as Ruth's mother.

"Ruth's gown for this evening," she announced, deftly unfolding the wrappings.

"Yellow!" exclaimed Mrs. Lewis, in surprise.

"Corn-color," corrected Mrs. Levice, playfully exact. "How do you think it will suit her?" She shook out the clinging silken crêpe.

"Charmingly; but I thought Ruth objected to anything but white."

"So she does; she thinks white keeps her unnoticed among the rest. This time, however, my will overrode hers. Didn't it, daughter?"

The girl made a mock courtesy.

"I'm only lady-in-waiting to your majesty, O queen!" she laughed, scarcely aware of what she said, wholly lost in a silent scrutiny of her mother's face.

"And how's our prime minister this afternoon?" Mrs. Levice was drawing off her gloves, and Ruth's searching look passed unnoticed.

"I haven't been down since luncheon," she said.

"What! Then go down at once and bring him up. I must see that he gets clothed in festive mind for this evening. Come to my sitting-room, Jennie, and we can have a comfortable chat."

Left to herself, Ruth hesitated before going to her father with her ill-boding tidings. None knew better than she of the great, silent love binding her parents. As a quiet, observant child, she had often questioned wherein could be any sympathy between her father, almost old, studious, and reserved, and her beautiful, worldly young mother. But as she matured, she became conscious that, because of this apparent disparity, it would have been still stranger had Mrs. Levice not loved him with a feeling verging nearer humble adoration than any lower passion. It seemed almost a mockery for her to have to tell him he had been negligent—not only a mockery, but a cruelty. However, it had to be done, and she was the only one to do it. Having come to this conclusion, she ran quickly downstairs, and softly, without knocking, opened the library door.

She entered so quietly that Mr. Levice, reading by the window, did not glance from his book. She stood a moment regarding the small, thoughtful-faced, white-haired man.

If one were to judge but by results, Jules Levice would have been accounted a fortunate man. Nearing the allotted three-score and ten, blessed with a loving, beloved wife and this one idolized ewe-lamb, surrounded by luxury, in good health, honored, and honorable—trouble and travail seemed to have passed him by. But this scene of human happiness was wholly the result of intelligent and unremitting effort. He had been thrown on the world when a boy of twelve. He had resolved to become *happy*. Many of us do likewise; but he had not overlooked the fact that men are provided with feet, not wings, and cannot fly to the goal. His dream of happiness had been ambitious; it had soared beyond contentment. Not being a lily of the field, he had known that he must toil; any honest work had been acceptable to him. He was possessed of a fine mind; he had found the means to cultivate it. He had a keen observation; he became a student of his fellowmen; and, being strong and untiring, he had become rich. This had been but the nucleus of his ambitions, and it came to him late, but not too late for him to build round it his happy home, and to surround himself with the luxuries of leisure for attaining that wide information which he had always craved. His was merely the prosperity of an intellectual, self-made man whose time for rest had come.

Ruth seated herself on a low stool which she drew up before him, and laid her hand upon his.

"You, darling?" He spoke in a full, musical voice with a marked French accent.

"Can you spare me a few minutes, father?"

"I am all ears." He shut the book, and his hand closed about hers.

"Jennie was here just now."

"And did not come in to see me?"

"She had something to tell me."

"A secret?"

"Yes; something I must repeat to you."

"Yes?"

"Father—Jennie thinks—she has reason to know that—dear, do you think mother is perfectly well?"

"No, my child; I know she is not."

This quiet assurance was staggering.

"And you allow her to go on in this way without calling in a doctor?" A wave of indignant color suffused her cheeks.

"Yes."

"But—but—why?" She became a little confused under his calm gaze, feeling on the instant that she had implied an accusa-tion unjustly.

"Because, Ruth, I wished to be quite sure before interfering, and I have become convinced of it only within the past week. Your mother knows it herself, and is trying to hide it from me."

"Did she admit it?"

"I have not spoken of it to her; she is very excitable, and as she wishes to conceal it, I don't care to annoy her by telling her of my discovery."

"But isn't it wrong—unwise—to allow her to dissipate so much?"

"I have managed within the past week to keep you as quiet as possible."

"But tonight—forgive me, father—you insist on our going to this reception."

"Yes, my sweet confessor; but I have a good reason—one not to be spoken of."

" 'Those who trust us educate us,' " she pleaded in wistful earnestness.

"Then your education is complete. Well, I knew your mother would resist seeing any physician, for fear of his measures going contrary to her desires, so I have planned for her to meet tonight a certain doctor whom I would trust professionally with my wife's life, and on whom I can rely for the necessary tact to hide the professional object of their meeting. What do you think of my way, dear?"

She stooped and kissed his hand.

"May I know his name?" she asked after a pause.

"His name is Kemp—Dr. Herbert Kemp."

"Why, he lives a few blocks from here—I've seen his sign. Is he—old?"

"I should judge him to be between thirty-five and forty. Not old certainly, but one with the highest reputation for skill. Personally he is a man of great dignity—he inspires confidence in everyone."

"Where did you meet him?"

"In the hospitals," said her father quickly. "But I will introduce him to you tonight. Don't lose your head when you talk to him."

"Why should I?"

"Because he is a magnificent fellow; and I wish my daughter to hold her own before a man whom I admire so heartily."

"Why, this is the first time you've ever given me worldly advice," she laughed.

"Only a friendly hint," he answered, rising and putting his book in its place with the precision of a spinster.

CHAPTER II

ERBERT KEMP stood looking down upon the golden-haired slip of a girl seated upon a divan near the conservatory. The soft strains of remote stringed instruments chimed in harmoniously with their low-voiced converse, and he listened with evident enjoyment to her incessant babble, the naïveté of which was somewhat belied by the bright-glancing search of her regard.

"And you don't feel like the proverbial square peg?" she insisted.

"Not a bit," he returned. "I feel singularly fit—and fitting. Won't I do?"

"But you're so—rare. How did Mrs. Merrill bait you?"

"Ah, that was a trick," he teased.

"I thought so. She has a knack in getting whomever she wants, and she so often wants the elusive and—unusual. She loves a *rara avis,* and you're one of them tonight. I think I met you out only once last winter. This must seem like a sort of début to you."

"It does—with you beside me."

"Thanks—and you who so hate débutantes!"

"Who's been maligning me?"

"No one. Everybody knows your good taste in the—more-seasoned."

He laughed his amazement. "That's queer," he said. "I didn't know I had any taste. But since you say so there must be something in it. Not everything, though."

She flushed delightedly under his eyes. She knew her own girlish charms.

"Well, then," she mused, "perhaps it's 'the marrieds' ' good taste in you. If you would look round now—but don't!—you'd see Mrs. Sherwood—is she a patient of yours?—gazing dreamily through us as if we were so much space, but all the while she's saying, 'You silly little thing, Dorothy Gwynne! Can't you see you're boring Dr. Kemp? Hand him over—pass him round—*I* want him!'"

Kemp's lips twitched at the corners. "Aren't you improvising?" he asked. "Nobody is of such importance to anyone."

"That depends on who's who. Now here comes the Queen of Sheba—and—and—shall we say King Solomon? You'll admit *they* are of some importance. At least she is—to me."

She broke off with an expectant smile as Ruth Levice approached with her cousin, Louis Arnold.

Singly, each would have attracted attention anywhere; together they were doubly striking-looking. Arnold, tall and slight, carrying his head high, fair of complexion as a peachy-cheeked girl, was a peculiarly distinguished-looking man. The delicate *pince-nez* he wore emphasized slightly the elusive air of supercilious courtliness he always conveyed. Now, as he spoke to Ruth, who, although a tall girl, was some inches shorter than he, he maintained a strict perpendicular from the crown of his head to his heels, only looking down with his eyes. Short women resented this trick of his, protesting that it made them stand on tiptoe to speak to him.

There was something faintly oriental about Ruth, with her colorless face, creamy as a magnolia blossom. Her dusky hair was loosely rolled from her forehead and temples; her eyes, soft and brown beneath delicately penciled brows, matched the pure oval of her face. But the languorous air of Eastern skies was wholly wanting in the sweet sympathy of her glance, and in a certain alertness about the poise of her head.

Arnold stopped perforce at Miss Gwynne's slight signal.

"Where are you going?" she asked as they turned to greet her. "One would think you saw the fates before you, you're so oblivious to the beauties lying in wait." She looked up at Arnold, after one comprehensive glance over the palely golden shimmer of Ruth's gown.

"We both wished to see the orchids of which one hears," he answered with pronounced French accent and idiom, adding, with a slight smile, "I did not overlook you, but you were so busily contemplating other ground that it would have been cruelty to disturb you." He spoke the language slowly, as a stranger upon foreign ground.

"Oh, yes; I forgot. Dr. Kemp, the Queen of Sheba and her sworn knight, Louis, surnamed Arnold." She paused a moment as the parties amusedly acknowledged the fantastic introduction, and then broke in, rather breathlessly: "There, doctor, I'll leave you with royalty; don't let your republican ignorance forget her proper title. Mr. Arnold, Mrs. Merrill wants us; will you come?" With an impish look at Ruth, she drew Arnold away before he could murmur an excuse.

At the flippant words the soft, rich blood suffused Ruth's face.

"Will you sit here a while and wait for Mr. Arnold, or shall we go and see the orchids?" The pleasant, deep voice broke in upon her confusion and calmed her self-consciousness. She raised her eyes to the dark face above her. It was a strong rather than a handsome face. From the broad sweep of the forehead above the steady scrutiny of the gray eyes to the grave lip and firm chin under the short pointed beard, strength and gentleness spoke in every line. His personality bore the stamp of a letter of credit.

"Thank you," said she; "I think I'll sit here. My cousin will probably be back soon."

The doctor seated himself beside her. Miss Gwynne's appellation was not inaptly chosen, still he would have preferred to know her more conventional title.

"This is a peaceful little corner," he said. "Do you notice how removed it seems from the rest of the room?"

"Yes," she answered, meeting and disconcerting his pleasantly questioning look with one of swift resolve. "Dr. Kemp, I want to tell you that my father has confided to me your joint secret."

"Your father?" he looked bewildered; his knowledge of the Queen of Sheba's progenitors was vague.

"My father, yes," she repeated, smiling over his perplexity. "Our name is not very common; I'm Jules Levice's daughter."

He was about to exclaim "No!" The kinship seemed ridiculous in the face of this lovely girl and the remembered picture of the little plain-faced Jew. What he did say was:

"Mr. Levice is an esteemed friend of mine. He's here this evening, isn't he?"

"Yes. Have you met my mother yet?"

The mother would probably unravel the mysterious origin of this beautiful face and this strange, sweet voice, whose tones held an uncommon charm.

"No; but your father is diplomat enough to manage that before the evening is over. So you know our little scheme. Pardon the 'shop' I'll have to bore you with, but have you seen any signs of illness in your mother?"

"No; I've been very blind and selfish," she replied, somewhat bitterly. "Everyone but myself seems to have seen that something was wrong. She has been very anxious to give me pleasure, and I'm afraid she's been burning the candle at both ends for my light. I wish I had known—probably it lay just within my hand to prevent this, instead of leading her on by my often expressed delight. What I want to ask you is that if you find anything serious, you'll tell me, and quiet my father's fears as much as possible. Please do this for me. My father isn't young, and I, I think, am trustworthy."

She had spoken rapidly, but with convincing sincerity, looking her companion full in the face.

The doctor quietly scrutinized the earnest young face before he answered. Then he slightly bowed in acquiescence.

"That's a pact," he said lightly, "but in all probability your father's fears are exaggerated."

" 'Where love is great, the littlest doubts are fears,' " she quoted, softly flushing. The doctor had a singular, impersonal habit of keeping his eyes intently bent upon the person with whom he conversed, which made his companion feel that they two were exclusively alone—a sensation slightly bewildering upon first acquaintance. By and by one understood that it was merely his air of interest which evoked the feeling, and so gradually got used to it as to one of his features.

"That's true," he replied cheerily; "and—I see someone is going to play. Mrs. Merrill told me we should have some music."

"It's Louis, I think; I know his touch."

"Your cousin? He plays?"

Ruth looked at him in questioning wonder. Truth to say, the doctor could not but betray his surprise over the idea of the cold-looking Arnold in the light of a musician. But his doubts took instant flight after the opening chords. He played Chopin, played him with all the poignant passion, all the poetic imagery and tragedy, of that tragic fount of music.

"An artist," said someone standing near.

"Something more," murmured Kemp, rising as he saw Ruth do so. He was about to offer her his arm when Mrs. Merrill, a gentle-faced woman, stepped up to them, and laying her hand upon Ruth's shoulder, said rather hurriedly:

"I'm sorry to trouble you, doctor, but Mrs. Levice—don't be alarmed, Ruth dear—has become somewhat hysterical, and we can't calm her. Will you come this way, please, and no one need know. She's in the study."

They turned with her, through the conservatory, and so across the hall.

"I'll be here, doctor, if you need anything," said Mrs. Merrill, standing without, as he and Ruth entered, and immediately shutting the door after them.

"Stay there," he said with quiet authority to Ruth, and she stood quite still where he left her. Mrs. Levice was seated in a large easy-chair, her back to the door. Her husband had drawn her head to his bosom. There was no one else in the room, and, for a second, not a sound, till Mrs. Levice began to sob in a frightened manner.

"It's nothing at all, Jules," she cried, trying to laugh and failing lamentably. "I—I'm only silly."

"There, dear, don't talk." Levice's face was white as he soothingly stroked her hair.

"O-o-oh!"

The doctor stepped in front of them, and laying both hands upon her shoulders, motioned Levice aside.

"Hush! Not a word!"

At the sound of his stern, brusque voice, the long, quivering shriek stopped halfway.

"Be perfectly still," he continued, holding her firmly. "Obey this instant." She began to whimper. "Not a sound now."

Ruth and her father stood spellbound at the effect of the stranger's measures. For a moment Mrs. Levice had started in affright to scream; but the cool, commanding tone, the powerful hands upon her shoulders, the impressive, unswerving eye holding hers, soon began to act hypnotically. The sobbing gradually ceased, the shaking limbs slowly regained their calm, and as she sank upon the cushions the strained look in her eyes melted. She was feebly smiling up at the doctor in response to his own persuasive smile which gradually succeeded the gravity of his countenance.

"That's right," he said, speaking soothingly as to a child, and still keeping his smiling eyes upon hers. "Now—just—close—your—eyes—for a minute; see—I have your hand—so. Go to sleep."

There was not a sound in the room; Ruth stood where she had been placed, and Mr. Levice was behind the doctor, his face quite colorless, scarcely daring to breathe. Finally the faint, even breathing of Mrs. Levice told that she slept.

Kemp turned to Mr. Levice and spoke in a low, but distinct, tone.

"Put your hand, palm up, under hers. I'm going to draw my hand away and go—I don't want to excite her. She'll probably open her eyes in a few moments. Take her home as quietly as you can."

"You'll call tomorrow?" whispered Levice.

He quietly assented.

"Now be quick." The transfer was deftly made, and nodding cheerfully, Dr. Kemp left the room.

Ruth came forward. Five minutes later Mrs. Levice opened her eyes.

"Why, what has happened?" she asked languidly.

"You fell asleep, Esther," replied her husband, gently.

"Yes, I know; but why is Ruth in that gown? Oh—ye-es!" Consciousness was returning to her. "And who was that handsome man who was here?"

"A friend of Ruth's."

"He is very dictatorial," she observed pensively. She lay back in her chair for a few minutes as if dreaming. Suddenly she started up.

"What thoughtless people we are! Let's go back to the drawing-room or they'll think something dreadful has happened."

"No, mamma; I don't feel at all like going back. Stay here with father while I get our wraps."

Before Mrs. Levice could demur, Ruth had left the room. As she turned in the direction of the stairs, she was startled by a hand laid upon her shoulder.

"Oh, you, Louis! I'm going for our wraps."

"Here they are. How is my aunt?"

"She's quite herself again. Thanks for the wraps. Will you call up the carriage? We'll go at once, but don't think of coming yourself."

"Nonsense! Tell your mother you have made your adieux to Mrs. Merrill—she understands. The carriage is waiting."

A few minutes later the Levices and Louis Arnold quietly stole away. Mrs. Merrill lightly explained to those inquiring that Mrs. Levice had had an attack of hysteria. "Nothing at all," the little world about her said, and dismissed it as carelessly as most of the quiet turning-points in a life-history are dismissed.

CHAPTER III

THE LEVICES' house stood well back upon its grounds, almost with an air of reserve in comparison with the rows of stately, bay-windowed houses facing it and hedging it in on both sides. But the broad, sweeping lawns, the confusion of exquisite roses and heliotropes, the open path to the veranda, whereon stood an hospitable garden settee and chair, the long French windows open this summer morning to sun and air, offered an unusually inviting aspect for a city home.

As Dr. Kemp ascended the few steps leading to the front door he looked around approvingly.

"Not a bad berth for the grave little bookworm," he mused as he rang the bell.

It was immediately answered by the "grave little bookworm" in person.

"I've been on the lookout for you for the past hour," he explained, leading him into the library and turning the key of the door as they entered.

It was a cosy room, not small or low, as the word might suggest, but large and airy; the cosyness was supplied by comfortable easy-chairs, two deep couches, a broad, low table with flowers, an open piano, a few soft prints and paintings on the walls, and books in cases, books on tables, books on stands, books everywhere. Two long deep-framed windows let in through their draperies a flood of searching sunlight which brought to light not an atom of dust in the remotest corner. It is almost an article of faith with many a Jewess that her house be kept as clean as if at any moment a search-warrant for dirt might be served upon her.

"Won't you be seated?" asked Levice, looking up at Kemp as the latter stood pulling off his gloves.

"Is your wife coming down here?"

"No; she is in her room yet."

"Then let's go up immediately. I'm not at leisure."

"I know. Still, I wish to ask you to treat whatever you may find wrong as lightly as possible in her presence; she has never known anxiety or worry of any kind. It will be necessary to tell only me, and every precaution will be taken."

Here was a second one of this family of three wishing to take the brunt of the trouble on his shoulders, and the third had been bearing it secretly for some time. Probably a very united family, loving and unselfish doubtless, but the doctor had to stifle an amused smile in the face of the old gentleman's dignified appeal.

"But she's not a child, I suppose; she knows of the nature of my visit?" He moved with some impatience toward the door.

"Ruth—my daughter, you know,—was about to tell her as I left the room."

"Then we'll go up directly."

Levice preceded him up the broad staircase. As they reached the landing, he turned to the doctor.

"Pardon my care, but I must make sure that Ruth has told her. Just step into the sitting-room a second," and the solicitous husband went forward to his wife's bedroom, leaving the door open.

Standing thus in the hallway, Kemp could plainly hear the following words:

"And being interested in nervous diseases," the peculiarly low voice was saying, "he told father he would call and see you—out of professional curiosity, you know. Besides we wouldn't like you to be often taken as you were last night, would we?"

"People with plenty of time on their hands," soliloquized the doctor, looking at his watch in the hallway.

"What is his name, did you say?"

"Dr. Herbert Kemp."

"What! Don't you know that Dr. Kemp is one of the best-known physicians in the city? Everyone knows he has no time for curiosity. Nervous diseases are his specialty, and do you think he would come without—"

"Being asked?" interrupted a pleasant voice; the doctor, with some respect for the flight of time, had walked in unannounced.

"Keep your seat," he continued, as Mrs. Levice started up, the excited blood springing to her cheeks.

"You hardly need an introduction, Esther," said Levice. "You remember Dr. Kemp from last night?"

"Yes. Don't go, Ruth, please. Jules, hadn't you something to do downstairs?"

Did she imagine for a moment that she could still conceal her trouble from his tender watchfulness? Great dark rings encircled her now feverishly bright eyes, her mouth trembled visibly, and as Ruth drew aside, her mother's shaking fingers held tight to her hand.

"I have nothing in the world to do," replied Levice, heartily. "I'm going to sit right here and get interested."

"You will have to submit to a friendly cross-examination, Mrs. Levice," said the physician.

He drew a chair up before her and took both her hands in his. Ruth, relinquishing her hold, encountered a pair of pleasantly authoritative gray eyes, and instantly divining their expression, left the room.

She descended a few steps to the windowed landing. Here she intended joining the doctor on his way down. Probably her father would follow him, but it was her intention to intercept any such plan. A fog had arisen, and the struggling, rosy beams of the sun glimmered opalescently through the density. Ruth thought it would be clear by noon, when she and her mother could go for a stirring tramp. She stood lost in thought till a firm footfall on the stairs aroused her.

"I see Miss Levice here; don't come down," Kemp was saying. "What further directions I have must be given to a woman."

"Stay with mother, father," called Ruth, looking up at her hesitating father. "I'll see the doctor out," and she quickly ran down the few remaining steps to Kemp, awaiting her at the foot. She opened the door of the library, and closing it quickly behind them, turned to him expectantly.

"Nothing to be alarmed at," he said, answering her mute inquiry. He seated himself at the table and drew from his vest-pocket pencil and blank. Without another glance at the girl, he wrote rapidly for some minutes. When he arose he handed her the two slips of paper.

"The first is a tonic which you will have made up," he explained, picking up his gloves and hat and moving toward the door, "the other is a diet which you are to observe. As I told her just now, she must stay in bed and see no one but her immediate family; you must see that she hears and reads nothing exciting. That's all, I think."

Indignation and alarm held riot in Ruth's face and arrested the doctor's departure.

"Dr. Kemp," she said, "you force me to remind you of a promise you made me last night. Won't you at least tell me why you have to use such strenuous measures?"

A flash of recollection came to the doctor's eyes.

"Why, this is an unpardonable breach, Miss Levice, but I'll tell you all the trouble. Your mother is suffering from a certain form of hysteria to a degree that would have prostrated her if we had not come forward in time. As it is, by prostrating her ourselves for awhile, say a month or so, she'll easily regain her equilibrium. You've heard of the food-and-rest cure?"

"Yes."

"Well, that's what she will undergo, mildly. Has she any duties that will suffer by her neglect?"

"No necessary ones but those of the house. Under no circumstances can I imagine her giving up their supervision."

"Well, she'll have to under the present state of affairs. Remember, her mind must be kept unoccupied, though time may be made to pass pleasantly for her. This isn't an easy job, Miss Levice, but, according to my promise, I've left you to undertake it."

"Thank you," she responded quietly.

Kemp looked at her with a pleasant sense of satisfaction.

"Good-morning," he said, and held out his hand with a smile.

As the door closed behind him, Ruth felt as if a burden had fallen from, unstead of upon, her. For the last twenty-four hours her apprehensions had been excessive. Now, though she knew positively that her mother's condition needed instant and constant care, which she must herself assume, all sense of responsibility fell from her. The few quiet words of this strange physician had made her trust his strength as she would a rock. She could not have explained why it was so, but as her father remarked once, she might have said, "I trust him implicitly, because, though a man of superiority, he implicitly trusts himself."

When she reëntered her mother's room her father regarded her intently.

"So we're going to make a baby of you, mamma," she cried playfully, coming forward and folding her arms around her mother who lay on the couch.

"So he says, and what he says one can't oppose." There was an apathetic ring to her mother's voice that surprised her. Quickly the thought flashed through her that she was too weary to resist, now that she was found out.

"Then we won't try to," Ruth decided, seating herself on the edge of the couch close to her mother. From his armchair, Mr. Levice noted with remorseful pride the almost matronly poise and expression of his lovely young daughter as she bent over her weary-looking mother and smoothed her hair.

"And if you're to be baby," she continued, smiling down, "I'll have to change places with you, and be mother. You'll see what a capital one I'll make. Let's see, what are the duties? First, baby must be fed—properly—I'm an artist at that; second, father, and the rest of us, must have a perfectly appointed *ménage*; third—"

"I don't doubt that you will make a perfect mother, my child." The gentle meaning of her father's words and glance made Ruth flush with delight. When Levice said, "My child," the words were a caress. "Just believe in her, Esther. One of her earliest lessons was 'Whatever you do, do thoroughly.' She'll have to learn it through experience. But as you trust me, trust my pupil."

The soft smile playing upon her husband's face found its reflection on Mr. Levice's.

"Oh, Ruth," she murmured tremulously, "it will be so hard for you!"

This was a virtual laying down of arms, and Ruth was satisfied.

CHAPTER IV

OUIS ARNOLD, the only other member of the Levice family, had been forced to leave town on business the morning after Mrs. Levice's attack at the Merrill reception. He was, therefore, much surprised and shocked on his return, a week later, to find his aunt in bed and such rigorous measures for quiet in vogue.

Arnold had been an inmate of the house for the past twelve years. He was a direct importation from France, which he had left just before attaining his majority, through Levice's urgent plea for "the arm of a son" in his declining years. He had no sooner taken up his abode with his uncle than he was regarded as the most useful and ornamental piece of foreign *vertu* in the beautiful house.

Being a business man by nature, keen, wary, and indefatigable, he was soon able to take almost the entire charge of Levice's affairs. After a few years his uncle had ceased to question his business capabilities. From the time he arrived, he naturally fell into the position of his aunt's escort, thus again relieving Levice, who preferred the quieter life.

When Ruth began to go into society, his presence was almost a necessity, as Jewish etiquette, or rather Jewish espionage, forbade, in those days, a young man unattached by blood or intentions to appear as the attendant of a single woman. This was one of the well-intentioned unwritten laws Jewish heads of families sternly held to—keeping the young people apart—making the young men graceless, and depriving the young girls of a great deal of innocent pleasure.

Arnold, however, was not an escort to be despised, as Ruth soon discovered. She very quickly felt a sort of family pride in his cool, quizzical manner and caustic repartee, which was wholly distinct from her more girlish admiration of his distinguished person. He and Ruth were great friends in a quiet, unspoken fashion.

They were sitting together alone in the library on the evening of his return. Mrs. Levice had fallen asleep, and her husband was sitting with her. Ruth had stolen down to keep Louis company, knowing he would feel lost in the changed order of the house.

Arnold lay at full length on a couch; Ruth was sunk in a deep, winged-backed chair.

"What I am surprised at," he was saying, "is that my aunt submits to this confining treatment." He pronounced the last word "tritment," but he never stopped at a word because of its pronunciation, thus adding a certain piquancy to his speech.

"You wouldn't be surprised if you knew Dr. Kemp; one follows his directions blindly."

"So I have heard from a great many—women."

"And not men?"

"I have never happened to hold a conversation with a man on the powers of Dr. Kemp. Women delight in such things."

"What things?"

"Why, giving in to the magnetic power of a strong man."

"You err slightly, Louis; it's the power, not the giving in, we delight in, counting it an attractive part of manliness."

"Will you allow me to differ with you? Besides, apart from this great first cause, I do not understand how, after a week of it, she has not rebelled."

"I think I can answer that satisfactorily," replied his cousin, a mischievous smile parting her lips and showing a row of strong white teeth. "She is in love."

"Also?"

"With father; and so does as she knows will please him best. Love is also something everyone loves to give in to."

"Everyone who loves, you mean."

"Everyone loves something or someone."

"Behold the exception, then." He moved his head so as to get a better view of her.

"I don't believe you."

"That—is rude." He kept his eyes meditatively fixed upon her.

"Have you made a discovery in my face?" she asked presently, slightly moving from his gaze.

"No," he replied calmly. "My discovery was made some time ago. I am merely going over beautiful and pleasant ground."

"Really?" she returned, flushing. "Then please look away now; you annoy me."

"Why should I, since you know it is done in admiration? You are a woman; don't pretend distaste for it."

"I'll certainly go upstairs if you persist in talking so hatefully."

"Indulge me a little; I feel like talking, and I promise not to be—hateful. Always wear white—it becomes you. Never forget that real beauty is most adorned when least adorned. Another thing, *ma belle cousine,* that little trick you have of blushing on the slightest provocation spoils your whole appearance. Your complexion should always retain its healthy whiteness, while—"

"You've been indulged quite enough, Louis. Do you know, if you often spoke to me in this manner I should soon detest you?"

"That would indeed be unfortunate. Never hate, Ruth; besides making enemies, hate is an arch enemy to the face, distorting the softest and loveliest."

"We can't love people who calmly sit and irritate us."

"That is exaggerated, I think. Besides, heaven forbid our loving everybody! Never love, Ruth; let liking be strong enough for you. Love only wears out the body and narrows the mind, all to no purpose. Cupid, you know, died young, or wasted to plainness, for he never had his portrait taken after he matured."

"A character such as you would have would be unbearable."

"But sensible and wise."

"Happily our hearts need no teaching; they love and hate instinctively before the brain can speak."

"Good—for some. But in me behold the anomaly whose brain always reconnoiters the field before-hand, and has never yet considered it worth while to signal either 'love' or 'hate.' "

He rose with a smile and sauntered over to the piano. The unbecoming blush mounted slowly to Ruth's face and her eyes were bright as she watched him. When his hands touched the keys, she spoke.

"No doubt you think it adds to your dominance to pretend independence of all emotion. But, do you know, I think feeling, instead of being a weakness, is often more clever than wisdom? At any rate, what you're doing now is proof sufficient that you feel, and perhaps more strongly than many."

He partly turned on the music-stool and regarded her questioningly, never, however, lifting his hands from the keys as he played a softly passionate minor strain.

"What am I doing?" he asked.

"Making love to the piano."

"It does not hurt the piano, does it?"

"No; but never say you don't feel when you can play like that."

"Is not that rather peremptory? Who taught you to read character?"

"You."

"I? What a poor teacher I was to allow you to show such bungling work! Will you sing?"

"No, I'm going to read; I've had quite enough of myself and of you for one night."

"Alas, poor me!" he retorted mockingly, and seeming to accompany his words with his music. "I am sorry for you, my child, that your emotions are so troublesome. You have just made your entrance into the coldest, most exciting arena—the world. Remember what I tell you—all the strong motives, love and hate and jealousy, are mere flotsam and jetsam. You are the only loser by their possession."

The quiet closing of the door was his only answer. Ruth had left the room.

She knew Arnold too well to be affected by his little affectation of cynicism. If she could escape a cynic, either in books or in society, she invariably did so. Life was still beautiful for her, and one of her father's untaught lessons was that the cynic is a one-sided creature, having lost the eye that sees the compensation balancing all things. As long as Louis attacked things, it did no harm, except to incite a friendly passage-at-arms; hence, most of such talk passed in the speaking. Not so his faint disparagement of Dr. Kemp.

During the week in which Ruth had established herself as nurse-in-chief to her mother she had seen him almost daily. Time in the quiet sick-room had passed monotonously; events, unnoticed in hours of well-being and activity, had assumed proportions of importance; meal-times were looked forward to as a break in the day; the doctor's visit, especially as it was the only one allowed, was an excitement. Dr. Kemp's visits were short, but the two had learned to look for his coming and the sound of his deep, cheery voice, as to a morning's tonic that would strengthen the whole day. Naturally, as he was a stranger, Mrs. Levice in her idleness had analyzed and discussed aloud his qualities, both personal and professional, to her satisfaction. She had small ground for basing her judgments, but comment and speculation upon the doctor formed a good part of her conversation.

Ruth's knowledge of him was somewhat wider—about the distance between Mrs. Levice's bedroom and the front door. She had a homely little way of seeing people to the door, and here it was the doctor gave her any new instructions. Instructions were soon given and taken, however, and there was always time for a word or two of a different nature.

In the first place, she had been attracted by his magnificent pair of black horses.

"I wonder if they'd despise a lump of sugar," she said one morning.

"Why should they?" asked Kemp.

"Oh, they seem to hold their heads so haughtily."

"Still, they're human enough to know sweets when they see them," their owner replied, taking in the beautiful figure of the young girl in her quaint, flowered morning-dress. "Try them once, and you won't doubt it."

She did try them, and as she turned a slightly flushed face to Kemp, who stood beside her, he held out his hand, saying gaily, "Let me thank you and shake hands for my horses."

One can even become eloquent, witty, or tender over the weather. The doctor became neither of these, but Ruth, whose spirits were mercurially affected by the atmosphere, always viewed the elements with the eye of a private signal-service reporter.

"This is the time for a tramp," she said, as they stood on the veranda, and the summer air, laden with the perfume of heliotrope, stole around them. "That's where the laboring man has the advantage over you, Dr. Kemp."

"Which, ten to one, he finds a disadvantage. But I agree with you—in such weather every healthy person of leisure should be gormandizing on this air. You, Miss Levice, should get on your walking togs instantly."

"Yes, but not conveniently. My father and I never failed to take our morning constitutional together when all was well. Father always gave me the dubious compliment of saying I walked as straight and took as long strides as a boy. Being a great lover of walking, I was sorry my *pas* was not ladylike."

"I'm sure you must be a capital pedestrian. Your father evidently remembered what a troublesome thing it is to conform one's length of limb to the dainty footsteps of a woman."

"Father has no trouble on that score," said Ruth, laughing.

The doctor laughed heartily in response, and raising his hat, said, "That's where he has the advantage over a tall man."

Reviewing several such scenes, Ruth could remember nothing in his manner but a sort of invigorating, friendly bluntness, totally at variance with the peculiarities of the mere woman's man Louis had insinuated he was accounted. She resolved to scrutinize him more narrowly the next morning.

Mrs. Levice's room was handsomely furnished and daintily appointed. Even from her pillows she would have detected any lapse in its exquisite order, and one of Ruth's duties was to leave none to be detected. The house was large, and with three servants the young girl had a deal of supervising. She took a naïve pride in having things move as smoothly as under her mother's administration; and Mr. Levice assured his wife it was well she had retired, as the new broom was a vast improvement.

Ruth had given the last touches to her mother's dark hair, and was reading aloud the few unexciting items one finds in the morning paper. Mrs. Levice, propped almost to a sitting position by many downy pillows, polished her nails and half listened. Her cheeks were no longer brightly flushed, but quite pale; but the expression of her eyes was placid, and her slight hand quite firm; the strain lifted from her, a great weariness had taken its place. The sweet morning air came in unrestrained at the open window.

Ruth's reading was interrupted by the entrance of the maid, carrying a dainty basket of Duchesse roses.

"For Madame," she said, handing it to Ruth, who came forward to take it.

"Read the card yourself," she said, placing it in her mother's hand as the girl retired. A pleased smile broke over Mrs. Levice's face; she buried her face in the roses, and then opened the envelope.

"From Louis!" she exclaimed delightedly. "Poor fellow! he was dreadfully upset when he came in. He didn't say much, but his look and handshake were enough as he bent to kiss me. Do you know, Ruth, I think Louis has a very loving disposition?"

"Yes, dear?"

"Yes. One wouldn't think so, judging from his manner, but I know him to be unusually sympathetic, for a man. I would sooner have him for a friend than many a woman; he hasn't many equals among the young men I know. Don't you agree with me, dear?"

"Oh, yes. I always liked Louis."

"How coldly you say that! And, by the way, it struck me as very queer last night that you didn't kiss him after his being away a whole week. Since when has this formal handshake come into use between you?"

A slight flush crimsoned Ruth's cheek.

"It's not my fault," she said, smiling ruefully. "I always kissed Louis even after a day's absence. But some few months ago he inaugurated the new régime, and holds me at arm's length. I can't ask him why, when he looks at me so matter-of-factly through his eye-glass, can I?"

"No; certainly not." A slight frown marred the complacency of Mrs. Levice's brow. Such actions were not at all in accordance with her darling scheme. Arnold was much to her, but she wished him to be more. This was a sidetrack upon which she had not wished her train to move.

Her cogitations took a turn when she heard a quick footfall in the hall.

Ruth anticipated the knock, and opened the door to greet the doctor.

Bowing slightly to her, he advanced somewhat hurriedly to the bedside. He had not taken off his gloves, and an intent air of troubled gravity replaced his usual leisurely manner.

"Good-morning, Mrs. Levice," he said, taking her hand in his, and looking searchingly down at her. "How are you this morning? Any starts or shakes of any sort?"

"No; I'm beginning to feel as impassive and stupid as a well-fed animal. Won't you sit down?"

"No, I have a consultation in a very short time. Keep right on as you've been doing. I don't think it will be necessary for me to call for several days now, probably not before Friday."

"And today is Tuesday! Am I to see no one till then?"

"No one but those you have seen. Please don't complain, Mrs. Levice," he said in sharp sternness. "You're a very fortunate invalid. Illness with you is cushioned in every conceivable corner. I wish I could make you divide some of your blessings. As I can't, I wish you would appreciate them as they deserve. Don't come down, Miss Levice." She had moved to follow him. "I'm in a great hurry. Good-morning."

"How harassed he looked! I wonder who is his patient!" murmured Mrs. Levice, as Ruth quietly returned to her seat. A sunbeam fell aslant the girl's preoccupied face. The doctor's few words had given her food for thought.

When, later, she remembered how she was going to disprove for herself Louis's innuendoes, she wondered if he could have found anything to cavil at, had he been present, in Kemp's abrupt visit of the morning.

CHAPTER V

Ruth Levice's taste in dress was part of her distinction. Indeed, any little jealousy her lovely presence might occasion was usually summed up in the terse truism,' "Fine feathers make fine birds."

She had discovered the art of dressing appropriately. Having a full purse, she could humor every occasion with a change of gown; being possessed of correct taste, her toilettes never offended; desiring to look pleasing, as every normal woman does, she studied what was becoming; having a mother to whom a good appearance was one of the most pressing duties, and who delighted in planning beautiful gowns for her beautiful daughter, there was nothing to prevent Ruth from being well-dressed.

On this summer afternoon she was clad from head to foot in soft gray. Every movement of her young body, as she walked toward town, betokened health and elastic strength. Her long, easy gait precluded any idea of hurry; she noticed everything she passed, from a handsome horse to a dirty child.

She was approaching that portion of Geary Street which the doctors had appropriated, and she carefully scanned each silvery sign-plate in search of Dr. Kemp's name. It was the first time she had had occasion to go, and with a little feeling of novel curiosity she ran up the steps leading to his office.

It was just three, the time stated as the limit of his office-hours, but when Ruth entered the handsome waiting-room two or three patients were still awaiting their turns. Seated in one of the easy-chairs near the window was an aristocratic-looking woman, whom Ruth recognized as a friend of one of her Christian friends, and with whom she had a speaking acquaintance. Nodding pleasantly in response to the rather frigid bow, she walked to the center of the room and, laying upon the table a bunch of roses she was carrying, she proceeded to select one of the magazines scattered about. As she sat down she found herself opposite a stout Irishwoman, coarsely but cleanly dressed, who, with undisguised admiration, was taking in every detail of Ruth's appearance. She overlooked the evident simplicity of the woman's stare, but the wistful, yearning gaze of a little girl who reclined upon the lounge caused her to sit with her magazine unopened. As soon as she perceived that it was her flowers the child was regarding so longingly, she bent forward, and holding out a few roses, said invitingly:

"Would you like these?"

There is generally something startling in the sudden sound of a voice after a long silence between strangers, but the pretty cadence of Ruth's gentle voice bore no suggestion of abruptness.

"Indeed, and she just do dote on 'em," answered the mother, in a loud tone, for the blushing child.

"So do I," responded Ruth; and leaning farther forward, she put them in the little hand.

But the child's hand did not close over them, and the large eyes turned piteously to her mother.

"It's paralyzed she is," hurriedly explained the mother. "Shall mamma hold the beautiful roses for ye, darlint?"

"Please," answered the childish treble.

Ruth hesitated a second, and then rising and bending over her said:

"No; I know of a much better way. Wouldn't you like to have me fasten them in your belt? There—now you can smell them all the time."

"Roses is what she likes mostly," proceeded the mother, garrulously, "and she's for giving the doctor one every time she can when he comes. Faith! it's about all he do get for his goodness, for what with—"

The sudden opening of the folding-door interrupted her flow of talk. Seeing the doctor standing on the threshold as a signal for the next in waiting to come forward, the poor woman arose, ready to help her child into the consulting-room.

"Let me help Mamie, Mrs. O'Brien," he said as he came toward her. At the same moment the elegant-looking woman rose from her chair and swept toward him.

"I believe it's my turn," she said, in response to his questioning salutation.

"Certainly, if you came before Mrs. O'Brien. If so, walk in," he moved aside for the other to enter.

"Sure, doctor," broke in Mrs. O'Brien, anxiously, "we came in together."

"Indeed?" He looked from the florid, flustered face to the haughtily impassive woman beside her.

"Well, then," said he, courteously, "I know Mrs. O'Brien is wanted at home by her little ones. Mrs. Baker, you won't object, I'm sure."

It was now the elegant woman's turn to flush as Kemp took up the child.

Ruth felt a leap of delight at the action. She could never have defined the sense of proud exultation thrilling through her, but she knew she would never see him in a better light than when he left the room holding the little charity patient in his arms.

She also noticed with a tinge of amusement the look of added hauteur on the face of Mrs. Baker, as she returned to her seat at the window.

"Haughtiness," mused Ruth, "is merely a cloak to selfishness. What sympathy with humanity does that woman know? Poor thing!"

The magazine article remained unread; she drifted into far thoughts and scarcely noticed when Mrs. Baker left the room.

"Well, Miss Levice."

She started up, slightly embarrassed, as the doctor's voice thus aroused her.

"I was day-dreaming," she said, coming forward and flushing under his amused smile. "It was so quiet here that I forgot where I was."

He stood aside as she passed into the room, bringing with her an exquisite fragrance of roses.

"Will you sit down?" he asked, turning from closing the door.

"No; it's not worth while."

"What's the trouble—you or your mother?"

There had been nothing disconcerting in the Irishwoman's stare, but she felt suddenly hot and uncomfortable under the doctor's intent gaze.

"Neither of us," she answered. "I broke the tonic bottle this morning and the number was destroyed, so I should like to have you give me another prescription, please."

"Directly. Take this chair for a moment."

She seated herself perforce, and he took the chair beside the desk.

"How is she since yesterday?" he asked, writing without looking up.

"Quite as comfortable."

He handed her the prescription presently, and she arose at once. He stepped forward to open the outer door for her.

"You're not worried about her now, are you?" he questioned, with a hand on the knob.

"No; you've made us feel there was no cause for it. If it weren't for you, I'm afraid there might have been."

"Thanks, but don't think anything of the sort. Your nursing was as big a part of the game as my directions. It isn't Congress, but the people, who make the country, you know."

"That's condescending, coming from Congress," she laughed gayly. "But both the comparison and—the association make me feel duly proud. Do I look terribly 'sot up?' "

"You look—just as you should look. Miss Levice, may I beg a rose of you? No, not all. Well, thank you, they'll look wonderful in a certain room I'm thinking of."

"Yes?" There was a quick note of inquiry in the little word in reply to the doctor's pointed remark.

"Yes," he continued, leaning his back against the door and looking earnestly down at the tall girl, "the room of a lad without even the presence of a mother to make it pretty." He paused as if to note the effect of his words. "He's as lonely and uncomplaining as a tree in a desert; these roses will be a peculiar godsend to him." He finished his sentence with added warmth at sight of the swift sympathy in her lovely brown eyes.

"Do you think he would care to see anyone?"

"Well," replied Kemp, slowly, "I think he wouldn't mind seeing you."

"Then will you tell me where he lives so that I can go there some day?"

"Some day? Why not today? Would it be impossible to arrange it?"

"Why, no," she faltered, looking at him in surprise.

"You'll forgive my urging you—the boy is in such pressing need of some pleasurable emotion that as soon as I looked at you and your roses I thought, 'Now, that wouldn't be a bad thing for Bob.' You see, I was simply answering a question that's been bothering me all day. Then you'll drive there with me now?"

"But there isn't room," she said, searching unaccountably for an excuse.

"I can easily dispense with my driver."

"But won't my presence be annoying?" she persisted, still hesitant.

"Not to me," he said, and turned quickly for his hat.

She followed him silently with a sensation of novel excitement. She knew it was not the simple adventure but the personality of the man that was lending to the moment its piquant charm.

Presently she found herself comfortably seated beside him. He drove off at a rapid pace.

"I think," he said, turning his horses westward, "I'll have to make a call out here on Jones Street before going to Bob. You won't mind the delay, Miss Levice, will you?"

"Oh, no. This is 'my afternoon off,' you know. Father's at home, and mother won't miss me in the least. I was just thinking—"

She came to a sudden pause. She had just remembered that she was about to become communicative to a comparative stranger; the intent, interested look in Kemp's eye as he glanced at her was the disturbing element.

"You were thinking what?" he prompted with his eye now to the horses' heads.

"Nothing," she said, flushing deeply. "I mean, they'll have a lovely long afternoon together—without me."

"They are great lovers, those two, aren't they?" There was a faint tinge of curiosity in the idle comment.

"Past-masters. They've been lovering for almost a quarter of a century. Don't you think they should be experts by this time?"

Kemp checked the easy irony rising to his lips. He felt anew, with stronger urge, the individuality of the girl beside him, a certain innocence, quite distinct from ignorance, a *je-ne-sais-quoi* of youthful outlook, not referable alone to her youth, which moved his steady pulses with illusive delight. He quoted softly a verse from the *Rubaiyat*. They spoke of the poets. . . . June's sun and wind danced along with them, to the beat of their hearts, to the beat of the horses' hoofs. The moment was winged, at least it seemed so to Ruth.

They suddenly drew up before a somewhat imposing house with its double bay-windowed front, and the doctor sprang out, placed the reins in her proffered hand, and with a quick, "I won't be long," sprang up the broad flight of steps. Ruth, holding the reins, did not follow him with her eyes.

He had been in the house about five minutes when she saw him come out hastily. His hat was pulled down over his brows, which were gathered in an unmistakable frown. At the moment when he reached the last step a stout woman hurrying along the sidewalk accosted him breathlessly.

He waited stolidly, his foot on the carriage step, till she came up.

"So sorry I had to go out!" she burst forth. "How did you find my husband? What do you think of him?"

"Madame," he replied between his teeth, "since you ask, I think your husband is little short of an idiot!"

Ruth felt herself flush as she heard.

The woman looked at him in consternation.

"What's the matter?" she asked.

"Matter? Stuffing's the matter. If a man with a weak stomach like his can't resist gorging himself with things he has been strictly forbidden to touch, he'd better admit he's irresponsible, and be done! It's nonsense calling me in when he persists in cutting up such capers as he has just confessed. Good-afternoon."

And abruptly raising his hat, he sprang in beside Ruth, taking the reins from her without a word.

She felt quite meek and small beside him, and he seemed to have forgotten her presence entirely. So they traveled in silence in all the intimacy of an uncontrolled mood shared together.

They were now driving northeast toward that section of the city known as the Latin Quarter. The sweet, fresh breeze on the western heights toward Golden Gate seemed here, in its agglomeration of crowded, poorer cosmopolitanism, to be charged with odors redolent of anything but the "shores of Araby the blest."

Kemp finally gave vent to his exasperation.

"Some men," he said deliberately, as if laying down an axiom, "have no more conception of the dignity of controlled appetites than savages. Here is one who couldn't withstand anything savory to eat, to save his soul; otherwise he's a strong, sensible man. I can't account for it."

"The force of habit, perhaps," suggested Ruth.

"Probably. Jewish appetite is known to dote on the fat of the land."

That he said this with as little vituperation as if he had remarked on the weather, Ruth knew; and she felt no inclination to resent the remark, although a vision of her cousin Jennie's protesting did present itself, for, along with many Jewish people of embittered imagination, Jennie regarded every adverse remark on the race as a personal calumny.

"We always make the reservation that the fat be clean," she laughed.

Kemp flashed around at her.

"Miss Levice," he exclaimed contritely, "I completely for-got—I hope I wasn't rude."

"Why, certainly not," she answered half merrily, half earnestly. "Why should you be?"

"As you say, why should I be? Jewish individuals, of course, have their faults like the rest of us. As a race, most of their characteristics redound to their honor, in my estimation."

"Thank you," said the girl, quietly. "I am very proud of many Jewish traits."

"Such as a high morality, loyalty, intelligence, filial respect, and countless other things."

"Yes."

"Besides, it's wonderful how they hold the balance of power in the musical and histrionic worlds. And yet, to be candid, in comparison with these, they don't seem to have made much headway in the other branches of art. Can you explain it, Miss Levice?"

He waited deferentially for a reply.

"I was trying to think of a proper answer," she responded with earnest simplicity; "and I think that their great musical and histrionic powers are the results not so much of art as of passion inherited from times and circumstances stern and sad since the race began. Painting and sculpture require other things."

"Which the Jew cannot obtain?"

A soft glow overspread her face and mounted to her brow.

"Dr. Kemp," she answered, "we have begun. We have even risen—artistically speaking—out of the thrall of the Second Commandment. I should like to quote you the beautiful illustration with which one of our rabbis was inspired to answer a clergyman asking the same question; but I should only spoil that which in his mouth seemed eloquent."

"You would not, Miss Levice. Tell the story, please."

They were on level ground, and the doctor could disengage his attention from the horses. He did not fail to note the emotion which lit up her expressive face and made her sweet voice tremble.

"It is the story of the Rose of Sharon. This is it briefly: A pilgrim was about to start on a voyage to the Holy Land. In bidding a friend good-bye, he said: 'In that far land to which I am journeying, is there not some relic, some sacred souvenir of the time beautiful, that I can bring to you?' The friend mused awhile. 'Yes,' he made answer finally; 'there is a small thing, and one not difficult to obtain. I beg of you to bring me a single rose from the plains of Sharon.' The pilgrim promised, and departed.

On his return he presented himself before his friend. 'You have brought it?' he cried. 'Friend,' answered the pilgrim, sadly, 'I have brought your rose; but, alas! after all this weary traveling it is now but a poor, withered thing.' 'Give it to me!' exclaimed the friend, eagerly. The other did so. True, it was lifeless and withered; not a vestige remained of its once fragrant glory. But, as the man held it tenderly in his hand, memory and love untold overcame him, and he wept in ecstasy. And as his tears fell on the faded rose, lo! the petals sprang up, flushed into life; an exquisite perfume enveloped it—it had revived in all its beauty. Sir, in the words of the rabbi, 'In the light of toleration and love, we too have revived, we too are looking up.' "

As the girl paused, Kemp slightly, almost reverentially, raised his hat.

"Miss Levice, that is exquisite," he said softly.

They had reached the old, poorer section of the city, and the doctor stopped before a weather-beaten cottage.

"This is where Bob receives," he said, holding out a hand to Ruth; "in all truth it can't be called a home."

Ruth had a singular, disturbing feeling of understanding with the doctor as she went in with him. She dimly realized that she had been an impressionable witness of some of his dominant moods, and that she herself had been led on to an unrestrained display of feeling.

CHAPTER VI

THEY WALKED directly into a bare, dark hallway. There was no one stirring, and Kemp softly opened the door of one of several rooms leading into the passage. Here a broad band of yellow sunlight fell unrestrained athwart the waxen face of a sleeping boy. The rest of the simple, meager room was in shadow. The doctor noiselessly closed the door behind them, and stepped to the bed, which was covered with a heavy gray blanket.

The boy on the bed, even in sleep, would not have been accounted good-looking; there was a heaviness of feature, a plenitude of freckles, a shock of lack-lustre hair, which made poor Bob Bard anything but a thing of beauty. And yet, as Ruth looked at him, and saw Kemp's firm white hand placed gently on the low forehead, a great wave of tender pity took possession of her. Sleep puts the strongest at the mercy of the watcher, and there was a loneliness about this particular boy, a silent, expressive plea for protection, irresistibly appealing. Ruth longed to raise the rough, lonely head to her bosom.

"It would be too bad to wake him now," said the doctor, in a low voice, coming back to her side. "He is sleeping restfully, and that's what he needs. I'm sorry our little plan is frustrated, but it would be senseless to wait; there's no telling when he'll wake up."

A shade of disappointment passed over the girl's face, which he noticed.

"But," he added hurriedly, "you might leave your roses where he can't help seeing them. His wondering over their mysterious appearance will rouse him sufficiently for one day."

He watched her move lightly across the room and fill a cup

with water from an earthenware pitcher. She looked about for a second as if hesitating where to place it, and then quickly drew up a high-backed wooden chair close to the bedside and placed the cup with the roses upon it so that they looked straight into the face of the slumbering lad.

"We'll go now," Kemp said, and opened the door for Ruth to pass before him. She followed him with lingering step, but on the threshold drew back, a thoughtful little pucker on her brow.

"I think I'll wait after all," she explained. "I should like to talk with Bob a little."

The doctor looked slightly annoyed.

"You'd better drive home with me," he objected.

"Thank you," she said, drawing farther back into the room. "The Jackson Street cars are very convenient."

"But I should prefer to have you come with me," he insisted.

"But I don't want to," she resisted gently. "I have decided to stay."

"That settles it, then," smiled Kemp, and shaking her hand, he went out alone.

"When my lady will, she will; and when she won't, she won't," he mused, gathering up his reins. But the terminal point to the thought was a very wistful smile.

Ruth, left alone, seated herself on the one other chair near the foot of the bed. Strange to say, though she gazed at Bob, her thoughts had flown out of the room. She was still conscious of a new intoxication in her veins. Had she cared to look the cause boldly in the face, she would have known that, to begin with, she was flattered by Dr. Kemp's unmistakable desire for her assistance. She did admit that he must at least have looked at her with friendly eyes—but here her modesty drew a line even for herself, and, giving herself a quick mental shake, she saw that two lambent brown eyes were looking wonderingly at her from the face of the sick lad.

"How do you feel now, Bob?" she asked, going to him and smiling down at him.

The boy forgot to answer.

"The doctor brought me here," she went on brightly; "but you were asleep and he couldn't wait. Are you feeling better, Bob?"

The soft, star-like eyes did not wander in their gaze.

"Why did you come?" he breathed finally. His voice was surprisingly musical.

"Why?" faltered Ruth. "Oh, to bring you these roses. Do you like flowers, Bob?" She lifted the mass of delicate buds toward him. Two pale, transparent hands went out to meet them. Tenderly as you sometimes see a mother press the cheek of her baby to her own, he drew them to his cheek.

Ruth looked on, wondering.

"Like them!" he murmured passionately, his lips pressed to the fragrant petals.

"Why, you love them, don't you!"

"Lady," replied the boy, raising himself to a sitting position, "there's nothing in the world to me like flowers."

"I never thought boys cared so for flowers," she said in surprise.

"I'm a gardener," he returned simply, and again buried his face in the roses. Sitting up, he looked fully seventeen or eighteen years old.

"You must have missed them during your illness," observed Ruth.

A long sigh answered her. The boy rested his glowing eyes upon her. He was no longer ugly, with his face thus illumined.

"Maréchal Niel," she heard him murmur, still with his eyes upon her. "You are like a Maréchal Niel! Lady, I'd like to put my Homer rose next to you!"

"What Homer rose?" asked Ruth, humoring the flower-poet's conceit.

Recalled to himself, the boy flushed shyly. "It's—it's a way I've got into," he stammered, "comparing people to flowers. You can find a flower for nearly everybody, if you're used to them— flowers, I mean. Sometimes I think some people and some weeds"—he laughed, excited by his own fantasy.

"So do I," exclaimed Ruth, responsive, "now that you make me think of it. But what about that Homer rose?"

"Oh, he—the doctor, of course. Strong and firm and—enduring. Can—" again his eyes glowed like stars while his words groped—"can a Maréchal Niel—understand—a Homer?"

The girl felt herself flushing strangely. "Not as you do," she said quickly. "But tell me where you suffer, Bob."

"I don't suffer, I'm only weak. But he's taking care of me, and Mrs. Mills brings me just what he orders."

"And is there anything you would like to have that you forgot to tell him?"

"I never tell him anything I want," replied the boy proudly. "He knows beforehand. He knows about me the way I know about flowers. He hears me think."

It was like listening to music to hear the slow, drawling words of the invalid. Ruth's hand closed softly over his.

"I've got some pretty stories at home about flowers," she said. "Would you like to read them?"

"I can't read—very well," answered Bob, in unabashed simplicity.

Yet his spoken words were flawless.

"Then I'll read them to you," she answered promptly. "To-morrow, Bob, say, at about three?"

"You are coming again?" The heavy mouth quivered in eager surprise.

"Why, yes; now that I know you, I'm going to know you better. May I come?"

"Oh, lady!"

Ruth went out enveloped in that look of gratitude. It was the most spontaneous expression of warm gratitude she had ever received, and as she walked down the steep hill, she longed to be doing something really helpful to the many Bobs. Social service was still in its infancy, unorganized, spasmodic, individual, still groping its way through rigid sectarianism, into a Fruit and Flower Mission here, a Pioneer Kindergarten there. Besides, Ruth had led, on the whole, so far, an egoistic life.

Up to the present, her parents, between them, had claimed or planned most of her time. During her school years she had been a sort of human reservoir for all her father's ideas, whims, and hobbies. True, he had given her an interest in most things within her line of vision. Hanging on his arm as they wandered off daily in their peripatetic school, he had informed her outlook with a certain essence of nobility, due to the potential beauty which the visionary finds in the meanest thing. But while this theoretic life had been immensely inspiring and interesting, she had, as yet, given it no practical testing. For the past six months, after a year's travel in Europe, her mother had led her on in a whirl of what constituted to Mrs. Levice a girl's acme of happiness. But Ruth, peculiarly grounded as she was, had soon gauged the worth of the tyranny Society has imposed upon its devotees, and now that a lull had come, she realized that she needed an interest outside and beyond herself.

So immersed was she in this call of her deeper being, she walked on, unconscious of her foreign and picturesque surroundings, the old gray Greek church with its dome and minarets, the long flights of wooden steps leading up to the tinder-box homes with their spindly balconies, the Italian fishermen and bambinos, the Negroes and gayly-garbed Negresses, the blue-smocked Chinese with their queues, trotting along imperturbably—the whole motley bouquet of the Latin quarter.

A hand suddenly laid upon her shoulder startled her roughly.

"What are you doing in this part of town?" broke in Louis Arnold's voice in evident anger.

"Oh, Louis, how you frightened me! What's the matter with this part of town?"

"You are on a very disreputable street. Where are you going?"

"Home."

"Then be so kind as to turn back with me and take the car."

She glanced at him quickly, unused to his tone of command, and turned with him.

"How do you happen to be here?" he demanded shortly.

"Dr. Kemp took me to see a poor patient of his."

"Dr. Kemp?" Surprise raised his eyebrows grotesquely.

"Yes."

"Indeed! Then," he continued in cool, biting displeasure,

"why didn't he carry his charity a little farther and take you home again?"

"Because I didn't choose to go with him," she returned, rearing her head and looking calmly at him as they walked along.

"Bosh! What had your choosing or not choosing to do with it? The man knew where he had taken you even if you did not know. This quarter is occupied by nothing but Negroes and Chinamen, and foreign immigrants and adventurers, and—and worse! It was decidedly ungentlemanly to leave you to return alone at this time of the evening."

"Probably he gave me credit for being able to take care of myself in broad daylight."

"Probably he never gave it a second's thought one way or the other. Hereafter you had better consult your natural protectors before starting out on quixotic excursions with indifferent strangers."

"Louis!"

She stamped her foot angrily.

"Well?"

"Stop that, please. You are not my keeper!"

Her cousin smiled quizzically. They took their seats on the dummy, just as the sun, a golden ball, was about to glide behind Lone Mountain. It was that quiet, dreamy time of late afternoon, and Ruth and Louis did not speak for a while.

The girl was experiencing a whirl of conflicting emotions—anger at Louis' interference, pleasure at his protecting care, annoyance at what he considered gross negligence on the doctor's part, and a sneaking pride, in defiance of his insinuations, in the thought that Kemp had trusted to her womanliness as a safeguard against any chance annoyance. She also felt ashamed of having shown temper.

"Louis," she ventured finally, rubbing her shoulder against his, as gentle animals conciliate their mates, "I'm sorry I was so cross, but it exasperates me to hear you cast slurs, as you've done before, upon Dr. Kemp—behind his back."

"Why should it, my dear, since it gives you a chance to uphold him?"

There is a way of saying "my dear" that is as mortifying as a slap in the face, and Arnold used that way.

The dark blood surged over the girl's cheeks. She drew a long, hard breath, then said in a low voice:

"I think we won't quarrel, Louis. Will you get off at the next corner with me? I have a prescription to be made up at the druggist's."

"Certainly."

Arnold was all-courteous again.

CHAPTER VII

M RS. LEVICE was slowly gaining the high-road to recovery, and many of the restrictions for her cure had been removed. As a consequence, and with an eye ever to Ruth's social duties, she urged her to leave her more and more to herself.

As a matter of course, Ruth laid the case of Bob and his neighborhood before her father's consideration. A Jewish girl's life was, at that epoch, an open page to her family. Matters of small as well as of larger moment were freely shared and discussed—a good clearing-house institution which guarded against many indiscretions. This may have been a relic of more restricted days, days sadly narrowing, but broadly beautiful in that they implanted an unconquerable love of home and family in the core of every Jewish heart, a love which lies at the root of all a Jew's best inspirations. It was as natural for Ruth to consult her father in this trivial matter, in view of Arnold's disapproval, as it was for her friend, Dorothy Gwynne, to sally anywhere as long as she herself felt justified in so doing.

Ruth ardently wished to go, and as her father, after considering the matter, could find no objection, she went. After that it was enough to tell her mother that she was going to see Bob. Mrs. Levice had heard the doctor speak of him to Ruth, and any little charity that came in her way she was only too happy to forward.

Bob's plain, ungarnished room soon began to show signs of beauty under Ruth's deft fingers. A pot of mignonette in the window, a small painting of exquisite chrysanthemums on the wall, a daily bunch of fresh roses, were the food she brought for his poet soul. But there were other substantial things.

The day after she had replaced the coarse horse-blanket with a soft quilt, the doctor made one of his bi-weekly visits to her mother.

As he stood taking leave of Ruth on the veranda, he turned, with his foot on the last step, and looked up at her as if arrested by a sudden thought.

"Miss Levice," said he, "I'd like to give you a friendly scolding. May I?"

"How can I prevent you?"

"Well, if I were you I wouldn't indulge Bob's love of luxury as you do. He positively refused to get up yesterday on account of the 'soft feel,' as he put it, of that quilt. Now, you know, he must get up; he's able to, and in a week I want to start him in to work again. Then he won't be able to afford such 'soft feels,' and he'll rebel. He's had enough coddling for his own good. I really think it's mistaken kindness, Miss Levice."

The girl was leaning lightly against one of the supporting columns. A smile played about her lips while she listened.

"Dr. Kemp," she replied, "may I give you a little friendly scolding?"

"You have every right." His tone was very earnest, despite his smiling eyes. For a fleeting moment Ruth let the new note in his voice possess her, then,

"Well, don't you think it's rather hard of you to deprive poor Bob of any pleasure today may bring, on the ground that tomorrow he may wish it too, and won't be able to have it?"

"As you put it, it does seem so; but I'm hard enough to want you to see it as practically as I do. Put sentiment aside, and the only sensible thing to be done now is to prepare him for the hard, uncushioned facts of a hard life."

"But why must it be so hard for him?"

"Why? In the face of the inevitable, that's a time-wasting, useless question. Life is so; even if we find the underlying cause, the discovery won't alter the fact."

"Yes, it will."

"How?"

"By its enabling us to turn our backs on the hard way and seeking a softer."

"You forget that strait-jacket to all inclination—circumstance."

"And aren't you forgetting that friendly hands may help to loosen the strait-jacket?"

Her lovely face looked very winning, there above him.

"Good!" said he, raising his hat and forgetting to replace it while he spoke. "That's a gentle truth; some day we'll discuss it further. For the present, use your influence in getting Bob upon his feet."

"Yes." She gave a hurried glance at the door behind her, and ran quickly down to the lowest step. "Dr. Kemp," said she, a little breathlessly, "I've wanted for some time to ask you to let me know when you have any cases that require assistance outside of a physician's—such as my father or I might lend. You must have an immense field for such opportunities. Will you think of me then, please?"

"I will," he replied, looking with musing joy into her flushed face. "Going in for philanthropy, Miss Levice?"

"No; going out for it, thank you;" and she put her hand into his outstretched one. She watched him step into his carriage; he turned and raised his hat again—their eyes met and held each other in sudden, sweet recognition. Then he was gone.

He did not fail to keep his promise, and once on the lookout for "cases" herself, Ruth soon found enough irons in the fire to occupy her spare hours.

Mrs. Levice, however, insisted upon her resuming her place in society.

"A young girl can't withdraw herself from her sphere, or people will either consider her eccentric or will forget her entirely. Don't be unreasonable, Ruth; there's no reason why you shouldn't enjoy every function in our circle, and Louis is always happy to take you. When he asked you if you'd go with him to the Art Exhibition on Friday night, I heard you say you didn't know. Now, why?"

"Oh, that? I never gave it a second's thought. I promised

father to go with him in the afternoon; I didn't consider it worth an explanation."

"But, you see, I did. It looks very queer for Louis to be traveling around by himself; couldn't you go again in the evening with him?"

"Of course, you over-thoughtful aunt. If the pictures are good, a second visit won't be thrown away,—that is, if Louis is really anxious to have me with him. But, 'I doubt it, I doubt it, I do.' "

"What nonsense!" returned her mother, testily. "Why shouldn't he be? You are always amiable together, aren't you?"

"Well," she said, knitting her brows and pursing her lips musingly, "that, methinks, depends on the limits and requirements of amiability. If disputation showeth a friendly spirit, then is my lord overfriendly; for it oft hath seemed of late to pleasure his mood to wax disputatious—though, in sooth, lady fair, I have always maintained a wary and decorous demeanor."

"I can imagine," laughed her mother, with a frown. "Then you'll go?"

"Why not?"

If Arnold really cared for the outcome of such maneuvers, Mrs. Levice's exertions bore some fruit.

CHAPTER VIII

THERE ARE few communities, comparatively speaking, with more enthusiastic theater-lovers than are to be found in San Francisco. The play was one of the few worldly pleasures Mr. Levice thoroughly enjoyed. When a great star was heralded, he was in a feverish delight until he had come and gone. When Bernhardt appeared, the quiet little man fully earned the often indiscriminately applied title of "crazy Frenchman." A Frenchman is never so much one as when confronted in a foreign land with a great French creation; every fiber in his body answers each charm with an appreciation worked to fever-heat by patriotic love; at such times the play of his emotions precludes any idea of reason to an onlooker. Bernhardt was one of Levice's passions. Booth was another, though he took him more composedly. The first time the latter appeared at the Baldwin Theater (his opening play was *Hamlet*) the Levices—that is, Ruth and her father—went three times in succession to witness his matchless performance, and every succeeding characterization but strengthened their enthusiasm.

Booth was coming again. The announcement had been rapturously hailed by the Levices.

"It will be impossible for us to go together, father," Ruth remarked at the breakfast-table. "Louis will have to take me on alternate nights, while you stay at home with mamma. Did you hear, Louis?"

"You will hardly need to do that," answered Arnold, lowering his cup. "If you and your father prefer going together, I shall enjoy staying with your mother on those nights."

"Thanks for the offer—and your evident delight in my company," laughed Ruth with a little grimace. "But there's one play to which you'll have to take me. Don't you remember we always wanted to see his *Merchant of Venice* and judge for ourselves his interpretation of the character? Well, I'm determined that we must see it together."

"When does he play it?"

"A week from Saturday night."

"Sorry to disappoint you, but I shall be out of town at the end of next week."

"Oh dear! Honestly? Can't you put it off? I want so much to go!"

"Impossible. Go with your father."

"You know very well neither of us would go off and leave mamma alone at night. It's horrid of you to go. I'm sure you could manage differently if—"

"Why, my child!"

She was almost crying, and her father's quiet tone of surprised reprimand just headed off two great tears that threatened to fall.

"I know," she said, trying to smile, and showing an April face instead, "but I had just set my heart on going, and with Louis too."

"That comes of being a spoilt only child," put in Arnold, teasingly. "You ought to know by this time that of the many plans we make with ourselves, nine out of ten come to nothing. Before you set your heart on a thing, be sure you will not have to give it up."

Ruth, still sore with disappointment, acknowledged this philosophic remark with a curled lip.

"There, save your tears for something more worthy," cut in Levice, briskly. "If you care so much about it, we, or chance, must arrange it for you."

But chance in this instance was not propitious. Wednesday came, and Arnold saw no way of accommodating her. He left town after taking her to see *The Fool's Revenge* as a compromise.

"You seemed to be enjoying the poor Fool's troubles last night," observed Dr. Kemp, in the morning. They were still standing in Mrs. Levice's room.

"I? Not enjoying his troubles; I enjoyed Booth, though—if you can call it enjoyment when your heart is ready to break for him. Were you there? I didn't see you."

"No, I don't suppose you did, or you would have been in the pitiable condition of the princess who had her head turned. I sat directly back of your box, in the dress-circle. Then you like Booth?"

"Take care! that's a dangerous subject with my family," broke in Mrs. Levice. "Ruth has actually exhausted every adjective in her admiration vocabulary. The last extravaganza I heard from her on that theme was after she had seen him as Brutus: she wished herself Lucius, that, in the tent scene, she might kiss Booth's hand."

"It sounds gushing enough for a schoolgirl now," laughed Ruth, blushing under his eyes, "but at the time, I meant it."

"Have you seen him in all his repertoire?" he asked.

"In everything but Shylock."

"You'll have a chance for that on Saturday night. It will be a great farewell performance."

"Undoubtedly, but I shall have to forego that last glimpse of him."

"Now, doctor," exclaimed Mrs. Levice, "will you please impress it on her that I'm not a lunatic and can be left alone without fear? She is wild to go Saturday night, but won't go with her father, on the ground that I'll be left alone. Mr. Arnold is out of town. Isn't that being unnecessarily solicitous?"

"Surely. But," he added, turning deferentially to Ruth, "in lieu of a better escort, how would I do, Miss Levice?"

"I don't understand."

"Will you come with me Saturday night to see Shylock?"

Ruth was embarrassed. The doctor had said neither "will you honor me" nor "will you please me," but he had more than pleased and honored her. She turned a pair of radiant eyes to her mother. "Come now, Mrs. Levice," laughed Kemp, noting the action, "will you let your little girl go with me? Don't detain me with a refusal; it will be impossible to accept one now, and I won't be around till then, you know. Good-morning."

Unwittingly, the doctor had caused an excitement in the

hearts both of mother and daughter. The latter was naturally surprised at his unexpected invitation, but surprise was soon obliterated by another and quite a different feeling, which she kept rigorously to herself. Mrs. Levice was frankly in a dilemma about it, and consulted her husband in the evening.

"By all means, let her go," replied he. "Why should you have had any misgivings about it? I'm sure I'm glad she is going."

"But, Jules, you forget that none of our Jewish friends let their girls go out with strangers."

"Is that part of our religion?"

"No; but custom is in itself a religion. People do talk so at every little innovation against convention."

"What will they say? Nothing detrimental either to Ruth or the doctor. Pshaw, Esther! you ought to feel proud that Dr. Kemp has asked the child. If she wishes to go, don't set an impossible bogy in the way of her enjoyment. Besides, you don't care to appear so silly as you would if you said to the doctor, 'I can't let her go on account of people's tongues,' and that is the only honest excuse you can offer." So, in his forthright way, he decided it.

On Saturday night Ruth stood in the drawing-room buttoning her pale suede glove. Kemp had not yet come in. She looked unusually well in her dull sage-green gown. A tiny toque of the same color rested on her soft dark hair. The creamy pallor of her face, the firm, white throat revealed by the broad rolling collar, her grave lips and dreamy eyes, hardly told that she was feeling a little shy. Presently the bell rang, and Kemp came in, his open overcoat revealing the evening dress which became him well. He came forward hastily.

"I'm a little late," he said, holding her hand, "but it was unavoidable. Ten minutes to eight—the horses must make good time."

"It's slightly chilly tonight, isn't it?" she asked, for want of something better to say, turning for her wrap.

"I didn't feel it," he replied, intercepting her. "But this furry thing will keep the cold off, if there is any." He held it for her, and quite unprofessionally bent his head to hook it at her throat.

A bewildering sensation shot through Ruth as his face approached so close to her own.

"How are your mother and father?" he asked, holding the door open, while she turned for her fan.

"They're as usual," she answered. "Father expects to see you after the play. You will come in for a little supper, won't you?"

"That sounds alluring," he responded lightly, his quick eye remarking, as she came toward him, the dainty femininity of her loveliness, which seemed to have caught a grace beyond the reach of art.

It thus happened that they took their places just as the curtain rose.

CHAPTER IX

EVERYBODY KNOWS the sad old drama, as differently interpreted in its graver sentiment as there are different interpreters. Ruth had seen one who made of Shylock merely a fawning, mercenary, loveless, bloodthirsty wretch. She had seen another who presented a man of quick wit, ready tongue, great dignity, greater vengeance, silent of love, wordy of hate. Booth, without throwing any romantic glamour on the Jew, showed him as God and man, but mostly man, had made him: an old Jew, grown bitter in the world's disfavor through fault of race; grown old in strife for the only worldly power vouchsafed him—gold; grown old with but one human love to lighten his hard existence; a man who, at length, shorn of his two loves through the same medium that had robbed him of his manhood's birthright, now turned fiend, endeavors with tooth and nail to wreak the smoldering vengeance of a lifetime upon the chance representative of an inexorable persecution.

All through the performance Ruth sat a silent, attentive listener. Kemp, with his ready laugh at Gratiano's sallies, would turn a quick look at her for sympathy; he was rather surprised at the grave, unsmiling face beside him. When, however, the old Jew staggered alone and almost blindly from the triumphantly smiling court-room, a little pinch on his arm decidedly startled him.

He lowered his glass and turned toward her so suddenly that Ruth started.

"Oh," she faltered, "I—I beg your pardon; I had forgotten you weren't Louis."

"I don't mind in the least," he assured her easily.

The last act passes merrily and quickly; only the severe, great things of life move slowly.

As the doctor and Ruth made their way through the crowded lobby, the latter thought she had never seen so many acquaintances, each of whom turned an interested look upon her stalwart escort. Of this she was perfectly aware, but the same human interest with which Kemp's acquaintances regarded her passed by her, unnoticed.

A moment later they were in the fresh, open air.

"How beautiful it is!" said Ruth, looking up at the stars. "How the stars glow; and the wind has entirely died away."

" 'On such a night,' " quoth Kemp, as they approached the curb, "a closed carriage seems out of season."

"And reason," supplemented Ruth, while the doctor reluctantly opened the door. She glanced at him hesitatingly.

"Would you—" she began.

"Right! I would!" The door was banged to.

"John," he said, looking up at his man in the box, "take this trap around to the stable; I won't need the horses again tonight."

John touched his hat, and Kemp drew his companion's little hand through his arm.

"Well," he said, as they turned the corner, "were you satisfied with the great man tonight?"

"Yes," she replied meditatively, "fully; there was no exaggeration—it was all quite natural."

"Except Jessica in boy's clothes."

"Don't mention her, please; I detest her."

"And yet she spoke quite prettily on the night."

"I didn't hear her."

"Why, where were you while all the world was making merry on the stage?"

"Not with them; I was with the weary, heartbroken old man who passed out when joy began."

"Ah! I fancied you didn't half appreciate Gratiano's jesting. Miss Levice, I'm afraid you allow the sorry things of life to take too strong a hold on you. It isn't right. I assure you for every tear there's a laugh, and you must learn to give each its deference due."

"I'm sorry," replied Ruth, quietly, "but I'm afraid I can't learn that—tears are always stronger than laughter. How could I listen to the others' nonsense when my heart was sobbing with that lonely old man? Forgive me, but I can't forget him."

They walked along silently for some time. Instinctively, each felt the perfect accord with which they kept step. Ruth's little ear was just about on a level with the doctor's chin. He hardly felt the soft touch of her hand upon his sleeve, but as he looked at the white profile of her cheek against the dark fur of her collar, the knowledge that she was there was a disturbingly pleasing one.

"Did you consider the length of our walk when you fell in so promptly with my wish?" he asked presently.

"I like a long walk in pleasant weather; I never tire of walking."

"You've found the essentials of a good pedestrian—health and strength."

"Yes; if everybody were like me, all your skill would be thrown away—I'm never ill."

"There's no reason why you should be, with common-sense to back your blessings. If common-sense could be bought at the drug-store, I should be rid of a great many patients."

"That reminds me of a snatch of conversation I once overheard between my mother and a doctor's wife. I'm reminded of it because the spirit of your meaning is so different from hers. After some talk my mother asked, 'And how is the doctor?' 'Oh,' replied her visitor, with a long sigh, 'he's well enough in body, but he's blue, terribly blue; everybody is so well, you know.' "

"More human than humane," laughed Kemp. He was glad to see that she had roused herself from her sad musings; but a certain set purpose he had formed robbed him now of his former lightness of manner.

He was about to broach a subject requiring delicate handling, but an intuitive knowledge of the womanly character of the girl aided him much. It was not so much what he had seen her do as what he knew she was, that led him to begin his recital.

"We have a good many blocks before us yet," he said, "and I'm going to tell you a little story. Why don't you take the full benefit of my arm? There," he proceeded, drawing her hand farther through his arm, "now you feel more like a big girl than a bit of thistledown. If I get tiresome, just call 'time,' will you?"

"All right," she assented. She was beginning to meet halfway this matter-of-fact, unadorned, friendly manner of his, and when she did meet it, she felt a comfortable security in it. From the beginning to the end of his short narrative he looked straight ahead.

"How shall I begin? Do you like fairy tales? Well, this is the soul of one without the fictional wings. Once upon a time—I think that's the very best introduction going—a woman was left a widow with one little girl. She lived in New Orleans, where the blow of her husband's death and the loss of her good fortune came almost simultaneously. She must have had little moral courage, for as soon as she could she left her home, not being able to face the inevitable falling off of friends that generally follows loss of fortune. She wandered over the intermediate States between here and Louisiana, stopping nowhere long, but endeavoring to keep together the bodies and souls of herself and child by teaching.

"They kept this up for years until the mother succumbed. They were on the way from Nevada to Los Angeles when she died. The daughter, then not eighteen, went on to Los Angeles, where she buried her mother, and endeavored to find private teaching, as she had been doing before. She was young, unsophisticated, sad, and in want, in a strange town. She applied for advice to a man highly honored and recommended by his fellow-citizens. The man played the brute. The girl fled—anywhere. Had she been less brave, she would have fled from herself. She came to San Francisco and took a position as nurse-maid; children, she thought, could not play her false, and she might outlive it. The hope was cruel. She was living near my home, had seen my sign probably, and, in the extremity of her distress, came to me. There's a good woman who keeps a lodging-house, and who delights in doing me favors. I left the poor child in her hands, and she's now fully recovered.

"As a physician I can do nothing more for her, and yet melancholy has almost made a wreck of her. Nothing I say has any effect; all she answers is, 'It isn't worth while.' I understand her perfectly, but I hoped to buoy her up with some of her old spirit of independence. So this morning I asked her if she intended letting herself drift on in this way. I may have spoken a little more harshly than necessary, for my words broke down completely the wall of dogged silence she'd built around herself.

" 'Oh, sir,' she cried, weeping like the child she is, 'what can I do? Can I dare to take little children by the hand, stained as I am? Can I go as an impostor where, if people knew, they would snatch their dear ones from me? Oh, it would be too wretched!' I tried to remonstrate with her, told her that the lily trampled in the dust is no less a lily than is her spotless sister held high above contamination. She looked at me miserably from her tear-stained face, and then said, 'Men may think so, but women don't; a stain with them is ineffaceable whether made by one's self or another. No woman knowing my story would think me free from dishonor, and hold out her clean hands to me.'

" 'Plenty,' I contradicted. 'Maybe,' she said humbly; 'but what would it mean? The hand would be held out at arm's length by women safe in their position, who would never fail to show me how low they think me. I'm young yet; can you show me a girl, like myself in years, but white as snow, kept safe from contamination, as you say, who, knowing my story, would hold out her hand to me and not feel herself tainted by the contact? Don't say you can—I know you can't.'

"She was crying so violently that she wouldn't listen to me. When I left her, I myself could think of none of my young friends to whom I could put the question. I know many sweet, kind girls, but I could count not one among them all who, in such a case, would be brave as she was womanly—until I thought of you."

Complete silence followed his words. He did not turn his glance from the street ahead of him. He had made no appeal, would make none, in fact. He had told the story with scarcely a reflection on its tenor, a reflection which would have arrested another man from introducing such an element into his gentle fellowship with a girl like Ruth. His lack of hesitancy was born of his knowledge of the outcast's blamelessness, of her dire necessity for help, and of a premonition that Ruth Levice would be as free from conventional surface modesty as was he, through the earnestness of the undertaking.

There is something very sweet to a woman in being singled out by a man for some exceptional courage. Ruth felt this so strongly that she could almost hear her heart beat with the intoxicating knowledge. No question had been asked, but she felt an answer was expected. Yet, had her life depended on it, the words could not have come at that moment. Was she indeed what he esteemed her? Had he indeed placed her on this pedestal? Did she deserve the high place he had given her, or—would she?

With many women the question would have been, did she care for Dr. Kemp's good opinion? Now, though Ruth was indeed put upon her mettle, her quick sympathy had instantly responded to the girl's miserable story. Perhaps the spokesman himself influenced her, but had the girl stood before her at the moment, she would have seized her hand with all her impulsive warmth of understanding.

As they turned the corner of the block where Ruth's house stood, Kemp said, deliberately:

"Well?"

"Thank you. Where does she live?"

Her quiet, natural tone told nothing of the tumult of sweet emotions within. They had reached the house, and the doctor opened the gate before he answered. When he did, after they had passed through, he took both her hands in his.

"I'll take you there," he said, looking down at her with grave, shining eyes. "I knew you wouldn't fail me. When shall I call for you?"

"Don't call for me at all. I think—I know it will be better for me to walk in alone, as of my own accord."

"Ah, yes!" he said, and told her the address. She ran lightly up the steps, and as he turned her key in the door for her, she raised a pair of starry eyes to his.

"Dr. Kemp," she said, "I've had an exceptionally lovely evening. I won't soon forget it."

"Nor I," he returned, raising his hat; holding it in his hand, he gently drew her gloved hand to his lips.

"My brave young friend!" he said; and the next minute his quick footfall was crunching the gravel of the walk. Neither of them had remembered that he was to have come in with her. She waited till the gate clicked behind him, and then softly closed the heavy door.

"My brave young friend!" The words mounted like wine to her head. She forgot her surroundings and stood in a sweet dream in the hall, slowly unbuttoning her gloves. She had been standing in this attitude for several minutes, when, raising her eyes, still shadowy with thought, she saw her cousin before her down the hall, his arm resting on the newel-post.

"Louis!" she cried in surprise, and without considering, she hurried to him, threw her arm around his neck, and kissed him on the cheek. Arnold, taken by storm, stepped slightly back.

"When did you get home?" she asked. The pale rose-flush mantling her cheeks made her face exquisite.

"A half-hour ago."

She looked at him quickly.

"Are you tired, Louis?" she inquired gently. "You're really pale, and you speak as though you were all in."

"Did you enjoy the play?" he asked quietly, ignoring her remarks.

"The play!" she echoed, and then a quick burning blush suffused her face. The epilogue had wholly obliterated the play from her recollection.

"Oh, of course," she responded, turning from the rather sardonic smile of his lips and seating herself on the stairs. "Do you want to hear about it now?"

"Why not?"

"Well," she began, laying her gloves in her lap and snuggling her chin in the palms of her hands, "shall I tell you how I felt about it? In the first place, I wasn't ashamed of Shylock; if his vengeance was distorted, the cause distorted it. But, oh, Louis, the misery of that poor old man! After all, his punishment was as fiendish as his guilt. Booth was great. I wish you could have seen the play of his wonderful eyebrow and the eloquence of his fine hand. Poor old, lonely Shylock! With all his intellect, how could he regret that wretched little Jessica?"

"He was a Jewish father."

"How singularly you say that! Of course he was a Jew; but Jewish hardly describes him—at least, according to the modern idea. Are you coming up?"

"Yes. Go on; I will lower the gas."

"Wouldn't you like something to eat or drink? You look so worn out; let me get you something."

"Thanks; I have dined. Good-night." The girl passed on to her pretty white-and-gold room. Shylock had again fled from her memory, but there was singing in her heart a man's grave voice saying:

"My brave young friend!"

CHAPTER X

"A HUMBLE BARD presents his respects to my Lady Maréchal Niel, and begs her to step down to the gate for about two minutes."

The penciled note was handed to Ruth early the next morning as she stood in the kitchen beating up eggs for an omelette for her mother's breakfast. A smile of mingled surprise and amusement overspread her face as she read, and, turning the card, she saw, "Herbert Kemp, M.D.," as she had surmised.

"Do I look all right, Mary?" she asked, hurriedly placing the bowl on the table and half turning to the cook as she walked to the door. Mary deliberately placed both hands on her hips and eyed her sharply.

"And striped flannel dresses and hairs in braids," she began, as she always did, as if continuing a thought, "being nice, pretty flannel and nice, pretty braids, Miss Ruth do look sweet-like, which is nothing out of the common, for she always do!"

The last was almost shouted after Ruth, who had run from her prolixity.

As she hurried down the walk, she recognized the doctor's carriage, with the doctor himself, and Bob in state beside him. Two hands went up to two respective hats as the gate swung behind her, and she came with hands extended to Bob.

"You're looking so much better," she exclaimed heartily, holding the bashfully outstretched hand. "Isn't this your first outing?"

"Yes, lady." It had been impossible for her to make him call her by name.

"He elected to pay his first devoirs to the Queen of Roses, as he expressed it," spoke up Kemp, his disengaged hand on the boy's shoulder, and looking with a puzzled expression at Ruth.

Last night she had been a young woman; this morning she was a young girl; it was only after he had driven off that he discovered the difference lay in the arrangement of her hair.

"Thank you, Bob; presently I expect to have you paying me a visit on foot, when we can come to a clearer understanding about my flower-beds."

"He says," returned the boy, turning a humbly devoted look upon Kemp, "that I mustn't think of gardening for some weeks. And so—and so—"

"Yes."

"And so," explained the doctor, briskly, "he's going to hold my reins on our rounds, and drink in an ocean of sunshine to expend on some flowers—yours or mine, perhaps—by and by."

Bob's eyes were luminous as they rested on the bearded face of his benefactor.

"Now say all you have to say, and we'll be off," said Kemp, tucking in the robe at Bob's side.

"I didn't have anything to say, sir; I only came to let her know."

"And I'm so glad, Bob," said Ruth, smiling up into the boy's shy, speaking eyes. And, as people always will try to add to the comfort of a convalescent, Ruth, in turn, drew the robe over the lad's hands. As she did so, her cousin, Jennie Lewis, passed hurriedly by. Her quick blue eyes took in, to a detail, the attitudes of the trio.

"Good-morning, Jennie," called Ruth, turning. "Are you coming in?"

"Not now." She bowed stiffly and hurried on.

"Cabbage-rose."

Bob delivered himself of his sentiment without the slightest change of expression.

The doctor gave a quick look at Ruth. She met it lightly.

"He can't help his inspirations," she remarked, and stepped back as the doctor pulled the reins.

"Come again, Bob," she called and, with a smile to Kemp, she ran in.

"And I was going to say," continued Mary, as she re-entered

the kitchen, "that a speck of aig splashed on your cheek, Miss Ruth, when you was making the omelette."

"Oh, Mary, where?"

"But not knowin' as you would see anybody, I didn't think to run after you; so it's just this side your mouth, like if you hadn't wiped it good after breakfast."

Ruth rubbed it off, wondering with vexation if the doctor had noticed it. Truth to say, the doctor had noticed it, and placed the same passing construction on it that Mary had suggested. Not that the little yellow splash occupied much of his attention. When he drove off, all he thought of Ruth's appearance was that her braided hair hung gracefully and heavily down her back; that she looked young—decidedly young and missish; and that he had probably spoken indiscreetly and impulsively to the wrong person on a wrong subject the night before.

An hour later, and Dr. Kemp could not have failed to recognize Ruth, the woman of his confidence. Something, perhaps a dormant spirit of worldliness, kept her from disclosing to her mother the reason of her going out. She herself felt no shame or doubt as to the advisability of her action; but the certain knowledge of her mother's disapproval of such a proceeding restrained the disclosure which, of a surety, would have cost her the nonfulfilment of a kindly act. A bit of subterfuge which hurts no one is often not only excusable, but commendable, and in this instance, it saved her mother an annoying controversy. So, with conscience fully satisfied, Ruth took her way down the street. The question as to whether the doctor had gone beyond the bounds of their brief acquaintance had, of course, presented itself to her mind; but if a slight flush came into her face when she remembered the nature of the narrative and the personality of the narrator, it was quickly banished by the precious assurance that in so doing he had honored her beyond the reach of current flattery.

A certain placid strength possessed her and showed in her grave brown eyes; with her whole heart and soul she wished to do this thing, and she longed to do it well. Her purpose robbed her of every trace of nervousness, and it was a very quiet, sweet-faced young woman who gently knocked at room Number 10 on the second floor of a respectable lodging-house on Polk Street.

Receiving no answer to her knock, she repeated it somewhat more loudly. At this a tired voice called, "Come in."

She turned the knob, which yielded to her touch, and found herself in a small, well-lighted, and neat room. Seated in an arm-chair near the window, but with her back toward it, was what on first view appeared to be a golden-haired child in black; one elbow rested on the arm of the chair, and a childish hand sup-ported the flower-like head. As Ruth hesitated after closing the door behind her, she found a pair of listless violet eyes regarding her from a small white face.

"Well?" queried the girl, without changing her position ex-cept to allow her gaze to travel to the floor.

"Are you Miss Rose Delano?" asked Ruth, coming a step nearer.

"What of that?" admitted the girl, lifelessly, her dull eyes wan-dering everywhere but to the face of her strange interlocutor.

"I'm Ruth Levice, a friend of Dr. Kemp's. Won't that introduc-tion be enough to make you shake hands with me?"

She advanced toward her, holding out her hand. A burning flame shot across Rose Delano's face, and she shrank farther back among her pillows.

"No," she said, putting up a repellant hand; "it isn't enough. Don't touch me, or you'll regret it. You *mustn't*, I say." She arose quickly from her chair and stood at bay, regarding Ruth. The latter, taller than she by head and shoulders, looked down at her wistfully.

"I know no reason why I mustn't," she replied gently.

"Then you don't know me."

"No; but I know of you."

"Then why did you come; why don't you go?" The blue eyes looked with passionate resentment at her.

"Because I've come to see you; because I want to know you."

"Why?"

"Why?"

"Why do you want to know me?"

"Because I want to be your friend. Mayn't we be friends? I'm not much older than you, I think."

"You're centuries younger. Who sent you here? Dr. Kemp?"

"No one sent me; I came of my own free will."

"Then go as you came."

"No."

She stood gracefully and quietly before her. Rose Delano moved farther from her, as if to escape her grave brown eyes.

"You don't know what you are doing," cried the girl, excitedly; "haven't you a father or a mother, no one to tell you what a girl shouldn't do?"

"I have both; but I have also a friend—Dr. Kemp."

"He's my friend too," affirmed Rose, proudly.

"Then we've one good thing in common; and since he's my friend and yours, why shouldn't we be friends?"

"Because he's a man, and you're a woman, and those things don't count with men. Then he's told you my story?"

"Yes."

"And you feel yourself free to come here—to such a creature as I?"

"I feel nothing but pity for you; how can I blame you? But, oh, little girl, I do so grieve for you because you won't believe that the world isn't all merciless. Won't you give me your hand?"

"No," she said, and clasped her hands behind her, retreating as the other advanced. "Go away, please. You're very good, but you're very foolish. Besides I want to be let alone. Please go."

"Not till I've held your hands in mine."

"Stop! I tell you I don't want you to come here; I don't want your friendship. Can't you go now, or are you afraid your sweetheart will upbraid you if you don't carry out his will?"

"My sweetheart?" she asked in questioning wonder.

"Yes; only a lover could make a girl like you so forget herself. I'm speaking of Dr. Kemp."

"But he isn't my lover," she stated, still speaking gently, but with a pale face turned to her companion.

"I—I—beg your pardon," faltered the girl, humbly drooping

her head, shamed by the cold pride in her tormentor's face. "But why, oh, why, then, won't you go?" she continued, wildly sobbing. "I assure you it's best."

"This is best," Ruth said, deliberately, and before Rose knew it she had seized her two hands, and unclasping them from behind her, drawn them to her own breast.

"Now," she said, holding them there tightly, "who's the stronger, you or I?" She looked brightly down at the tear-stained face so close to hers.

"O God!" breathed the girl, her storm-beaten eyes held by the spell of her captor's firmness.

"Now we're friends," said Ruth. "Let's sit down and talk."

Still holding the slender hands, she drew up a chair, and seating the frail girl in the armchair, sat down beside her.

"Oh, wait!" whispered Rose. "Let me tell you everything before you make me hope again."

"I know everything; and truly, Rose, nothing you can say could make me budge an inch."

"How wonderfully he must have told you!"

"He told me nothing but the truth. I know you—blameless—a victim, not a culprit. And now, tell me, do you feel perfectly strong?"

"Oh, yes." The little hand swept in agony over the sad, childish face.

"Then you ought to go out for a nice walk. You have no idea how pleasant it is this morning."

"I can't, indeed I can't! and, oh, why should I?"

"You can and you must, because you must get to work soon."

Two frightened eyes flew up to hers, beseeching.

"Yes," Ruth added, patting the hand she held; "you're a teacher, aren't you?"

"I was—" The catch in her voice was audible.

"What were you used to teaching?"

"Spanish, and English literature."

"Spanish—with your blue eyes!" The sudden outburst of surprise sent a faint April beam into the other's face.

"*Sí, señorita.*"

"Then you must teach me. Let—me—see. Wednesdays—Wednesday afternoons, yes?"

Again the frightened eyes appealed to her; but Ruth ignored them.

"And so many of my friends would like to speak Spanish. Will you teach them too?"

"Oh, Miss Levice, how can I go with such a past?"

"I'm telling you," said Ruth, proudly rearing her head, "if I present you as my friend, you are, you must be, presentable."

The pale lips strove to answer her.

"Tomorrow I'll come with a number of names of girls who are 'dying,' as they say, to speak Spanish, and then you can go and make arrangements with them. Will you?"

Thus pushed to the wall, Rose's tear-filled eyes were her only answer.

Ruth's own filled in turn.

"Dear little Rose," she said, her usual sweet voice coming back to her, "won't it be lovely to do it? You'll feel so much better when you once get out and are earning your independent, pleasant, living again. And now, will you forgive me for having been so insistent?"

"Forgive you!" A red spot glowed on each pallid cheek; she raised her eyes and said with simple fervor, "I would die for you."

"No, but you may live for me," laughed Ruth, rising. "Will you promise me to go out this morning, just for a block or two?"

"I promise you."

"Well, then, good-bye." She held out her hand meaningly and a little fluttering one was placed in hers. Ruth bent and kissed the wistful little face. The girl looked up in adoration.

"I'll see you tomorrow surely," Ruth called back, turning a radiant face to the lonely little figure in the doorway. She felt deliriously happy as she ran down the stairs; her eyes shone like stars; a buoyant joyfulness spoke in her step.

"It is so easy to be happy when one has everything," she mused, forgetting to add, "and gives much." There is so much happiness derived from a kind action that were it not for the motive, charity might be called supreme selfishness.

Down noisy Polk Street, with its clanging, transferring cable cars, its cobbles ringing to the heavy hoofs of truck-horses, its markets and gay bazaars, its children and candy shops, Ruth moved, on the wings of joyous romance.

CHAPTER XI

S HE TOLD her mother in a few words at luncheon that she had arranged to take Spanish lessons from a young protégé of Dr. Kemp's who had been ill and was in want.

"And I was thinking," she added with naïve policy, "that I might combine a little business with pleasure this afternoon—pay off some of those ever-urgent calls you accuse me of outlawing, and at the same time try to get up a class of pupils for Miss Delano. What do you think?"

"That would be nice; don't forget Mrs. Bunker. I know you don't like her, but you must pay a call for the musicale which we didn't attend; and she has children who might like to learn Spanish. I wonder if I could take lessons too; it wouldn't be exciting, and I'm not too old to learn."

"You might ask the doctor. He's almost dismissed himself now, and after we get back from the country perhaps Jennie would join us two in a class. Mother and daughter can then go to school together."

"It's very fortunate," Mrs. Levice observed pensively, sipping her necessary glass of port, "that Celeste sent your hat this morning to wear with your new gown. Isn't it?"

"Fortunate!" Ruth exclaimed. "It's destiny."

So Mrs. Levice slipped easily into Ruth's plan from a social standpoint, as Ruth slipped out, trim and graceful, from her mother's artistic surveillance.

Meanwhile Mrs. Levice intended writing some delayed letters till her husband's return, which promised to be early in the afternoon.

She had just about settled herself at her desk when Jennie Lewis came bustling in. Mrs. Lewis always brought in a sense of importance; one looked upon her presence with that exhilarating feeling with which one anticipates the latest number of a society journal.

"Go right on with your writing, Aunt Esther," she said after they had exchanged greetings. "I've brought my work, so I won't mind the quiet in the least."

"As if I would bore you in that way!" returned Mrs. Levice, with a kind glance at her, as she closed her desk. "Take off your things, and let's have an old-fashioned, comfortable afternoon. Don't forget a single sensation; I'm actually starving for one."

Mrs. Lewis smiled grimly as she fluffed up her bang with her hat-pin. She drew up a second cosy rocking-chair near her aunt's, drew out her needle and crochet-work, and as the steel hook flashed in and out, her tongue soon acquired its accustomed momentum.

"Where's Ruth?" she began, winding her thread round her chubby, ring-bedecked finger.

"She's paying off some calls for a change."

"Indeed! Got down to conventionality again?"

"You wouldn't call her unconventional, would you?"

"Oh, well; everyone has a right to an opinion."

Mrs. Levice glanced at her inquiringly. Without doubt there was an underground mine beneath this non-committal remark. Mrs. Lewis rocked violently backward and forward without raising her eyes. Her face was beet-red, and it looked as if an explosion were imminent. Mrs. Levice waited with no little speculation as to what act of Ruth's her cousin could disapprove of so seriously. She liked Jennie; everyone who knew her recognized her sterling good heart, but almost everyone who knew her agreed that a grain of flour was a whole cake, baked and iced, to Mrs. Lewis's imagination, and these airy comfits were passed around promiscuously to whoever was at hand. Not a sound broke the portentous silence but the decided snap with which Mrs. Lewis pulled her needle through, and the hurricane she raised with her rocking.

"I was at the theater last night."

The blow drew no blood.

"Which theater?" asked Mrs. Levice, innocently.

"The Baldwin. Booth played *The Merchant of Venice*."

"Did you enjoy it?" queried her aunt, either evading or failing to perceive the meaning.

"I did." A pause, and then, "Did Ruth?"

Mrs. Levice saw a flash of daylight, but her answer hinted at no perturbation.

"Very much. Booth is her actor-idol, you know."

"So I've heard." She spread her crochet-work on her knee as if measuring its length, then with striking indifference picked it up again and adjusted her needle.

"She came in rather late, didn't she?"

"Did she?" questioned Mrs. Levice, parrying with enjoyment the indirect thrusts. "I didn't know. Had the curtain risen?"

"No; there was plenty of time for everyone to recognize her."

"I had no idea she was so well known."

"Those who didn't know her knew her escort. Dr. Kemp is very well known, and his presence is naturally remarked."

"Yes, his appearance is very striking."

"Aunt Esther!" The vehemence of Mrs. Lewis's feelings sent her ball of cotton rolling to the other end of the room.

"My dear, what is it?" Mrs. Levice turned a pair of bright, interested eyes upon her niece.

"You know very well what I want to say: everybody wondered to see Ruth with Dr. Kemp."

"Why?"

"Because everyone knows that she never goes out with anyone but Uncle or Louis, and we all were surprised. The Hoffmans sat behind us, and Miss Hoffman leaned forward to ask what it meant. I met several acquaintances this morning who had been there, and each one made some remark about Ruth. One said, 'I had no idea the Levices were so intimate with Dr. Kemp;' another young girl laughed and said, 'Ruth Levice had a new escort last night, didn't she?' Still another asked, 'Anything on the *tapis* in your family, Mrs. Lewis?' And what could I say?"

"What *did* you say?"

Mrs. Levice's quiet tone did not betray her vexation. She had feared just such a little disturbance from the Jewish community, but her husband's views had overruled hers, and she was now bound to uphold his. Nevertheless, she hated anything of the kind.

"I simply said I knew nothing at all about it, except that he was your physician. Even if I had known, I wouldn't have said more."

"There's no more to be said. Dr. Kemp and Ruth have become friendly through their mutual interest in several poor patients; and in the course of conversation one morning he heard that Ruth was anxious to see this play, and had no escort. So he asked her, and her father saw no objection to her going. It's a pity she didn't think to hand round a written explanation to her different Jewish friends in the audience."

"There you go, Aunt Esther! Jewish friends! I'm sure that no matter how indifferent Uncle is to such things, you must remember that our Jewish girls never go alone to the theater with anyone outside of the family, and certainly not with a Christian."

"What has that to do with it, so long as he is a gentleman?"

"Nothing. Only I didn't think you cared to have Ruth's name coupled with one."

"No, nor with anyone. But as I can't control people's tongues—"

"Then I wouldn't give them cause for wagging. Aunt Esther, *is* there anything between Ruth and Dr. Kemp?"

"Jennie, you surprise and anger me. Do you know what you insinuate?"

"I can't help it. Either you are crazy, or ignorant of what is going on, and I consider it my duty to enlighten you"—a gossip's duties are always enlightening—"unless, of course, you prefer to remain in blissful or wilful ignorance."

"Speak out, please."

"Of course I knew you must have sanctioned her going last night, though, I must confess, I still think you did very wrong; but do you know where she went this morning?"

Mrs. Levice was exasperated. She was enough of a Jewess to realize that if you dislike Jewish comment, you must never step out of the narrowly conventional Jewish pathway. That Ruth, her only daughter, should be the subject of vulgar bandying was more bitter than wormwood to her, but that her own niece could come with these wild conjectures incensed her beyond endurance.

"I do know," she said in response to the foregoing question. "Ruth is not a sneak,—she tells me everything; but her adventures are so mild that there would be no harm if she left them untold. She called on a poor young girl who, after a long illness, is looking for pupils in Spanish."

"A friend of Dr. Kemp's."

"Exactly."

"A young girl, unmarried, who, a few weeks ago, through a merciful fate, lost her child at its birth."

The faint flush on Mrs. Levice's cheek receded.

"Who told you this?" she questioned in an even, low voice.

"I *thought* you couldn't know. Mrs. Blake, the landlady where the girl lives, told me."

"And how, pray, do you connect Ruth with this girl?"

"I'll tell you. Mrs. Blake does my white sewing. I was there this morning, and just as I went into her room, I saw Ruth leaving another farther down the hall. Naturally I asked Mrs. Blake who had the room, and she told me the story."

"Naturally." The cutting sarcasm drove the blood to Mrs. Lewis's face.

"For me it was; and in this case," she retorted with rising accents, "my vulgar curiosity had its vulgar reward. I heard a scandalous account of the girl whom my cousin was visiting, and, outside of Dr. Kemp, Ruth is the only visitor she has had."

"I'm sorry to hear this, Jennie."

"I know you are, Aunt Esther. But what I find so very queer is that Dr. Kemp, who pretends to be her friend—and I've seen them together many times—should have sent her there. Don't you?"

"I don't understand it at all—neither Ruth nor him."

"Surely you don't think Ruth knew anything of this?" questioned Mrs. Lewis, leaning forward and raising her voice in horror.

"Of course not," returned Mrs. Levice, rather lamely. She had long ago acknowledged to herself that there were depths in her daughter's nature which she had never gauged.

"I know what an idol his patients make of him, but he's a man nevertheless, and though you may think it horrible of me, it struck me as very suggestive that he was that girl's *only* friend."

"Therefore he must have been a good friend."

Mrs. Lewis bounded from her chair and turned a startled face to Mr. Levice, who had thus spoken, standing in the doorway. Mrs. Levice breathed a sigh of hysterical relief.

"Good-afternoon, Jennie," he said, coming into the room and shaking her hand; "sit down again. Good-afternoon, Esther." He stooped to kiss his wife.

Mrs. Lewis's hands trembled; she looked, to say the least, ashamed. She had been caught scandal-mongering by her uncle, Jules Levice, the head and pride of the whole family.

"I'm sorry I heard what I did, Jennie; sorry to think that you are so poor as to lay the vilest construction on an affair of which you evidently know nothing, and sorry you couldn't keep your views to yourself." It was the habit of all of Levice's relatives to listen in silence to any personal reprimand the dignified old man might offer.

"I heard a good part of your conversation, and I can only characterize it as—petty. Can't you and your friends see anything without springing at shilling-shocker conclusions? Don't you know that people sometimes enjoy themselves without any further design? So much for the theater talk. What is more serious is the fact that you could so misjudge my honorable friend, Dr. Kemp. Such a thing, Jennie, my girl, would be as remote from Dr. Kemp's possibilities as—murder. Remember, what I say is indisputable. Whether Ruth knew the story of this girl or not, I can't say, but, either way, I feel assured that what she did was well done—if innocently; if with knowledge, so much the better. And I venture to assert that she is not a whit harmed by the action. In all probability she will tell us all the particulars if we ask her. Otherwise, Jennie, don't you think you have been unnecessarily alarmed?" The benign gentleness of his question calmed Mrs. Lewis.

"Uncle," she replied earnestly, "in my life such things are not trivial; perhaps because my life is narrower. I know you and Ruth take a different view of everything."

"Don't disparage yourself; people generally do that to be contradicted or to show that they know their weaknesses and have never cared to change them. A woman of your intelligence need never sink to the level of a spiteful chatterbox; everyone should keep his tongue sheathed, for it is more deadly than a sword. Your higher interests should make you overlook every little action of your neighbors. You only see or hear what takes place when the window is open; you can never judge from that what takes place when the window is shut. How are the children?"

By dint of great tenderness he strove to make her more at ease.

Ruth, confronted with their knowledge, confessed, with flushed cheeks and glowing eyes, the details of the incident.

"And," she said in conclusion, "father, mamma, nothing you can say will make me retract anything I have done, or purpose doing."

"Nothing?" repeated her father.

"I hope you won't ask me to, but that's my decision."

"My darling, I dislike to hear you call yourself a mule," said her father, looking at her with something softer than disapproval; "but in this case I won't use the whip to turn you from your purpose. Shall we, Esther?"

"It's quixotic," affirmed Mrs. Levice, "but since you've gone so far, there's no reasonable way of getting out of it. When next I see the doctor I shall speak to him of it."

"There will be no occasion, dear," remonstrated the indulgent father, at sight of the annoyed flash in Ruth's eyes. "I shall."

By which it will be seen that the course of an only child is not so smooth as one of many children may think; every action of the former assumes such prominence that it is examined and cross-examined, and very often sent to Coventry; whereas, in a large family, the happy-go-lucky offspring has his little light dimmed, and therefore less remarked, through the propinquity of others.

But Mr. Levice failed to "speak to" Dr. Kemp about the little tempest in a teapot. Ruth, trusting to his sensitive understanding, had no further fears on that score.

CHAPTER XII

IF RUTH, in the privacy of her heart, realized that she was sailing toward dangerous rapids, the premonition gave her no unpleasant fears. Possibly she was reckless, content to glide forever on her smooth stream of delight. When the sun blinds us we cannot see the warning black lurking in the far horizon. Without doubt the girl's spirit and sympathies were receiving their proper food. Life was full for her, not because she was occupied—a busy life does not always prove a full one—but because she was beginning to enter thoroughly into the lives of others, to struggle with their struggles, to triumph in their triumphs, and so she was beginning to see in everything, good or bad, its cause for existence. Under ordinary circumstances one cannot see much misery without experiencing a world of disillusion and futile rebellion of spirit, but Ruth was not living just at that time under ordinary circumstances.

Something of the nature of electricity which she could not fathom seemed to envelop her, which made her pulses bound, her lips quick to smile, and her eyes shine like twin dream-stars. She seemed to be moving to some rapturous music unheard save by herself. At night, alone with her heart, she dared hardly name to herself the meaning of it all—a certain puritanic modesty withheld her. Yet all the sweet humility of which she was possessed could not banish from her memory the lingering clasp of a hand, the warm light that fell from eyes that glanced at her. For the present, these were grace sufficient for her daily need. Given the perfume, what need to name the flower?

Her family, without understanding it, noted the difference in their different ways. Mrs. Levice saw with a thrill of delight that she was growing more softly beautiful. Her father, holding his hands a few inches from her shoulders, said, one morning, with a drolly puzzled look, "I'm afraid to touch you; sparks might fly."

Arnold surprised her standing in the gloaming by a window, her hands clasped over her head, a smile parting her lips, her eyes haunting in the witchery of their expression. By some drawing power her glance fell unconsciously upon him, and he beheld, with mingled amazement and speculation, a rosy hue overspread her face and throat, her hands went swiftly to her face as if she would hide something it might reveal, and she passed quickly from the room. Arnold sat down to solve this problem of an unknown quantity.

Ruth's birthday came in its course, a few days after her meeting with Rose Delano. The family celebrated it in their usual fashion, which consisted only in making the day pass pleasantly for the one whose day of days it was—their simple way of showing that her birth had been a happy one for all concerned.

On this evening of her twenty-second anniversary, Ruth seemed to be in her element. She had donned, in a spirit of mischief, a gown she had worn five years before on the occasion of some youthful festivity. The girlish fashion of the white frock, with its straight, full skirt to her ankles, the round baby waist, and short puffs on her shoulders made a very child of her.

"Who can imagine me seventeen?" she asked gayly as she entered the library, softly lighted by many wax candles. Her mother, who was again enjoying the freedom of the house, and who was now snugly ensconced in her own particular chair, looked up at her.

"That little frock makes me long to take you in my lap," said she, brightly.

"One—two—three—and here I am!" Ruth threw herself into her mother's arms and twined her arms about her neck.

"Well, Mr. Arnold, you can't scare me tonight with your sarcastic disapproval!" she invited, glancing over at her cousin seated in a deep, blue-cushioned chair.

"I have no desire to scare you, little cousin," he answered pleasantly. "I only do that to children or grown-up people."

"And what am I, pray, good sir?"

"You are neither; you are neither child nor woman; you are neither flesh nor spirit; you are unknowable."

"Dear me! In other words, I'm a conundrum. Who will guess me?"

"You are the Sphinx," added her cousin.

"I won't be that ugly-faced thing," she retorted; "guess again."

"Impossible. Once acquire a sphinx's elusiveness, and you are a mystery perpetual. You alone can unriddle the riddle."

"I can't. I give myself up."

"Not so fast, young woman," broke in her father, shutting his magazine and settling his glasses more firmly upon his nose, "that's an office I alone can perform. Who has been hunting on my preserves?"

"Alas! They're not tempting, so be quite calm on that score." She sat up with a forlorn sigh, adding, "Think of it, father, twenty-two, and not a heart to hang on my belt."

"Hands are supposed to mean hearts nowadays." said Louis, reassuringly. "I am sure you have mittened one or two."

"Oh, yes," she answered, laughing evasively, "both of little Toddie Flynn's. Mamma, don't you think I'm too big a baby for you to hold so long?" She sprang up, and drawing a stool before her father's chair, exclaimed restlessly—

"Now, father, a grown-up Mother-Goose story for my birthday; make it short and sweet and with a moral—like you."

Mr. Levice patted her head and rumpled the loosely gathered hair.

"Once upon a time," he began, "a little boy went into his father's warehouse and ate up all the sugar in the land. He did not die, but he was so sweet that everybody wanted to bite him. That is short and sweet; and what is the moral?"

"Selfishness brings misery," answered Ruth, promptly. "Clever of both of us, but what's the analogy? Louis, you look lonesome over there. I feel as if I were play-acting and can't get near you. Come nearer the footlights."

"And get scorched for my pains? Thanks; this is very comfortable. Distance adds to illusion."

"Thanks. But you don't mean to admit *you* have any illusions,

do you? Why, those glasses of yours could see through a diplomat, I truly believe. Did you ever see anything you didn't consider a delusion and a snare?"

"Yes; there's a standing institution the honest value of which
there is no doubt."

"And that is?"

"My bed."

"There's inspiration for you! But after all, it's a lying institution, my friend; and aren't you deposing your masculine muse—
your cigar? Oh, that reminds me of the annual peace-pipe."

She jumped up, snatched a candle, and left the room. As she
turned toward the staircase she was arrested by the ringing of the
doorbell. She stood quite still, holding the lighted candle while
the maid opened the door.

"Is Miss Levice in?" asked the voice which made the little
candle-light seem like myriads of swimming stars. As the maid
answered in the affirmative, she came mechanically forward and
met the bright-glancing eyes of Dr. Kemp.

"Good-evening," she said, and held out her disengaged hand,
which he grasped and held close.

"Is it Santa Filomena?" he asked, smiling into her eyes.

"No, only Ruth Levice, who is delighted to see you. Will you
come into the library? We are having a little home evening together."

"Thank you. Directly." He slipped out of his overcoat, and
turning quietly to her, said, "But before we go in, and I enact the
odd number, I should like to say just a few words to you alone,
please."

She gave him a quick look of inquiry, and meeting his compelling eyes, led him across the hall into the drawing-room. He
noticed how the soft light she held made her the only white spot
in the dark room, till, touching a tall silver lamp, she threw a
rosy halo over everything. That it was an exquisite, graceful
apartment he felt without seeing.

She placed her candle upon a tiny rococo table, and seated
herself in a quaint chair with high, carved ebony back and arms
in which she seemed to sit enthroned. The doctor declined to

sit. He stood with one hand upon the fragile table and looked down at her.

"I'm inclined to think, after all," he said slowly, "that you are, in truth, the divine lady with the light. It's a pretty name and a pretty fame—that of Santa Filomena."

What had come over her eyelids that they refused to be raised?

"I think," he continued with a low laugh, "that I shall always call you so, and have all rights reserved. May I?"

"I'm afraid," she faltered, finally looking up, "that your poem would be without rhyme or reason—a candle is too slight a thing for such beautiful flattery."

"But not a Rose Delano. I saw her today, and at least one sufferer would turn to kiss your shadow. Do you know what a wonderfully beautiful thing you've done? I came tonight to thank you—anyone who makes good our ideals is a subject for thanks. Of course, the thing had no personal bearing upon myself; but being an officious fellow, I thought it proper to let you know that I know. That's my only excuse for coming."

"Did you need an excuse?"

"That, or an invitation."

"Oh, I never thought of you—as—as—"

"As a man?"

How to answer this? Then, finally, she said:

"As caring to waste an evening."

"Would it be a waste? There's an old adage that one might adapt, then, 'A wilful waste makes woful want.' Want's a miserable thing, so I thought a little plunging wouldn't be a half-bad idea. Shall we go in to your family now? Won't they think you've been spirited away?"

He took the candle from her, and they retraced their steps. As she turned the handle of the door, she said:

"Will you give me the candle, please, and go in? I'm going upstairs."

"Aren't you coming down again?" He stood stolidly still.

"Oh, yes. Father, mother," she called, opening wide the door, "here is Dr. Kemp."

With this announcement she fled up the staircase.

She had come up for some cigars; but when she reached her father's room she seated herself blindly, looking aimlessly down at her hands. What a blessed reprieve this was! If she could but stay here! She could, if it were not for the peace-pipe. Such a silly performance that! Father kept those superfine cigars over in the cabinet there. Should she bring them? Should she bring only two, as usual? Then she was going? Of course. Only a minute to quiet down in! She wondered what they were talking about. She supposed she looked very foolish in that gown with her hair all mussed! How his eyes— She rose suddenly and walked to the dressing-table with her light. After all, it was not very unbecoming. Had her face been so white all the evening? Louis liked her face to be colorless. Oh, she had better hurry down.

"Here comes the chief!" greeted her mother as she entered. "Now, doctor, you can see the native celebrating her natal day."

"She enacts the enchantress," said her father, "and sends us, living, to the happy hunting-grounds. Will you join us, doctor?"

"If Circe thinks me worthy. Is the metamorphosis as happy as it promises?"

He received no answer as Ruth came forward with a box of tempting Havanas. She selected one, and placing the box on a chair, reached to the high-tiled mantel-shelf, and taking a tiny pair of scissors from the tray, deftly cut off the point of the cigar. She seemed quite unconscious that all were watching her. Louis handed her a lighted match, and putting the cigar between her lips, she lit it into life. The doctor was amused.

She blew up a wreath of the fragrant smoke and handing it to her father, said:

"With this year's love, father."

The doctor grew interested.

She took another, and lighting it as gracefully, and without the slightest suggestion of haste, gave it into Louis's outstretched hand.

"Well?" he prompted, holding it from his lips till she had spoken.

"I can think of nothing you care enough for to wish you."

"Nothing?"

"Unless," she recalled with sudden mischief, "I wish you a comfortable bed all the year round—and pleasant dreams, Louis."

"That is much," he answered dryly as he drew a cloud of smoke.

The doctor became anticipative.

Ruth's embarrassment was evident as she turned and offered him a cigar.

"Do you smoke?" she asked, holding out the box.

"Like a chimney," he replied, looking at her, but taking none, "and in the same manner as other common mortals."

She stood still, but withdrew her hand a little as if repelling the hint his words conveyed. Whereupon he immediately selected a cigar, saying as he did so, "So you were born in summer—the time of all good things. Well. 'Thy dearest wish, wish I thee,' and may it not pass in the smoking!"

She swept him a playful courtesy.

After this, Ruth sat a somewhat silent listener to the conversation. She knew that they were discussing the pros and cons of the advantages, for a bachelor, of club life over home life. She knew that Louis was making some habitual, cynical remarks—asserting that the apparent privacy of the latter was delusive, and that the reputed publicity of the former was deceptive, as it was even more isolated than the latter. All of which the doctor laughed down as untruly epigrammatic.

"Then there's only one loophole for the poor bachelor," Mrs. Levice summed up, "and that is to marry. Louis complains of the club, and thinks himself a sort of cynosure in a large household. And you, doctor, complain of the want of homeliness in a bachelor establishment. It's evident you need a wife."

"And oust my Pooh-ba! You can't imagine what a treasure that old soldier of mine is. If I call him a veritable Martha, I'm only paying him a doubtful compliment for the neatness with which he keeps my house and linen; he entertains my palate as deliciously as a Recamier her salon, and—he's never in my way—or thoughts. Can you recommend me any woman so self-abnegatory?"

"Many women, but no wife, I'm glad to say. But you need one."

"So! That sounds cryptic, but maybe an explanation—"

"Oh, not to me, but—"

"You mean you consider a wife an adjunct to a doctor's certificate."

"It's a great guarantee with women," put in Louis, "as a voucher against impatience with their own foibles. They think only home practice can secure the adequate tolerance. Is that it, Aunt Esther?"

"Nonsense, Louis!" interrupted Mr. Levice. "What has that to do with a man's skill?"

"Skill is one thing; the *manner* of doctor is another—with women."

"That's worth considering—or adding to the requirements," observed Kemp, turning his steady, quiet gaze upon Arnold.

Ruth noticed that the two men had taken the same position—*vis-à-vis* to each other in their respective easy-chairs, their heads thrown back upon the cushions, their arms resting on the chair-arms. Something in Louis's veiled eyes caused her to interpose.

"Will you play, Louis?" she asked.

"Not tonight, *ma cousine*," he replied pleasantly, glancing at her from lowered lids.

"It's not optional with you tonight, Louis," she insisted lightly, rising as she spoke, "we—desire you to play."

"Or be punished for *lèse majesté?* Has your Majesty any other command?"

"No. I'll even turn the leaves for you."

"The leaves of what—memory. You know I don't need that."

He strolled over to the piano and sat down. He struck a few random chords, some soft, some florid, some harsh, some melting; he strung them together and glided into a dreamy, melodious rhythm, which faded into a birdlike hallelujah—swelling now into grandeur, fainting into sobs, rushing into an allegro so brilliantly bewildering that when the closing, crashing chords came like the pealing tones of a great organ, Ruth drew a long sigh with the last lingering vibrations.

"What is that?" asked Levice, looking curiously at his nephew, who, turning about on his music-stool, took up his cigar again.

"That," he replied, flecking an ash from his coat lapel, "has no name that I know of; merely vagaries which some poetic people call 'Soul.' "

A pained denial shot through Ruth at his careless words—he had plainly been improvising, and she knew he must have felt the turmoil he had evoked.

"Here, Ruth, sing this," he continued, turning round and picking up a sheet of music.

"What?" she asked without moving.

" 'The Bugle;' I like it."

Kemp looked at her expectantly. He said, in a low voice, he had not known she sang; but since she did, he was sure her voice was contralto.

"Why?" she asked.

"Because your face is contralto."

She turned from his eyes and voice as if they hurt her, and moved to Louis's side.

It could hardly be called singing. Louis had often said her voice needed merely to be set to rhythmic time to be music; in pursuance of which idea he had often put into her hand some poem which touched his fancy, told her to read it, and as she read, he would adapt to it an accompaniment according to the meaning and measure of the lines—grandly solemn, daintily tripping, wildly inspiriting, as the spirit of the lines chanced to be. It was more a chant than a song. Tonight he chose Tennyson's Bugle-song. Her voice was subservient to the accompaniment shaking its faint, sweet bugle-notes, at first, as in a rosy splendor; it rose and swelled and echoed and reverberated and died away slowly as if loath to depart. Arnold's playing was the poem, Ruth's voice the music the poet might have heard as he wrote, sweet as a violin, deep as the feeling evolved—for when she came to the lines beginning, "Oh, love, they die in yon rich sky," she might have stood alone with one, in some high, clear place, so mellow was the lingering thrill of her voice, so rapt the expression of her face. Kemp looked as if he would not tire if the sound should "grow forever and forever."

Mrs. Levice was wakeful after she had gone to bed. Her husband also seemed inclined to prolong the night, for he made no move to undress.

"Jules," said she in low-voiced confidence, "do you realize that our daughter is twenty-two?"

He looked at her with a half-smile.

"Isn't this her birthday?"

"Her twenty-second. And she is still unmarried."

"Well?"

"It's time she were. I should like to see it."

"So should I," he acquiesced with peculiar decision.

Mrs. Levice straightened herself up in bed and looked at her husband eagerly.

"Is it possible," she exclaimed, "that we have both thought of the same possibility?"

It was now Mr. Levice's turn to start into an interested position.

"Of whom," he asked with some constraint, "are you speaking?"

"Sh—sh! Come here. I have longed for it for so long, but have never breathed it to a soul—Louis."

Levice had become quite pale. As she pronounced the familiar name, the color returned to his cheek, and a surprised look sprang to his eyes.

"Louis? Why do you think of such a thing?"

"It is a most logical thought. I think them particularly well suited. Ruth, pardon me, dear, has gotten hold of some very peculiar and idealistic notions. No merely commonplace young man would make her happy. A man must have some ideas outside of what his daily life brings him, if she is to spend a moment's interested thought on him. She has repelled some of the most eligible advances for no obvious reasons whatever. Now, she doesn't care a rap for society, and goes only because I exact it. That's no condition for a normal girl to allow herself to sink into; she owes a duty to her future. I'm telling you this because, of course, you see nothing dangerous in such a course. But it's time you were roused; you know one look from you is worth a whole sermon from me. Do you want her to be an old maid? As to my thinking of Louis, well, in running over my list of eligibles, I find he fulfills every condition—good-looking, clever, cultivated, well-to-do, and—of course, of good family! Why shouldn't it be? They like each other, and see enough of each other to learn to love. We, however, must help to bring it to a head."

"First provide the hearts, little woman. What can I do—ask Louis or Ruth?"

"Jules," she returned with vexation, "how childish! Don't you feel well? Your cheeks are so flushed."

"I am a bit warm. I'm going in to kiss the child good-night. She ran off while I saw Dr. Kemp out."

Ruth sat in her white dressing-gown, her heavy dark hair about her, her brush idle in her hand. Her father stood silently in the doorway, regarding her, a great dread tugging at his heart. Jules Levice was a keen reader of the human face, and he had caught a faint glimpse of something in the doctor's eyes while Ruth sang. He knew the look had been harmless, for her back had been turned, but he wished to reassure himself against a nameless dread.

"Not in bed yet, my child?"

She started up in confusion as he came in.

"Of what were you thinking, darling?" He put his hand under her soft white chin and looked deep into her eyes.

"Well," she answered almost instantly, "I wasn't thinking of anything important—I was thinking of you! We're going to Beacham's next week—and *have* you any soft silk shirts?"

He laughed an almost relieved laugh.

"Well, no," he answered; "I leave all such fancies to your care. So we go next week. I am glad. And you?"

"I? Oh, I love the country in its summer dress, you know."

"Yes. Well, good-night, love." He took her face between his hands, and drawing it down to his, kissed it. Still holding her, he suddenly invoked with sweet solemnity, the age-old blessing:

" 'The Lord bless thee and keep thee.

" 'The Lord make his face to shine upon thee, and be gracious unto thee.

" 'The Lord lift up his countenance upon thee, and give thee peace.' "

He released her slowly. Ruth stood where he left her, with lowered head.

CHAPTER XIII

I T WAS August. The Levices had purposely postponed leaving town until the gay, merry-making crowds had disappeared, when Mrs. Levice, in the quiet of autumn, could put a crown to her recovery.

Ruth had a busy time getting all three ready, as she was to continue the management of the household affairs until their return, a month later. Besides which, numerous little private incidentals had to be put in running order for a month, and she realized, with a pang at parting with some of her simple, sincere protégés, that, were this part of her life withdrawn, the rest would pall insufferably.

The evening before their departure she stood bareheaded upon the steps of the veranda with Louis, who was enjoying his after-dinner smoke. Her father and mother, in the soft golden gloaming of late summer, were strolling arm-in-arm among the flower-beds. Mrs. Levice, without obviously looking toward them, felt with satisfaction that Ruth was looking well in a plain black gown which she had had no time to change after her late shopping. She did not know that, close and isolated as the young man and woman stood, not only were they silent, but each appeared oblivious of the other's presence.

Ruth, with her hands clasped behind her, and Arnold, blowing wreaths of blue smoke into the heliotrope-scented air, looked as if under a dream-spell.

As Mrs. Levice passed within earshot, Ruth heard snatches of the broken sentence—

"Jennie—good-bye—today—she'd have been so—"

This roused her from her revery, and she called to her mother:

"Why, I forgot to drop in at Jennie's this afternoon, as I promised."

"How annoying! when you know how sensitive she is and how angry she gets over any neglect."

"I can run out there now. It's light enough."

"But it will be dark in less than an hour. Louis, will go out to Jennie's with you, Ruth, I'm sure."

"What? Oh, certainly, if she cares to have me."

"Goodness, Louis! Why shouldn't I want you? I'll get my hat and jacket while you decide."

Ruth came back in a few minutes with a small sailor-hat on and a jaunty tan jacket, which she handed to Louis to hold for her.

"New?" he asked, pulling it into place in the back.

"Yes," she answered; "do you like it for traveling?"

"Under a duster. Otherwise its delicate complexion will be rather freckled when you arrive at Beacham's."

He pulled his hat on from ease to respectability and followed her down to the gate. They turned the corner, walking southward down the hill. Mrs. Levice and her husband stood at the gate and watched them saunter off. When they were quite out of sight, Mrs. Levice turned around and sang softly to Mr. Levice, "Ça va bien!" a gay little French song of the day.

The other two walked on silently. The evening was perfect. To the west and sweeping toward Golden Gate a hazy glory flushed the sky rose-color and molten gold, purple and silver; to the northward seas of glinting pale green held the eye with strange beauty. The air was soft and languorous after a very warm day; now and then a piano, violin, or mandolin sounded through open windows; the peace and beauty of evening went with them.

They continued down Van Ness Avenue a few blocks, and carelessly turned into one of the dividing streets toward Franklin. Suddenly Arnold felt his companion start, and saw she had taken her far-off gaze from the landscape. Following the direction of her eyes, he straightened up stiffly. The disturbing object was a small black sign-plate attached above a garden fence and bearing in gilt letters the name of Dr. Herbert Kemp.

Approaching nearer, Arnold felt of a certainty that there would be more speaking signs of the doctor's proximity. His premonition was not at fault.

Dr. Kemp's quaint, dark-red cottage, with its flower-edged lawn, was reached by a flight of low granite steps, at the top of which lounged the medical gentleman in person. He was not heaven-gazing, but seemed plunged in tobacco-inspired meditation of the flowers beneath him. Arnold's quick eye detected the pink flush rising to the little ear of his cousin. The sound of their footsteps on the stone sidewalk came faintly to Kemp; he raised his eyes slowly and indifferently. The indifference vanished as he recognized them.

With a hasty movement he threw the cigar from him and ran down the steps.

"Good-evening," he called, raising his old sombrero and arresting their evident intention of proceeding on their way. They came up, perforce, and met him at the foot of the steps.

"A beautiful evening," he said, holding out a cordial hand to Arnold and looking with happy eyes at Ruth. She noticed a diverting change in his appearance, he seemed different from anything she had been used to, looking particularly tall and easy in a loose dark velvet jacket, thrown open from his chest. The old sombrero hat which had settled on the back of his head left to view his dark hair brushed carelessly backward; an unusual color was on his cheek, an unusual glow in his gray eyes.

"I hope," he went on, frankly transferring his attention to Ruth, "this weather will continue. We are going to have a magnificent autumn; the woods must be beginning to look gorgeous."

"I'll know better tomorrow."

"Tomorrow?"

"Yes; we leave for Beacham's tomorrow, you know."

"No, I didn't know;" a frank shadow clouded his face, but he said quickly—

"That's an old hunting-ground of mine. The river is full of trout. Are you a disciple of old Walton, Mr. Arnold?" he turned with interest toward the silent Frenchman.

"You mean fishing? No; life is too short to hang my humor of a whole day on the end of a line. I have never been to Beacham's."

"Then you've missed it. But you'll probably go down there this year?"

"My business keeps me tied to the city just at present. A professional man has no such check; his will is his master."

"Hardly, or I should have slipped cables long ago. A restful night is an unknown indulgence sometimes for weeks."

His gaze moved from Arnold's peachy cheek, and falling upon Ruth, surprised her dark eyes resting upon him in anxious questioning. He smiled.

"We'll have to be moving on," she said hurriedly, holding out a gloved hand.

"Will you be gone long?" he asked, pressing it close.

"About a month."

"You'll be missed—by the Flynns. Good-bye." He raised his hat, looking steadily at her.

Arnold drew her arm within his, and they walked off.

It is said that the first thing a Frenchman learns when studying the English language is the use of that highly expressive outlet of emotion, "Damn." Arnold was an old-timer, but he had not outgrown the charm of his first linguistic victory, and now as he replaced his hat in reply to Kemp, he distinctly, though coolly, said, "Damn him."

Ruth looked at him, startled, but the composed, non-committal expression of his face led her to believe that her ears had deceived her.

A few more blocks were passed, and they stopped at a pretentious, many-windowed, Queen Anne house. Ruth ran lightly up the steps, her cousin following leisurely.

She had scarcely rung the bell when the door was opened by Mrs. Lewis herself.

"Good-evening, Ruth; why, Mr. Arnold doesn't mean to say that he does us the honor?"

Mr. Arnold had said nothing of the kind, but he offered no disclaimer, and giving her rather a loose handshake walked in.

"Come right into the dining-room," she continued. "I suppose you were surprised to find me in the hall; I had just come from putting the children to bed. They were in mischievous spirits and annoyed their father, who wanted them to be very quiet this evening."

By this time they had reached the room at the end of the hall, the door of which she threw invitingly open.

The apartment they entered was large and contained the regulation chairs, tables, and silver- and crystal-loaded sideboard.

Upon the mantelpiece, the unflickering light from a waxen taper, burning in a glass of oil, lent an unusual air of Sabbath quiet to the room.

"I have '*Yahrzeit*' for my mother," explained Jo Lewis, glancing toward the taper, after greeting his visitors. He sat down quietly again.

"Do you always burn the light?" asked Arnold.

"Always. A light once a year to a mother's memory isn't much to ask of a son."

"How long is it since you lost your mother?" questioned Ruth, gently.

Jo Lewis was a man with whom she had little in common. To her he seemed to have but one idea—the amassing of wealth. With her more intellectual cravings, the continual striving for this, to the exclusion of all higher aspirations, put him on a plane too narrow for her. Unpolished he certainly was, but the rough, exposed grain of his unhewn nature showed many strata of virility. In this gentle mood a tenderness had come to view which drew her to him with a touch of strong, racial kinship.

"Thirty years," he answered musingly—"thirty years. It's a long time, Ruth, but every year, when I light the taper, it seems as if it was only yesterday I was a boy crying because my mother had gone away forever." The strong man wiped his eyes, unashamed.

"The little light casts a long ray," observed Ruth. "Love builds its own lighthouse, and by its gleaming we travel back, as at a leap, to that which seemed eternally lost."

Jo Lewis sighed. Presently the thoughts so strongly possessing him found an outlet.

"There was a woman for you!" he cried with glowing eyes. "Why, Arnold, you talk of men being great financiers; I wonder what you would have said to the abilities my mother showed. We were poor, but poor to a degree of which you can know nothing. Well, with a large family of small children she struggled on alone, and managed to keep us not only alive, but educated and respectable. In our village Sara Lewis was a name every man and woman honored as if it belonged to a princess. Jennie is a good woman, but life's made easy for her. I often think how grand my mother would feel if she were here, and I were able to give her every comfort. God knows how proud and happy I would have been to say, 'You've struggled enough, mother; life is going to be a heaven on earth to you now.' Well, well, what's the good of thinking of it? Tomorrow I'll go down town and deal with men, not memories; it's more profitable."

"Not always," said Arnold, dryly. The two men drifted into a business discussion which neither Mrs. Lewis nor Ruth cared to follow.

"Are you quite ready?" asked Mrs. Lewis, drawing her chair closer to Ruth's.

"Entirely," she replied; "we start on the eight-thirty train in the morning."

"You'll be gone a month, won't you?"

"Yes; we want to get back for the holidays. New Year falls on the twelfth of September, and we must give the house its usual holiday cleaning."

"I've begun already. Somehow, I never thought you would mind being away."

"Why, we always go to the Temple, you know. And I wouldn't miss the Atonement services for a great deal."

"Why don't you say 'Yom Kippur,' as everybody else does?"

"Because 'Atonement' is English and means something to me. Is there anything odd about that?"

"I suppose not. By the way, if there's anything you would like to have done while you are away, let me know."

"I think I have seen to everything. You might run in and see Louis now and then."

"Louis," Mrs. Lewis called instantly, "be sure to come in often for dinner while the folks are gone."

"Thank you; I shall. The last dinner I ate with you was delicious enough to do away with any verbal invitation to another."

He rose, seeing Ruth had risen and was kissing her cousins good-bye.

Mrs. Lewis beamed with pleasure at his words.

"Now, won't you take something before you go?" she asked. "Ruth, I have the loveliest cakes!"

"Oh, Jennie," remonstrated Ruth, as her cousin bustled off, "we've just dined."

"Let her enjoy herself," observed her husband, "she's never so happy as when she's feeding somebody."

The clink of glasses was soon heard, and Mrs. Lewis's rosy face appeared behind a tray with tiny glasses and a plate of rich, brown little cakes.

"Jo, get the Kïrsch. You *must* try one, Ruth; I made them myself."

When they had complimented her on her cakes and Louis had drunk to his next transaction—suggested by Jo Lewis—the visitors departed.

They had been walking in almost total silence for a number of blocks, when Ruth turned suddenly to him and said, with great earnestness:

"Louis, whatever is the matter with you? For the last few days you have hardly spoken to me. Have I done anything to annoy you?"

"You? Why, no, not that I remember."

"Then, please, before we go off, be decent to me again."

"I am afraid I am not of a very hilarious temperament."

"Still, you manage to talk to others."

"Have you cared very much who has talked to you lately?"

Her cheek changed color in the starlight.

"What do you mean?" she demanded.

"Anything—or nothing."

Ruth looked at him haughtily.

"If nothing," he continued, observing her askance from lowered lids, "what I am about to say will be harmless. If anything, I still hope you will find it pardonable."

"What are you about to say?"

"It won't take long. Will you be my wife?"

And the stars still shone up in heaven!

Her face turned white as a niphetos rose.

"Louis," she said finally, speaking with difficulty, "why do you ask me this?"

"Why does any man ask a woman to be his wife?"

"Generally because he loves her."

"Well?"

If he had spoken outright, she might have answered him, but the simple monosyllable, implying a world of restrained avowal, confronted her like a wall, before which she stood silent.

"Answer me, Ruth."

"If you mean it, Louis, I am very, very sorry."

"Why?"

"Because I can never be your wife."

"Why not?"

"I don't love you—like that."

Silence for half a block, the man's lips pressed hard together under his mustache, the girl's heart beating suffocatingly. When he spoke, his voice sounded oddly clear in the hushed night air.

"What do you mean by, 'like that'?"

Her little hand was clinched tight as it lay within his arm. The perfect silence following the words of each made every movement significant.

"You know—as a woman loves the man she would marry, not as she loves a brotherly cousin."

"The difference is not clear to me—but—how did you learn the difference?"

"How dare you?" she cried, flashing a pair of dark, wet eyes upon him.

"In this case, 'I dare do all that may become a man.' Besides, even if there is a difference, I still ask you to be my wife. You would not regret it, Ruth, I think."

His voice was not soft, but there was a certain strained plead-
ing about it which pained her inexpressibly.

"Louis," she said, with slow distinctness, her hand moving
down until it touched his, "I never thought of this as a possibility. You know how much I've always loved you, dear; but, oh
Louis! will it hurt you very much, will you forgive me if I have to
say no, I cannot be your wife?"

"Wait. I ask you to consider this well. I am offering you all
that I have in the world; it is not despicable. Your family, I know,
would be pleased. Besides, it would be well for you—God knows,
not because I am what I am, but for other reasons. Wait. I beg of
you not to answer me till you have thought it over. You know
me; I am no saint, but a man who would give his life for you. I
ask of you nothing but the right to guard yours. Don't answer me
now."

They had turned the corner of their block.

"I need no time," said Ruth, with a quick sob in her voice. "I
can't marry you, Louis. My answer would be the same tomorrow
or at the end of all time—I can never, never be your wife."

"It is then as I feared—anything."

The girl's bowed head was the only answer to his bitter divina-
tion.

"Well," he said, with a hard laugh, "that ends it, then. Don't
let it bother you. Your answer has put it entirely from my mind.
I should be pleased if you would forget it as readily as I shall try
to. I hardly think we shall meet in the morning. I am going down
to the club now. Good-bye; enjoy yourself."

He held out his hand lightly; Ruth carried it in both hers to
her lips. Being at the gate, he lifted his hat with a smile and
walked away. Ruth did not smile; neither did Arnold when he
had turned from her.

CHAPTER XIV

BEACHAM'S LIES in a dimple of the inner coast range, and was reached then through what was, in that day, one of the finest pieces of engineering skill in the State. The tortuous route through the mountains, over trestle-bridges which span what seem, from the car-windows, like bottomless chasms, had need to hold some compensation at the end to counterbalance the fears engendered on the way. The higher one goes, the more beautiful becomes the scenery among the wild, marvelous redwoods which stand like mammoth guides pointing heavenward—and Beacham's realizes expectation.

It is a quiet, unpretentious little place, with its one hotel and two attached cottages, its old, disused sawmill, its tiny school-house beyond the fairy-like woods, its one general merchandise store, where cheese and calico, hats and hoes, ham and hominy, are forthcoming upon solicitation. It is by no means a fashion-able resort; the Levices had searched for something as unlike Del Monte and Coronado as milk is unlike champagne. They were looking for a pretty, healthful spot, with good accommodations and few social attractions, and Beacham's offered all this.

They were not disappointed. Ruth's anticipation was fulfilled when she saw the river. Russian River is about as pretty a stream as one can view upon a summer's day. Here at Beacham's it is very narrow and shallow, with low, shelving beaches on either bank. In the tiny rowboat which she immediately secured, Ruth pushed her way into enchantment. The river winds in and out through exquisite coves entangled in a wilderness of brambles and lacelike ferns almost transparent as they bend and dip toward the silvery waters; while, climbing over the rocky cliffs, run bracken and the fragrant yerba-buena, till, on high, they creep as if in awe about the great redwoods and pines of the forest.

Morning and night Ruth, in her little boat, wooed the lisping waters. Often of a morning her mother was her companion; later on, her father or little Ethel Tyrrell; in the evening one of the Tyrrell boys, generally Will, was her gallant cavalier. But it was always Ruth who rowed—Ruth in her pretty sailor blouse, with her strong round arms and steadily browning hands; Ruth, whose creamy face and neck remained provokingly unreddened, and took on only a little deeper tint, as if a dash of bistre had been softly applied. It was pleasant enough rowing down-stream with Ruth; she always knew when to sing "Nancy Lee," and when "White Wings" sounded prettiest. There were numerous coves, too, where she loved to beach her boat—here to fill a flask with honey-sweet water from a rollicking little spring which came merrily dashing over the rocks, there to gather some delicate ferns or maiden-hair with which to decorate the table, or the trailing yerba-buena for festooning the boat. But Ethel Tyrrell, aged three, thought they had the "dolliest" time when she and Ruth, having rowed a space out of sight, jumped out, and taking off their shoes and stockings and making all the other necessary preliminaries to wading, pattered along over the pebbly bottom, screaming when a sharp stone came against their tender feet, laughing gleefully when the water rose a little higher than they had bargained for; then, when quite tired, they would retire to the beach or the boat and dry themselves in the soft damask of the sun.

Ruth was happy. There were moments when the remembrance of her last meeting with Louis came like a summer cloud over the ineffable brightness of her sky, and she felt a sharp pang at heart. Still, she thought, it was different with Louis. His feeling for her could not be so strong as to make him suffer poignantly over her refusal. She was almost convinced that he had asked her more from a whim of good-fellowship, a sudden desire, perhaps a preference for her close companionship when he did marry, than from any deeper emotion. And yet—No, how could he know! In consequence of which conclusion, her musings were not so sad as they might otherwise have been.

Her parents laughed to see how she reveled in the freedom of the old-fashioned little spot, which, though on the river, was decidedly "out of the swim." It was late in the season, and there were few guests at the hotel. The Levices occupied one of the cottages, the other being taken by a pair of belated turtledoves, the wife a blushing dot of a woman, the husband an overgrown youth who bent over her in their walks like a devoted weeping-willow; there was a young man with a consumptive cough, a natty little stenographer off on a solitary vacation, and the golden-haired Tyrrell family, little and big, for Papa Tyrrell could not enjoy his hard-earned rest without one and all. They were such a gentle, happy, sweet family, for all their pinched circumstances, that the Levices were attracted to them at once. To be with Mrs. Tyrrell one whole day, Mrs. Levice said, was a liberal education—so bright, so uncomplaining, so ambitious for her children was she, and such a help and inspiration to her hardworked husband. Mr. Levice tramped about the woods with Tyrrell and brier-wood pipes, and appreciated the moral bravery of a man who struggled on with a happy face and small hope for any earthly rest. But the children! Floy with her dreamy face and busy sketchbook, Will with his halo of golden hair, his manly figure and broad, open ambitions, Boss with his busy step and fishing-tackle, and baby Ethel, the wee darling, who ran after Ruth the first time she saw her and begged her to come and play with her; ever since, she had formed a part of the drapery of Ruth's skirt or a rather cumbersome necklace about her neck. Every girl who has been debarred the blessing of babies in the house loves them promiscuously and passionately, and Ruth was no exception. It amused the mothers to watch her cuddle the child and wonder aloud at all her baby-talk.

Will was her next favorite satellite. A young girl with a winsome, sympathetic face and hearty manner may easily become the confidante of a manly fellow of fourteen. Will, with his arm tucked through hers, would saunter around after dusk and tell her all his ambitions. The soft, starry evenings up in the mountains, where heaven seems so near, were just the time for such talks.

They were walking thus one evening toward the river, Ruth in a creamy gown and a white scarf thrown over her head, Will without a hat, letting the sweet air play through his hair, as he loved to do.

"What do you think are the greatest professions, Miss Ruth?" asked the boy suddenly.

"Well, law is one—" she began.

"That's the way papa begins," he interrupted impatiently; "but I'll tell you what I think is the greatest. Guess, now."

"The ministry?" she ventured.

"Oh, of course; but I'm not good enough for that—that takes exceptions. Guess again."

"Well, there are the fine arts, or soldiery—that's it. You would be a brave soldier, Willikins, my man."

"No, sir!" he replied, flinging back his head. "I don't want to take lives; I want to save them."

"You mean—a physician, Will?"

"That's it—but not exactly—I mean a surgeon. Don't you think that takes bravery? And it's a long sight better than being a soldier; he draws blood to kill, we do it to save. What do you think, Miss Ruth? We're not going to have any war, you know. And if we do—won't I be able to do something for my country?"

"Indeed, you are right," she answered dreamily, her thoughts wandering beyond the river. So they walked along, and as they were about to descend the slope, a man in overalls, carrying a leather bag, came suddenly upon them in the gloaming. He stood stock-still, his mouth gaping wide.

When Ruth saw it was Ben, the steward, she laughed.

"Why, Ben!" she exclaimed.

The man's mouth slowly closed, and his hand went up to his cap.

"Begging your pardon, Miss—I mean Her pardon—the Lord forgive me, I took you for the Lady Madonna and the blessed Boy with the shining hair. Now, don't be telling of me, will you?"

"Indeed, we won't; we'll keep the pretty compliment to ourselves. Have you the mail? I wonder if there's anything for me."

Ben immediately drew out his little pack, and handed her two.
It was still light enough to read, and as the man moved on, she
stood and opened them.

"This," she announced in matter-of-course openness, "is from
Miss Dorothy Gwynne, who requests the pleasure of my company at a tea next Saturday. That, or the hay-ride, Will? And
this—this—"

It was a simple envelope addressed to

> Miss Ruth Levice—
> Beacham's—
> Sonoma County—
> Cal.

It was the sight of the peculiar use of the dashes which caused
the hiatus in her sentence, and made her heart give one great
rushing bound. The enclosure was to the point.

> SAN FRANCISCO, Aug. 18, 189—.

Miss Ruth Levice:

> My dear Friend—That you may not denounce me as too
> presumptuous, I shall at once explain that I am writing this at
> Bob's urgent desire. He has at last got the job at the florist's,
> and tells me to tell you that he is now happy. I dropped in
> there last night, and when he gave me this message, I told him
> that I feared you would take it as an advertisement. He merely
> smiled, picked up a Maréchal Niel lying on the counter, and
> said, "Drop this in. It's my mark; she'll understand." So here
> are Bob's rose and my apology.
>
> HERBERT KEMP.

She was pale when she turned round to the courteously waiting boy. It was a very cold note, and she put it in her pocket to
keep it warm. The rose she showed to Will, and told him the
story of the sender.

"Didn't I tell you," he cried, when she had finished, "a doctor has the greatest opportunity in the world to be great—and a surgeon comes near it. I say, Miss Ruth, your Dr. Kemp must be a brick. Isn't he?"

"Boys would call him so," she answered, shivering slightly.

It was so like him, she thought, to fulfil Bob's request in his hearty, friendly way—and nothing more. She supposed he wanted her to understand that he wrote to her only as Bob's amanuensis—it was plain enough. And yet, and yet, she thought passionately, it would have been no more than simple etiquette to send a friendly word from himself to—her mother. However, the note was not thrown away. Like all girls, since she could not have the handshake, she had to content herself with a sight of the glove.

And Ruth, in the warm, throbbing, summer days, was happy. She was not always active; there were long afternoons when mere existence was intensely beautiful. To lie at full length upon the soft turf in the depths of the small, enchanted woods, and hear and feel herself at one with the countless spells of nature, was unspeakable rapture.

"Ah, Floy," she cried one afternoon, as she lay with her face turned up to the great green boughs which seemed penciled against the azure sky, "if one could paint what one feels! Look at these silent, living trees that stand in all their grandeur as if under some mighty spell; see how the wonderful heaven steals through the leaves and throws its blue softness upon this twilight gloom; here at our feet—look at these soft, green ferns, and over it all is the indescribable fragrance of the redwoods. Turn there, to your right, little artist, high up on that mountain. Can you see through that shimmering haze a great team moving as if through the air? It's like the vision of the Bethshemites in Doré's mystic work, 'when, in the valley, they lifted up their eyes and beheld the ark returning.' Oh, Floy, it isn't nature; it's God. And who can paint God?"

"No one. If one could paint Him—the Vision—He would no longer be God," answered the girl, resting her sober eyes upon Ruth's enraptured countenance.

One afternoon Ruth took a book and Ethel over the tramway to this fairy spot. It was very warm and still. Mrs. Levice had swung herself to sleep in the hammock, and Mr. Levice was dozing and talking in snatches to the Tyrrells, who were likewise resting on the Levices' veranda. All nature was drowsy, as Ruth wandered off with the little one, who chatted on as was her wont.

"Me and you's yunnin' away," she laughed; "we's goin' to a fowest, and by and by two 'ittle birdies will cover us up wid leaves. My! won't my mamma be sorry! No darlin' 'ittle Ethel to pank and tiss no more. Poor mamma!"

"Does Ethel think mamma likes to spank her?"

"Yes; mammas does des what dey likes."

"But it is only when Ethel's naughty that mamma spanks her. Here, sweetheart, let me tie your sunbonnet tighter. Now Ruth is going to lie here and read, and you can play hide-and-seek all about these trees."

"Can I go wound and sit on dat log by a bwook?"

"Yes."

"Oh, I's afwaid. I's dweffully afwaid."

"Why, you can turn round and talk to me all the time."

"But nobody 'll be sitting by me at all."

"I'm here, just where you can see me. Besides, you know, God will be right next to you."

"Will He? Den a' yight."

Ruth took off her hat and prepared to enjoy herself. As her head touched the green knoll, she saw the little maiden seat herself on the log, and turning her face sideways, say in her pleasant, piping voice:

"How-de-do, Dod?" And having made her acknowledgments, all her fears vanished.

Ruth laughed softly to herself at her strategy, and straightway began to read. The afternoon burned itself away. Ethel played and sang and danced about her, quite oblivious of the heat. But, tired out at last, she threw herself into Ruth's arms.

"Sing by-low now," she demanded sleepily; "pay it's night, and you and me's in a yockin'-chair goin' to by-low land."

Ruth, nothing loath, and realizing that the child was weary, drew the little head to her bosom, threw off the huge sunbonnet and ruffled up the damp, golden locks.

"What shall I sing, sweetheart?" she mused: she was unused to singing babies to sleep. Suddenly a little kindergarten melody she had heard came to her, and she sang softly in her rich, tender contralto the lingering, swinging cradle-song:

> In a cradle, on the treetop,
>   Sleeps a tiny bird;
> Sweeter sound than mother's chirping
>   Never yet was heard.
> See, the green leaves spread like curtains
>   Round the tiny bed,
> While the mother's wings, outstretching,
>   Shield—the—tiny—head.

As her voice died slowly into silence, she found Ethel looking over her shoulder and nodding her head.

"No; I won't tell," the child said loudly.

"Tell what?" asked Ruth, amused.

"Hush! He put his finger on his mouf—sh!"

"Who?" asked Ruth, turning her head hurriedly. Not being able to see through the tree, she started to her feet, still holding the child.

Between two trees stood the stalwart figure of Dr. Kemp—Dr. Kemp in loose, light gray tweeds and white flannel shirt; on the back of his head was a small, soft felt hat, which he lifted as she turned—a wave of color springing to his cheek with the action. As for Ruth—her woman's face dared not speak.

"Did I frighten you?" he asked, coming slowly forward, hat in hand, the golden shafts of the sun falling upon his head and figure.

"Yes," she answered, trying to speak calmly, and failing, dropped into silence.

She made no movement toward him. She had let the child glide softly down till she stood at her side.

"I interrupted you," he continued. "Won't you shake hands with me, nevertheless?"

She put her hand into his proffered one, which lingered in the touch. Without looking at her again, he stooped and spoke to the child. In that moment she had time to compose herself.

"Do you often come up this way?" she ventured.

He turned from the child, straightening himself, and leaned one arm against the tree.

"Once or twice every summer I run away from humanity for a few days, and generally find myself in this part of the country. This is one of my sacred spots. I knew you would ferret it out."

"It's very lovely here. But we're going home now; the afternoon is growing old. Come, Ethel."

A shadow fell upon his dark eyes while she spoke, scarcely looking at him. Why should she hurry off at his coming?

"I'm sorry I've disturbed you so," he said quietly; "but I can easily go away again."

"Was I so rude?" She looked up with a frowning smile. "I did not mean it so, but Ethel's mother will want her now."

"Ethel wants to be tarried," begged the child.

"All right; Ruth will carry you." She stooped to raise her, but as she did so, Kemp's strong hand lightly touched her arm and held her back.

"Ethel will ride home on my shoulder," he said in the gay, winning voice he knew so well how to use with children. The baby's blue eyes smiled in response to his as he swung her lightly to his broad shoulder. There is nothing prettier to a woman than to see the confidence a little child reposes in a strong man.

So, through the mellow, golden sunlight, they strolled slowly homeward. Truly summer went with them, the phantom spirit, all light, all glory, without a shadow in its eyes.

CHAPTER XV

M R. LEVICE, sauntering down the garden-path, saw the trio approaching. For a moment he did not recognize the newcomer in his summer attire. When he did, surprise, then pleasure, then a spirit of inquietude, took possession of him. He had been unexpectedly startled on the night of Ruth's birthday by a vague something in Kemp's eyes. The feeling, however, had vanished gradually in the knowledge that the doctor always had a peculiarly intent gaze, and, moreover, no one could have helped appreciating the girl's loveliness that night. This, of itself, will bring a softness into a man's manner, he knew, and without doubt his fears had been groundless— fears he had not dared to put into words. For, old man as he was, he realized that Dr. Kemp's personality was such as would prove dangerously seductive to any woman whom he cared to honor with his favor. But with a "Get thee behind me, Satan" desire, he had put the foreboding from him. He could have taken his oath upon Ruth's heart-wholeness; yet now, as he recognized her companion, his misgivings returned threefold. The courteous gentleman, however, was at his ease as they came up.

"This is a surprise, doctor," he exclaimed cordially, opening the gate and extending his hand. "Who would have thought of meeting you here?"

Kemp grasped his hand heartily.

"I *am* a sort of surprise-party," he answered, swinging Ethel to the ground and watching her scamper off to the hotel; "and what's more," he continued, turning to him, "I didn't even wire for accommodations."

"You calculate without your host," responded Levice. "The

place is half empty now. But come up and listen to my wife rhapsodize. She'll be delighted to see you."

"How is she?" he asked, turning with him and catching a glimpse of Ruth's figure at the door.

"Feeling quite well," replied Levice. "She's all impatience now for a delirious winter season."

"I thought so," smiled the doctor. "But if you take my advice, you'll draw the bit slightly."

Mrs. Levice was unfeigned in her delight at sight of him; she said it was like the sight of a cable-car in a desert. He protested at such a stupendous comparison, and insisted that she make clear that the dummy was not included. The late afternoon glided soon into evening, and Dr. Kemp went over to the hotel and dined at the Levices' table.

Ruth, in a white wool gown, sat opposite him. It was the first time he had dined with them, and he enjoyed a singular feeling in the situation. He noticed that although Mrs. Levice kept up a flow of talk, she ate heartily, and that Ruth, very quiet, tasted scarcely anything. Her father also observed it, and resolved upon a course of strict surveillance. He was glad to hear that the doctor had to leave on the early morning train, though, of course, he did not voice his relief. As they strolled about afterward, he managed to keep his daughter with him and allowed Kemp to appropriate his wife.

They finally drifted to the cottage-steps, and were enjoying the beauty of the night when Will Tyrrell presented himself before them.

"Good-evening," he said, standing slim and straight as an arrow at the foot of the steps. "Mr. Levice, father says he has at last scared up two other gentlemen; and will you please come over and play a rubber of whist?"

Mr. Levice felt himself a victim of circumstances. He and Mr. Tyrrell had been looking for a couple of opponents, and had almost given up the search. Now, when he decidedly objected to moving, it would have been heartless not to go.

"Don't consider me," put in the doctor, observing his hesitancy. "If it will relieve you, I assure you I won't miss you in the least."

"Go right ahead, Jules," urged his wife; "Ruth and I will take care of the doctor."

If she had promised to take care of Ruth, it would have been more to the point, but since his wife was there, what harm could arise that his presence would prevent? So, with a sincere apology, he went over to the hotel.

He hardly appreciated what an admirable aide he had left behind him in his wife.

Kemp sat upon the top step, leaning his back against the railing. Although outwardly he kept up a constant low run of conversation with Mrs. Levice, swaying to and fro in a wicker rocking-chair, he was intently conscious of Ruth's white figure perched above on a broad window-sill.

How Mrs. Levice happened to broach the subject, Ruth never knew, but she was quite unprepared when she perceived that Kemp was addressing her.

"I should like to show my prowess to you, Miss Levice."

"In what?" she asked, altogether dazed.

"Ruth, Ruth," laughed her mother, "do you mean to say you haven't heard a word of all my glowing compliments on your rowing?"

"And I was telling your mother that, in all modesty, I was considered a fine oar at my Alma Mater."

"And I hazarded the suggestion," added Mrs. Levice, "that as it's such a beautiful night, there's nothing to prevent your taking a little row, and then each can judge of the other's boasted superiority."

"My claim has never been really established," said Ruth. "I've never allowed anyone to usurp my oars."

"As yet," corrected Kemp. "Then will you wrap something about you and come down to the river?"

"Certainly she will," answered her mother; "run in and get some wraps, Ruth."

"Of course you are coming too, mamma?"

"Of course; but considering Dr. Kemp's length, a third in your little boat will be the proverbial trumpery. But I suppose I can rely on you two crack oarsmen, though you know the slightest tremble in the boat in the fairest weather is likely to create a squall on my part."

If Dr. Kemp wished to row, he should row; and since the Jewish Mrs. Grundy was not on hand, anything harmlessly enjoyable was permissible, reasoned Mrs. Levice.

Ruth went indoors. This was certainly something she had not bargained for. How could her mother be so blind as not to know or feel her desire to evade Dr. Kemp? She felt a wild contempt for herself that his presence should affect her as it did; yet she dared not look at him lest her heart should flutter to her eyes. Probably the display flattered him. What was she to him after all but a girl with whom he could flirt in his idle moments? Well, with a passionate flinging out of her arms, she admonished herself to control the swift beating of her heart—surely she could meet and answer every one of his long, flirtatious glances in the same spirit.

She threw a black lace scarf over her hair and, with some wraps for her mother, came out.

"Hadn't you better put something over your shoulders?" he asked deferentially as she appeared.

"And disgust the night with lack of appreciation?"

She turned to a corner of the porch and lifted a pair of oars to her shoulder.

"Why," he exclaimed in surprise, coming toward her, "you keep your oars at home?"

"On the principle of 'neither a borrower nor a lender be.' We find it saves both time and spleen."

She held them lightly in place upon her shoulder.

"Let me have them," he said, placing his hand upon the oars.

A spirit of contradiction took possession of her.

"Indeed, no," she answered, "why should I? They're not at all heavy."

He gently lifted her resisting fingers one by one and raised the broad bone of contention to his shoulder. Then, without a look for her caprice, he turned and offered his arm to Mrs. Levice.

The crickets chirped in the hedges; now and then a firefly flashed before them; the trees seemed wrapped in silent awe at the majesty of the bewildering heavens. As they approached the river, the faint susurra came to them, mingled with the sound of a guitar and someone singing in the distance.

"Others are enjoying themselves too," he remarked as their feet touched the pebbly beach. A faint crescent moon shone over the water. Ruth went straight to the little boat aground on the shore.

"It looks like a cockle-shell," he said, as he put one foot in after shoving it off. "Will you sit in the stern or the bow, Mrs. Levice?"

"In the bow; I dislike to see dangers before we come to them."

He helped her carefully to her place; she thanked him laughingly for his exceptionally strong support, and he turned to Ruth.

"I was waiting for you to move from my place," she said in defiant mischief, standing motionless beside the boat.

"Your place? Oh, yes. Now," he said, holding out his hand to her, "will you step in?"

She took his hand and stepped in; they were both standing, and as the little bark swayed he made a movement to catch hold of her.

"You had better sit down," he said, motioning to the rower's seat.

"And you?" she asked.

"I'll sit beside you and use the other oar," he answered nonchalantly, smiling into her eyes.

With a half-pleased feeling of discomfiture, Ruth seated herself in the stern, whereupon Kemp sat in the contested throne.

"You'll have to excuse my turning my back on you, Mrs. Levice," he said pleasantly. "The oarsman's seat imposes it."

"That's no hindrance to my volubility, I'm glad to say; a back isn't very inspiring or expressive, but Ruth can tell me when you look bored, if I wax too discursive."

It was a tiny boat, and seated thus Kemp's knees were not half a foot from Ruth's white gown.

"Will you direct me?" he said, as he swept around. "I haven't rowed on this river for two or three years."

"You can keep straight ahead for some distance," she said, leaning back in her seat.

She could not fail to notice the easy motion of his body as he rowed lightly down the stream. His flannel shirt, low at the throat, showed his throat, rising firm and strong above his broad shoulders, and his dark face with the steady gray eyes looked across at her with grave sweetness. She would have been glad enough to be able to turn from the short range of vision between them; but the stars and river afforded her good vantage-ground, and upon them she fixed her gaze.

Mrs. Levice was in bright spirits, and seemed striving to outdo the night in brilliancy. For a while Kemp maintained a sort of Roland-for-an-Oliver conversation with her; but, with his eyes continually straying to the girl before him, it soon became spasmodic. Some merry rowers down the river were singing college songs harmoniously, and Mrs. Levice began to hum with them, her voice gradually subsiding into a faint murmur. The balmy, summer-freighted air made her drowsy. She listened absently to Ruth's occasional warnings to Kemp, and to the swift, responsive dip of the oars.

"Now we have clear sailing for a stretch," said Ruth, as they came to a broad curve. "Did you think you were going to be capsized when we shot over that snag, mamma?"

She leaned farther forward, looking past Kemp.

"Mamma!"

Then she straightened herself back in her seat. Kemp, noting the stiffening of her figure, turned halfway to look at Mrs. Levice. Her head was leaning against the flag-staff; her eyes were closed. In the manner of more wary chaperones—Mrs. Levice slept.

He moved quietly back to his former position.

Far across the river a woman's silvery voice was singing the ever-sweet old love-song, "Juanita"; overhead, the golden crescent moon hung low from the floor of heaven pulsating with stars. It was a passionate, tender night, and Ruth, with her face raised to the holy beauty, was a beautiful part of it. Against the black lace about her head her face shone like a cameo, her eyes were dreamy wells of starlight; she scarcely seemed to breathe, so still she sat, her slender hands loosely clasped in her lap.

Dr. Kemp sat opposite her—and Mrs. Levice slept.

Slowly and more slowly sped the tiny boat; long, gentle strokes touched the water; and presently the oars lay idle in their locks—they were unconsciously drifting. The water dipped and lapped about the sides; the tender woman's voice across the water stole to them, singing of love; their eyes met—and Mrs. Levice slept.

Ever, in the after time, when Ruth heard that song, she was again rocking in the frail rowboat upon the lovely river, and a man's deep, grave eyes held hers as if they would never let them go, till, under his worshipping eyes, her own filled with slow, ecstatic tears.

"Doctor," called a startled voice, "row out; I'm right under the trees."

They both started. Mrs. Levice, was, without doubt, awake. They had drifted into a cove, and she was cowering from the overhanging boughs.

"I don't care to be Absalomed. Where were your eyes, Ruth?" she complained sleepily, as Kemp pushed out with a happy, apologetic laugh. "Didn't you see where we were going?"

"No," answered the girl a little breathlessly. "I believe I'm growing—far-sighted."

"It must be time to sight home now," said her mother; "I'm dreadfully chilly."

In five minutes Kemp had grounded the boat and helped Mrs. Levice out. When he turned for Ruth, she had already sprung ashore and started up the slope. For the first time the oars lay forgotten in the bottom of the boat.

"Wait for us, Ruth," called Mrs. Levice, and the slight white figure stood still till they came up.

"You're so slow," she said with a reckless little laugh. "I feel as if I could fly home."

"Star-struck, Ruth?" asked her mother, but the girl had fallen behind them. She could not yet meet his eyes again.

"Come, Ruth, either stay with us or just ahead of us." Mrs. Levice, awake, was an exemplary duenna.

"There's nothing abroad here but the stars," she answered, flitting before them.

"And they are stanch, silent friends—on such a night," remarked Kemp, softly.

She kept before them till they reached the gate and was standing inside of it as they drew near.

"Then you won't be home till Monday," he said, taking Mrs. Levice's hand and raising his hat; "and I'm off on the early morning train. Good-bye."

As she turned in at the gate, he held out his hand to Ruth. His fingers closed softly, firmly, over hers; she heard him say meaningly, though almost inaudibly—

"Till Monday."

She raised her shy eyes for one brief second to his glowing ones, and he passed, a tall, dark figure, down the shadowy road.

When Mr. Levice returned from his game of whist he quietly opened the door of his daughter's bedroom and looked in. All was well; the wolf had departed, and his lamb slept safe in the fold.

But in the dark his lamb's eyes were mysteriously bright. Sleep! With this new crown upon her! Humble as the beautiful beggar-maid felt when the king raised her, she wondered why she had been thus chosen by one whom she had held immeasurably above her. She was only Ruth Levice, a little, unknown girl—while he! And this is another phase of woman's love—it exalts the beloved beyond all measure. It never studies proportion.

CHAPTER XVI

AT SIX o'clock the hills in their soft carpet of dull browns and greens were gently warming under the sun's first rays. At seven the early train which Dr. Kemp purposed taking would leave. Ruth, with this knowledge at heart, had noiselessly risen and left the cottage. Close behind the depot rose a wooded hill. She had often climbed it with the Tyrrell boys, and what was to prevent her doing so now? It afforded an excellent view of the station.

It was very little past six, and she leisurely began to ascend the hill. The sweet morning air was in her nostrils, and she pushed the broad hat from her happy eyes. She paused a moment, looking up at the wooded hilltop, which the sun was jeweling in silver.

"What do you see so beautiful up there?"

With an uncontrollable cry she wheeled about and faced Dr. Kemp within a hand's-breadth of her.

"Oh," she cried, stepping back with burning cheeks, "I didn't mean—I didn't expect—"

"Nor did I," he said in a low voice. "Chance is kinder to us than ourselves—beloved."

She turned quite white at the low, intense endearment.

"You understood me last night—and I wasn't—self-deceived?"

Her head drooped lower till the broad brim of her hat hid her face.

With a quick step he stood close beside her.

"Ruth, look at me."

She never had been able to resist his compelling voice, and now with a swift-drawn breath she threw back her head and looked up at him fairly, all her soul in her eyes.

"Well, are you satisfied?" she asked tremulously.

"Not yet." With one movement he had drawn her to him and his lips claimed hers.

"Santa Filomena," he murmured, tenderly pushing back her hat, his cheek against her hair, "this is worth a lifetime of waiting. Oh, Ruth, Ruth, my sweet!"

In his close embrace her face was hidden; she hardly dared meet his eyes when he finally held her from him.

"Why, you're not afraid to look at me? No one in the world knows you better than I, dear. You can trust me, I think."

"I know," she said, her hands fluttering in his. "But isn't—the train coming?"

"So anxious to have me go?"

Her fingers wound themselves tightly about his.

"Because"—he drew her close again—"I have something to ask you."

"To ask me?"

"Yes; you're not surprised, surely you can guess? Ruth, will you bless me still further? Will you be my wife?"

A great thrill took her; his voice had assumed a bewildering tenderness. "If you really want me," she managed to say, with a sobbing laugh.

"Soon?" he persisted.

"Why?"

"Because—I need you. You'll find me a tyrant in love, Ruth."

"I'm not afraid of you."

"Then you should be. Think, child, I'm an old man, already thirty-five. Did you remember that when you made me king among men?"

"Then I'm an old lady—I am twenty-two."

"As ancient as that? Then you should be able to answer me. Make it soon, sweetheart."

"Why, how you beg—for a king. Besides, there's father, you know; he decides everything for me."

"I know; and I've already asked him—in writing. There's a note waiting for him at the hotel; you'll see I took a great deal for granted last night, and— Ah, the whistle! What day is this, Ruth?"

"Friday."

"Good Friday, sweet, I think."

"Oh, I'm not at all superstitious."

"And Monday is four days off; well, it must make up for all we lose. Monday will be four days rolled into one.

"Remember," he continued hurriedly, "you're doubly precious now, and take good care of yourself until I have you safe again."

"And—and—you will remember that for me too, d-doctor?"

"Who?"

"Herbert."

"God bless you for that, dear!" he whispered in passionate farewell.

Mr. Levice, sleepily turning on his pillow, heard the whistle of the out-going train with benignant satisfaction. It was taking Dr. Kemp where he belonged—to his busy practice—and leaving his child's peace undisturbed. Confound the man anyway! he mused; what had possessed him to drop down upon them in that unexpected manner and rob Ruth of her appetite and happy talk? No doubt she had been flattered by the interest he had shown in her; but he was too old and too dignified a man to resort to flirtation, and anything deeper was out of the question. He must certainly have a little plain talk with the child that morning, and—well, he could cry "Ebenezer!" upon his departure. With this conclusion he softly rose, taking care not to disturb his placidly sleeping wife who never dreamed of waking till nine.

The morning, serenely beautiful, greeted him, and as he wandered over to the hotel, the serenity of the young day caught him as into a sudden haven of dreamy security and, yielding to its charm, all sense of disturbance fell from him while his eye unconsciously sought its daily thrill—the sight of his child.

Ruth generally waited for him for breakfast, but not seeing her around, he went in and took a solitary meal. Sauntering out afterward toward the hotel porch, his hat on, his stick under his

arm, busily lighting a cigar, he was met at the door of the bil-
liard-room by one of the clerks.

"Dr. Kemp left this for you this morning," said he, holding out
a small envelope. A flush rose to the old gentleman's sallow
cheek as he took it.

"Thank you," he said; "I believe I'll come in here for a few
minutes."

He passed by the clerk and seated himself in a deep, cane-
bottomed chair near the window. He fumbled for the cord of his
glasses in a slightly nervous manner, and adjusted them hastily.
The missive was addressed to him, certainly; and with no little
wonder he tore the envelope open and read:

BEACHAM'S, FRIDAY MORNING.

MY DEAR MR. LEVICE—Pardon the hurried nature of this
communication, but I must leave shortly on the in-coming
train, having an important operation to undertake this morning—otherwise I should have liked to prepare you more fully,
but time presses. Simply, then, I love your daughter. I told her
so last night upon the river, and she has made me the proudest
and happiest of men by returning my love. I am well aware
what I am asking of you when I ask you to let her be my wife.
You know me personally; you know my financial standing; I
trust you will remember my failings with mercy, in the knowledge of our great love. Till Monday night, then, I leave her
and my happiness to your consideration and love.

With the greatest respect, dear sir,
Yours sincerely,
HERBERT KEMP.

"My God!"

The clerk standing near him in the doorway turned hurriedly.

"Any trouble?" he asked, moving toward him and noticing
the ashy pallor of his face.

The old man's hand closed spasmodically over the paper.

"Nothing," he managed to answer, waving the man away;
"don't notice me."

The clerk, seeing his presence was undesirable, took up his position in the doorway again.

Levice sat on. No further sound broke from him; he had clinched his teeth hard. It had come to this, then. She loved him; it was too late. If the man's heart alone were concerned, it would have been an easy matter; but hers, Ruth's—God! If she really loved, her father knew only too well how she would love. Was the man crazy? Had he entirely forgotten the gulf which lay between them? Great drops of perspiration rose to his forehead. Two ideas held him in a desperate struggle—his child's happiness; the prejudice of a lifetime. Something conquered finally, and he arose quietly and walked off.

Through the trees he heard laughter. He walked round and saw her swinging Will Tyrrell.

"There's your father," cried Boss, from the limb of a tree.

She looked up, startled. With a newborn shyness she had endeavored to put off this meeting with her father. She gave the swing another push and waited his approach with beating heart.

"The boys will excuse you, Ruth, I think; I would like you to come for a short walk with me."

At his voice, the gentle seriousness of which penetrated even to the Tyrrell boys' understanding, she felt that her secret was known.

She laid her arm about his neck and gave him his usual morning kiss, reddening slowly under his long, searching look as he held her to him. She followed him almost blindly as he turned from the grounds and struck into the lane leading to the woods. Mr. Levice walked along, aimlessly knocking off with his stick the dandelions and camomile in the hedges. It was with a wrench he spoke.

"My child," he said, and now the stick acted as a support, "I was just handed a note from Dr. Kemp. He has asked me for your hand."

In the pause which followed Ruth's lovely face was hidden in her hat.

"He also told me that he loves you," he continued slowly,

had never failed before, to mark the wearied voice, pale face, and sad eyes of her father.

"Your mother will soon be awake," he said, "hadn't you better go back?"

Something she had expected was wanting in this meeting; she looked at him reproachfully, her mouth visibly trembling.

"What is it?" he asked gently.

"Why, father, you're so cold and hard, and you haven't even—"

"Wait till Monday night, Ruth. Then I will do anything you ask me. Now go back to your mother, but understand, not a word of this to her yet. I shall not recur to this again. Meanwhile we shall both have something to think of."

That afternoon Dr. Kemp received the following brief note:

BEACHAM'S, AUG. 25, 189—.

DEAR DR. KEMP—Have you forgotten that my daughter is a Jewess; that you are a Christian? Till Monday night I shall expect you to consider this question from every possible point of view. If then both you and my daughter can satisfactorily override the many objections I undoubtedly hold, I shall raise no obstacle to your desires.

Sincerely your friend,

JULES LEVICE.

In the meantime Ruth was thinking it all out. Love was blinding her, dazzling her; and the giants which rose before her were dwarfed into pigmies, at which she tried to look gravely, but succeeded only in smiling at their feebleness. Love was an Armada, and bore down upon the little armament thought called up, and rode it all to atoms.

Small wonder, then, that on their return on Monday morning, as little Rose Delano stood in Ruth's room looking up into her friend's face, the dreamy, starry eyes, the smiles which crept in thoughtful dimples about the corners of her mouth, the whole air of a mysterious something, baffled and bewildered her.

Upon Ruth's writing-table rested a basket of delicate Maré-chal Niel buds, almost veiled in tender maiden-hair; the anonymous sender was not unknown.

"It has agreed well with you, Miss Levice," said Rose, in her gentle, patient voice, which seemed so at variance with her young face. "You look as if you had been dipped in a love-elixir."

"So I have," laughed Ruth, her hand straying to the velvety buds; "and it has made a 'nut-brown mayde' of me, hasn't it, Rosebud? But tell me the city news. Everything in running order? Tell me."

"Everything is as your kind help has willed it. I have a pleasant little room with a middle-aged couple on Post Street. Altogether I earn ten dollars over my actual monthly expenses. Oh, Miss Levice, when shall I be able to make you understand how deeply grateful I am?"

"Never, Rose; believe me, I never could understand deep things; that is why I'm so happy."

"You're teasing now, with that mischievous light in your eyes. Yet the first time I saw your face I thought that either you had or would have a history."

"Sad?" The sudden poignancy of the question startled Rose.

She looked quickly up at her to note if she were as earnest as her voice sounded. The dark eyes smiled daringly, defiantly, at her.

"I'm no sorceress," she answered evasively but lightly; "look in the glass and see."

"You remind me of Floy Tyrrell—Pooh! Let's talk of something else. Then it can't be Wednesdays?"

"It can be any day. The Page children can have Friday."

"Do you know how Mr. Page is?"

"Didn't you hear of the great operation he—Dr. Kemp—performed Friday?"

"No." She could have shaken herself for the tell-tale, inevitable rush of blood overspreading her face. If Rose saw, she made no sign; she had had one lesson.

"I didn't know such a thing was in his line. It was done right there at the house. I had been giving Miss Dora a lesson in the nursery. The old nurse had brought the two little ones in there, and kept us all on tenter-hooks running in and out. One of the doctors, Wells, I think she said, had fainted; it was a very delicate and dangerous operation. When my lesson was over, I slipped quietly out. I was passing through the corridor when Dr. Kemp came out of one of the rooms. He was quite pale. He recognized me immediately, and though I wished to pass straight on, he stopped me and shook my hand so very friendly. And now I hear it was a great success. Oh, Miss Levice, he has no parallel but himself!"

It did not sound exaggerated to Ruth to hear him thus ex-tolled. It was only very sweet and true.

"I knew just what he must be when I first saw him," the girl babbled on; "that was why I went to him. I knew he was a doctor by his carriage, and his strong, kind face was my only inspiration. But there, you must forgive me if I tire you; you see he sent you to me."

"You can't tire me, Rose," she said gravely. And the same ex-pression rested upon her face till evening.

CHAPTER XVII

ONDAY NIGHT had come. As Ruth half hid a pale-yellow bud in her heavy, low-coiled hair, the gravity of her mien seemed to deepen. This was partially the result of her father's expressive countenance and voice. If he had smiled, it had been such a faint flicker that it was forgotten in the look of repression which had followed. In the afternoon he had spoken a few disturbing words to her:

"I have told your mother that Dr. Kemp is coming to discuss a certain project and desires your presence. She intends to go to bed early, and there is nothing to prevent your receiving him."

At the distantly courteous tone she raised a pair of startled eyes. He was regarding her patiently, as if awaiting some remark.

"Surely you don't want me to be present at this interview?" she questioned, her voice slightly trembling.

"Not only that, but I want your most earnest attention and calm reasoning powers to be brought with you. You have not forgotten what I told you to consider, Ruth?"

"No, father."

She felt, though in a greater degree, as she had often felt in childhood, when, in taking her to task for some naughtiness, he had worn this same sad and distant look. He had never punished her nominally; the pain he himself showed had always affected her as the severest reprimand never could have done.

She looked like a peaceful, sweet-faced nun in her simple white gown, which fell in long, straight folds to her feet; not another touch of color was upon her.

A calmness pervaded her whole person as she paced the softly lighted drawing-room and waited for Kemp.

When he was shown into the room, her tranquillity struck him immediately.

She stood quite still as he came toward her. Without doubt he had some old-time manners, for, first of all, he raised her hand in reverence to his lips. The curious, well-known flush rose slowly to her sensitive face at the action. When he had caught her swiftly to him, a long sigh escaped her.

"What is it?" he asked, drawing her down to a seat beside him. "Tired of me already, love?"

"Not of you; of waiting," she said, half-shyly meeting his look.

"I hardly hoped for this moment," he said after a pause. "Has your father flown bodily from the enemy and left you to face him alone?"

"Not exactly. But it really was kind of him to keep away for a while, wasn't it?" she asked naïvely.

"It was surprisingly kind. But I suppose you will have to make your exit on his entrance."

"No," she laughed softly, "I am going to play the role of audience tonight. He expressly wants me to stay. But if you differ—"

He looked at her curiously. The earnestness with which she had greeted him settled like a mask upon his face. The hand which held hers drew it quickly to his breast.

"I think it's well that you stay," he said, "because we agree at any rate on the main point—that we love each other. Always that, darling?"

"Always that—love."

The low, sweet voice which, for the first time, so caressed him thrilled him madly, but a measured step was heard in the hall, and Ruth moved like a bird to a chair. He could not know that the sound of the step had given her the momentary courage to address him thus.

He arose deferentially as Levice entered. The two men formed a striking contrast. Kemp stood tall, stalwart, straight as an arrow; Levice, with his short stature, his stooping shoulders, and his silvery hair falling about and softening somewhat his plain Jewish face, served as a foil to the other's bright, handsome address.

Kemp came forward to meet him and grasped his hand. Nothing is more thoroughly expressive than this cordial shaking of hands between men. It is a freemasonry which women, in their careless hand-touch, lack, and are the losers thereby. The kiss is a sign of emotion; the hand-clasp bespeaks strong esteem or otherwise. Levice's hand closed tightly around the doctor's; there was a great feeling of mutual respect between these two.

"How are you and your wife?" asked the doctor, seating himself in a low easy-chair as Levice took one opposite him.

"She is well, but tired this evening, and has gone to bed. She asked to be remembered to you." As he spoke, he half turned his head to where Ruth sat in a corner, a little removed.

"Why do you sit back there, Ruth?"

She arose, and seeing no other convenient seat at hand, drew up the low, high-backed ebony chair. Thus seated, they formed the figure of an isosceles triangle, with Ruth at the apex, the men at the angles of the base. It is a rigid outline, the isosceles, bespeaking each point an alien from the others.

There was an uncomfortable pause for some moments after she had seated herself, during which Ruth noted how, as the candlelight from the sconce behind fell upon her father's head, each silvery hair seemed to speak of quiet old age.

Kemp was the first to speak, and, as usual, came straight to the point.

"Mr. Levice, there's no use disguising or beating around the bush the thought uppermost in all our minds. I ask you now, in person, what I asked you in writing last Friday—will you give me your daughter to be my wife?"

"I will answer you as I did in writing. Have you considered that you are a Christian; that she is a Jewess?"

"I have."

It was the first gun and the answering shot of a strenuous battle.

"And you, my child?" he addressed her in the old sweet way which she had missed in the afternoon.

"I have also done so to the best of my ability."

"Then you have found it raised no barrier to your desire to become Dr. Kemp's wife?"

"None."

The two men drew a deep breath at the sound of the little decisive word, but with a difference. Kemp's face shone exultantly. Levice pressed his lips hard together as a shuddering breath left him; his heavily-veined hands were tightly clinched; when he spoke, however, his voice was quite peaceful.

"It is an old and just custom for parents to be consulted by their children upon their choice of husband or wife. In France the parents are consulted before the daughter; it is not a bad plan. It often saves some unnecessary pangs—for the daughter. I am sorry in this case that we are not living in France."

"Then you object?" Kemp almost hurled the words at him.

"I crave your patience," answered the old man, slowly; "I have grown accustomed to doing things deliberately, and will not be hurried in this instance. But as you have put the question, I may answer you now. I do most solemnly and seriously object."

Ruth, sitting intently listening to her father, paled slowly. The doctor also changed color.

"My child," Levice continued, looking her sadly in the face, "by allowing you to fall blindly into this trouble, without warning, with my apparent sanction for any relationship with Christians, I have done you a great wrong; I admit it with anguish. I ask your forgiveness."

"Don't, father!"

Dr. Kemp's clinched hand came down with force upon his knee. He was white to the lips, for though Levice spoke so quietly, a strong decisiveness rang unmistakably in every word.

"Mr. Levice, I trust I'm not speaking disrespectfully," he began, his full voice plainly agitated, "but I must say that it was a great oversight on your part when you threw your daughter, equipped as she is, into Christian society—put her right in the way of loving or being loved by any Christian, knowing all along that such a state of affairs could lead to nothing. It wasn't only wrong—holding such views, it was cruel."

"I acknowledge my culpability; my only excuse lies in the fact that such an event never presented itself as a possibility to my imagination. If it had, I should probably have trusted that her own Jewish conscience and bringing-up would protest against her allowing herself to think seriously upon such an issue."

"But, sir, I don't understand your exception; you are not orthodox."

"No; but I am intensely Jewish," answered the old man, proudly regarding his antagonist. "I tell you I object to this marriage; that is not saying I oppose it. There are certain things connected with it of which neither you nor my daughter have probably thought. To me they are all-powerful obstacles to your happiness. Being an old man and more experienced, will you permit me to suggest these points? My friend, I am seeking nothing but my child's happiness; if, by opening the eyes of both of you to what menaces her future welfare, I can avert what promises but a sometime misery, I must do it, late though it may be. If, when I have stated my view, you can convince me that I am wrong, I shall be persuaded and admit it. Will you accept my plan?"

Kemp bowed his head. The dogged earnestness about his mouth and eyes deepened; he kept his gaze steadily and attentively fixed upon Levice. Ruth, the beloved cause of the whole painful scene, seemed remote and shadowy.

"As you say," began Levice, "we are not orthodox; but before we become orthodox or reformed, we are born, and being born, we are invested with certain hereditary traits that are unconvertible. Every Jew bears in his blood the glory, the triumph, the misery, the abjectness of Israel. The farther we move in the generations, the fainter grows the inheritance. In most countries, in these times, the abjectness is vanishing; we have been set upon our feet; we have been allowed to walk; we are beginning to smile—that is, some of us. Those whose fathers were helped on are nearer the man as he should be than those whose fathers are still groveling. My child, I think, stands a perfect type of what freedom and culture can give. She is not an exception; there are thousands like her among our Jewish girls. Take any intrinsically pure-souled Jew from his coarser surroundings and give him the highest advantages, and he will stand forth the equal, at least, of any man; but he could not mix forever with pitch and remain undefiled."

"No man could," observed Kemp, as Levice paused. "But what are these things to me?"

"Nothing; but to Ruth, much. That is part of the bar-sinister between you. Possibly your sense of refinement has never been offended in my family; but there are many families, people we visit and love, who, though possessing all the substrata of goodness, have never been moved to cast off the surface distinctions which would prick your good taste as sharply as any physical pain. This, of course, is not because they are Jews, but because they lack refining influences in their surroundings. We look for and excuse these signs; many Christians take them as the inevitable marks of the race, and without looking further, conclude that a socially-desirable Jew is an impossibility."

"Mr. Levice, I am only an atom in the Christian world, and you who number so many of them among your friends shouldn't make such sweeping assertions. The world is narrow-minded; individuals are broader."

"True; but I speak of the majority, who decide the vote, and by whom my child would be, without doubt, ostracized. This only by your people; by ours it would be worse—for she will have raised a terrible barrier by renouncing her religion."

"I shall never renounce my religion, father."

"Such a marriage would mean only that to the world; and so you would be cut adrift from both sides, as all women are who move from where they rightfully belong to where they are not wanted."

"Sir," interrupted Kemp, "allow me to show you wherein such a state of affairs would, if it should happen, be of no consequence. The friends we care for and who care for us will not drop off if we remain unchanged. Because I love your daughter and she loves me, and because we both wish our love to be honored in the sight of God and man, how have we erred? We shall still remain the same man and woman."

"Unhappily the world would not think so."

"Then let them hold to their bigoted opinion; it's valueless, and having each other, we can dispense with them!"

"You speak in the heat of passion; and at such a time it would be impossible to make you understand that the honeymoon of life is made up of more than two, and a third, being inimical, can make it wretched. The knowledge that people we respect hold aloof from us is bitter."

"But such knowledge," interrupted Ruth's low voice, "would be robbed of all bitterness when surrounded and hedged in by all that we love."

Her father looked in surprise at the brave face raised so earnestly to his.

"Very well," he responded; "count the world as nothing. You have just said, my Ruth, that you would not renounce your religion. How could that be when you have a Christian husband who would not renounce his?"

"I should hope he would not; I should have little respect for any man who would give up his sacred convictions because I have come into his life. As for my religion, I am a Jewess, and will die one. My God is fixed and unalterable; He is one and indivisible; to divide His divinity would be to deny His omnipotence. He is the potential perfection in all humanity. As to forms, you, father, have bred in me a contempt for all but a few. Saturday will always be my Sabbath, no matter what convention would make me do. We have decided that writing or sewing or pleasuring, since it hurts no one, is no more a sin on that day than on another; to sit with idle hands and gossip or slander is more so. But on that day my heart always holds its Sabbath. But all this is the force of custom. Any day would do as well if we were used to it—for who can tell which was the first and which the seventh counting from creation? On our New Year I should still feel that a holy cycle of time had passed; but I live only according to one record of time, and my New Year falls always on the first of January. Atonement is a sacred day to me; I could not desecrate it. Our services are magnificently beautiful, and I should feel like a culprit if debarred from their holiness. As to fasting, you and I have agreed that any physical punishment which keeps our thoughts one moment from God, and puts them on the feast that is to come, is mere sham and vanity. After these, father, wherein does our religion show itself?"

"Surely," he replied with some bitterness, "we hold few Jewish rites. Well, and so you think you can keep these up? And you, Dr. Kemp?"

Dr. Kemp had been listening attentively while Ruth spoke. His eyes kindled brightly as he answered:

"Why should she not? If all her orisons have made her as beautiful, body and soul, as she is to me, what is to prevent her from so continuing? And if my wife would permit me to go with her upon her holidays to your beautiful Temple, no one would listen more reverently than I. Loving her, what she finds worshipful could find nothing but respect in me."

Plainly Mr. Levice had forgotten the wellspring which was to enrich their lives; but he perceived that an impregnable armor encased them which made every shot of his harmless.

"I can understand," he ventured, "that no gentleman with self-respect would, at least outwardly, show disrespect for any person's religion. You, doctor, might even come to regard with awe a faith which has withstood everything and has never yet been sneered at, however its followers have been persecuted. Many of its minor forms are slowly dying out and will soon be remembered only historically; this history belongs to everyone."

"Certainly. Let us, however, stick to the point in question. You are a man who has absorbed the essence of his religion, and cast off most of its unnecessary externals. You have done the same for my—for your daughter. This distinguishes you. If I were to say the characteristic has never been unbeautiful in my eyes, I should be excusing what needs no excuse. Now, sir, I, in turn, am a Christian—broadly speaking; more formally, a Unitarian. Our faiths are not widely divergent. We are both liberal; otherwise marriage between us might be a grave experiment. As to forms, for me they are a show, but for many they are a necessity—a sort of moral backbone without which they might fall. Sunday is to me a day of rest, if my patients do not need me. I enjoy hearing a good sermon by any noble, broad-minded man, and when I go to church I go not only for that, but for the pleasure of having my spiritual tendencies given a gentle stirring up. There is one holiday that I keep and love to keep. That is, Christmas."

"And I honor you for it; but loving this day of days, looking for sympathy for it from all you meet, how will it be when in your own home the wife whom you love above all others stands coldly by and watches your emotions with no answering sympathy? Will this not breed dissension, if not in words, at least in spirit? Will you not feel the want and resent it?"

Kemp was silent. The question was a telling one, and required thought; therefore he was surprised when Ruth answered for him. Her quiet voice carried no sense of hysteric emotion, but one of grave grace.

She addressed her father; each had refrained from appealing to the other. The situation in the light of their new, great love was strained and unnatural.

"I should endeavor that he should feel no lack," she said, "for, so far as Christmas is concerned, I am a Christian also."

"I do not understand." Her father's lips were dry, his voice husky.

"Ever since I have been able to judge," explained the girl, quietly, "Christ has been to me the loveliest and one of the best men that ever lived. You yourself, father, honor and reverence his life."

"Yes?" His eyes were half closed as if in pain; he motioned to her to continue.

"And so, in our study, he was never anything but what was great and good. Later, when I had read his 'Sermon on the Mount,' I grew to see that what he preached was beautiful. It did not change my religion; it made me no less a Jewess in the true sense, but surely it helped me to gentleness. To me he became the embodiment of Love in the highest—Love perfect, though warm and *human*; human Love so glorious that it needs no divinity to augment its power over us. He was God's attestation, God's symbol of what *Man* might be. As a teacher of brotherly love, he is sublime. So I may call myself a christian, though I spell it with a small letter. It is right that such a man's birthday should be remembered with love; it shows what a sweet power his name is, when, as that time approaches, everybody seems to love everybody better. Feeling so, would it be wrong for me to participate in my husband's actions on that day?"

She received no answer. She looked only at her father with loving earnestness, and the look of adoration Kemp bent upon her was quite lost.

"Would this be wrong, father?" she urged.

He straighted himself in his chair as if under a load. His dark, sallow face seemed to have grown worn and more haggard.

"I have always imagined myself just and liberal in opinion," he responded; "I have sought to make you so. I never thought you could leap so far. It were better had I left you to your mother. Wrong? No; you would be but giving your real feelings expression. But such an expression would grieve—Pardon—I am to consider your happiness." He seemed to swallow something, and hastily continued:

"While we are still on this subject, are you aware, my child, that you could not be married by a Jewish rabbi?"

She started perceptibly.

"I should love to be married by Doctor C———." As she pronounced the distinguished old rabbi's name, a tone of reverential love accompanied it.

"I know. But you would have to take a justice as a substitute."

"A Unitarian minister would be breaking no law in uniting us, and I think would not object to do so; that is, of course, if you had no objection." The doctor looked at him questioningly. Levice answered by turning to Ruth. She passed her hand over her forehead.

"Do you think," she asked, "that, after a ceremony had been performed, Dr. C——— would bless us? As a friend, would he have to refuse?"

"He would be openly sanctioning a marriage which, according to the rabbinical law, is no marriage at all. Do you think he would do this, notwithstanding his friendship for you?" returned her father. They both looked at him intently.

"Ah, well," she answered, throwing back her head, a half-smile coming to her pale lips, "it's only a sentiment, and I could forego it, I suppose. One must give up little things sometimes for great."

"Yes; and this would be only the first. My children, there is something ineradicably wrong when we have to overlook and excuse so much before marriage. 'Sufficient unto the day is the evil thereof'; and why should we add trouble to days already burdened before they come?"

"We should find all this no trouble," said Kemp; "and what is to trouble us after? We have now the wherewithal for our happiness. What, in God's name, do you ask for more?"

"As I have said, Dr. Kemp, we are an earnest people. Marriage is a step not entered into lightly. Divorce, for this reason, is seldom heard of with us, and for this reason we have few unhappy marriages. We know what we have to expect from every quarter. No question I have put would be necessary with a Jew. His ways are ours, and, with few exceptions, a woman has nothing but happiness to expect from him. How am I sure of this with you? In a moment of anger this difference of faith may be flung in each other's teeth, and what then?"

"You mean you cannot trust me."

The quiet, forceful words were accompanied by no sign of emotion. His deep eyes rested as respectfully as ever upon the old gentleman's face. But the attack was a hard one upon Levice. A vein on his temple sprang into blue prominence as he quickly considered his answer.

"I trust you, sir, as one gentleman would trust another in any undertaking; but I have not the same knowledge of what to expect from you as I should have from any Jew who would ask for my daughter's hand."

"I understand that," admitted the other; "but a few minutes ago you imputed a possibility to me that would be an impossibility to any gentleman. You may have heard of such happenings among some, but an event of that kind would be as removed from us as the meeting of the poles. Everything depends on the parties concerned."

"Besides, father," added Ruth, her sweet voice full with feeling, "when one loves greatly, one is great through love. Can true married love ever be divided and sink to that?"

The little white-and-gold clock ticked on; it was the only sound. Levice's forehead rested upon his hand over which his silvery hair hung. Kemp's strong face was as calm as a block of granite; Ruth's was pale with thought.

Suddenly the old man threw back his head. They both started at the revelation: great dark rings were about his eyes; his mouth was set in a strained smile.

"I—I," he cleared his throat as if something impeded his utterance—"I have one last suggestion to make. You may have children. What will be their religion?"

The little clock ticked on; a dark hue overspread Kemp's face. Ruth scarcely seemed to hear; her eyes were riveted upon her father's changed face.

"Well?"

The doctor gave one quick glance at Ruth and answered:

"If God should so bless us, I think the simple religion of love enough for childhood. Later, as their judgment ripened, I should let them choose for themselves, as all should be allowed."

"And you, my Ruth?"

A shudder shook her frame; she answered mechanically:

"I should be guided by my husband."

The little clock ticked on, backward and forward, and forward and back, dully reiterating, "Time flies, time flies."

"I have quite finished," said Levice, rising.

Kemp did likewise.

"After all," he said deferentially, "you have not answered my question."

"I—think—I—have," replied the old man, slowly. "But to what question do you refer?"

"The simple one—will you give me your daughter?"

"No, sir; I will not."

Kemp drew himself up, bowed low, and stood waiting some further word, his face ashy white. Levice's lips trembled nervously, and when he spoke it was in a gentle, restrained way, half apologetically and in strange contrast to his former violence.

"You see, I am an old man rooted in old ideas; my wife, not so old, holds with me in this. I do not know how wildly she would take such a proposition. But, Dr. Kemp, as I said before, though I object, I shall not oppose this marriage. I love my daughter too dearly to place my beliefs as an obstacle to what she considers her happiness; it is she who will have to live the life, not I. You and I, sir, have been friends; outside of the one great difference there is no man to whom I would more gladly trust my child. I honor and esteem you as a gentleman who has honored my child in his love for her. If I have hurt you in these bitter words, forgive me; as my daughter's husband, we must be more than friends."

He held out his hand. The doctor took it, and holding it tightly in his, made answer somewhat confusedly:

"Mr. Levice, I thank you. I can say no more now, except that no son could love and honor you more than I shall."

Levice bent his head, and turned to Ruth, who sat, without a movement, looking straight ahead of her.

"My darling," said her father, softly laying his hand upon her head and raising her lovely face, "if I have seemed selfish and peculiar, trust me, dear, it was through no lack of love for you. Do not consider me; forget, if you will, all I have said. You are better able, perhaps, than I to judge what is best for you. Since you love Dr. Kemp, and if, after all this thought, you feel you will be happy with him, then marry him. You know that I hold him highly, and though I cannot honestly give you to him, I shall not keep you from him. My child, the door is open; you can pass through without my hand. Good-night, my little girl."

His voice quavered sadly over the old-time pet name as he stooped and kissed her. He wrung the doctor's hand again in passing, and abruptly turned to leave the room. It was a long room to cross. Kemp and Ruth followed with their eyes the small, slightly stooped figure of the old man passing slowly out by himself. As the heavy portière fell into place behind him, the doctor turned to Ruth, still seated in her chair.

CHAPTER XVIII

SHE WAS perfectly still. Her eyes seemed gazing into vacancy.

"Ruth," he said softly. But she did not move. His own face showed signs of the emotions through which he had passed, but was peaceful as if after a long, triumphant struggle. He came nearer and laid his hand gently upon her shoulder.

"Love," he whispered, "have you forgotten that I am here?"

His hand shook slightly, but Ruth gave no sign that she saw or heard.

"This has been too much for you," he said, drawing her head to his breast. She lay there as if in a trance, her eyes closed, her face lily-white against him. They remained in this position for some minutes till he became alarmed at her passivity.

"You're tired, darling," he said, stroking her cheek. "Shall I go?"

She started up as if alive to his presence for the first time, and sprang to her feet. She turned giddy and swayed toward him. He caught her in his arms.

"I'm so dizzy," she laughed in a broken voice, looking with dry, shining eyes at him; "hold me for a minute."

A feeling of glad surprise took him as she clasped her arms around his neck; Ruth had been very shy with her caresses.

His eyes met hers in a long, gripping look.

"Of what are you thinking?" he asked in a low voice.

"There's a German song I used to sing," she replied musingly. "Will you think me very foolish if I say it is repeating itself to me now, over and over again?"

"What is it, dear?" he asked, humoring her.

"Do you understand German? Oh, of course, my student; but

this is a sad old song; students don't sing such things. These are some of the words: '*Behüt' dich Gott! es wär zu schön gewesen.*' I wish—"

"It's a miserable song," he said lightly. "Forget it."

She disengaged herself from his arms and sat down. Some late roisterers passing by in the street were heard singing to the twang of a mandolin. It was a full, deep song, and the casual voices blended in perfect accord. As the harmony floated out of hearing, she looked up at him with a haunting smile.

"People are always singing to us; I wish they wouldn't. Music is so sad; it's like a heart-break."

He knelt beside her.

"You're pale and tired," he said; "and I'm going to take a doctor's privilege and send you to bed. Tomorrow you can answer better what I so long to hear. You heard what your father said: your answer rests entirely with you. Will you write, or shall I come?"

"Do you know," she answered, her eyes burning in her pale face, "you have very pretty, soft dark hair? Does it feel as soft as it looks?" She raised her hand, and ran her fingers lingeringly through his short, thick hair.

"Why," she said brightly, "here are some silvery threads on your temples. Troubles, darling?"

"You shall pull them out," he answered, drawing her slender hand to his lips.

"There, go away," she said quickly, snatching it from him and moving from her chair as he rose. She rested her elbow on the mantel-shelf, and the candles from the silver candelabra shone on her face—it looked strained and weary. Kemp's brows gathered in a frown as he saw.

"I'm going this minute," he said, "and I want you to go to bed at once. Don't think of anything but sleep. Promise me you will go to bed as soon as I leave."

"Very well."

"Good-night, sweetheart," he said, kissing her lingeringly. "Dream happy dreams." He stooped again to kiss her hands, and moved toward the door.

"Herbert!" His hand was on the portière, and he turned in alarm at her raucous call.

"What is it?" he asked, taking a step toward her.

"Nothing. Don't—don't come back, I say. I just wanted to see your face. I'll write to you. Good-night."

And the curtain fell behind him.

As he passed down the gravel walk, a coupé drew up and stopped in front of the house. Louis Arnold sprang out. The two men came face to face.

Arnold recognized the doctor immediately and drew back. When Kemp saw who it was, he bowed and passed on. Arnold did likewise, but he went in where the other went out.

It was late, after midnight. He had just arrived on a delayed southern train. He knew the family had come home that morning. Dr. Kemp was rather early in making a visit; it had also taken him long to make it.

Louis put his key in the latch and opened the door. It was very quiet; he supposed everyone had retired. He flung his hat and overcoat on a chair and walked toward the staircase. As he passed the drawing-room, a stream of light came from beneath the portière. He hesitated in surprise—everything was so quiet. Probably the last one had forgotten to put out the lights. He stepped noiselessly up and entered the room. His footfall made no sound on the soft carpet as he moved about putting out the lights. He walked to the mantel to blow out the candles, but stopped, dumfounded, within a foot of it. The thing that disturbed him was the motionless white form of his cousin. It might have been a marble figure, so lifeless she sat, though her face was hidden in her hands.

For a moment Arnold was terrified; but the feeling was immediately succeeded by one of exquisite pain. He was a man not slow to conjecture; by some intuition he understood.

He quickly regained his presence of mind and turned quietly to quit the room; he hoped she had not heard him. He had but turned when a low, moaning sound arrested him. He came back irresolutely.

"Did you call, Ruth?"

Silence.

"Ruth, it is I, Louis, who is speaking to you. Do you know how late it is?"

With gentle force he drew her fingers from her face. The mute misery there depicted was appalling.

"Come, go to bed, Ruth," he said as to a child.

She made a movement to rise, but sank back again.

"I'm so tired, Louis," she pleaded in a voice of tears, like a weary child indeed.

"Yes, I know; but I will help you." The unfamiliar, gentle quality of his voice penetrated even to her numbed senses.

She had not seen him since the night he had asked her to be his wife. No remembrance of this came to her, his presence held only something very restful. She allowed him to draw her to her feet, and as calmly as a brother he led her upstairs and into her room. Without a question he lit the gas for her.

"Good-night, Ruth," he said, blowing out the match. "Go right to bed; your head will be better by morning."

"Thank you, Louis," she said, feeling dimly grateful for something his words implied. "Good-night."

Arnold noiselessly closed the door behind him. She quickly locked it and sat down in the nearest chair.

Her hands were interlaced so tightly that her nails left imprints in the flesh. She had something to consider. Oh dear, it was such a simple thing: was she to break her father's heart, or her own—and—his? Her father's—or his?

It was so stupid to sit and repeat it. Surely it had been decided long ago. Such a long time ago, when her father's loving face had put on its misery. Would it look that way always? No, no, no! She would not have it; she dared not; it was too utterly wretched.

Still, there was someone else, at the thought of whom her temples throbbed wildly. It would hurt him; she knew it. The thought for a moment was a miserable ecstasy. For he loved her—her, simple Ruth Levice—beyond all doubting she knew he loved her. And, oh, father, father, how she loved him! Why must she give it all up? she questioned fiercely. Did she owe no duty to herself? Was she to drag out all the rest of her weary life without his love? Life! It would be a lingering death, and she was young yet—in years. Other girls had married with graver obstacles, in open rupture with their parents, and they had been happy. Why could not she? It was not as if he were at fault; no one dared breathe a word against his fair name. To look at his strong, grave face meant confidence. That was why, when he left the room—

Someone else had left the room also. Someone who had loved her all her life, someone who had grown accustomed in more than twenty years to listen gladly for her voice, to anticipate every wish, to hold her as in the palm of a loving hand, to look for and trust in her unquestioned love. He, too, had left the room; but he was not strong and handsome, poor, poor old father with his small bent shoulders. What a wretched thing it is to be old and have the heart-strings that have so confidently twisted themselves all these years around another rudely cut off—and that by one's only child!

At the thought an icy quiet stole over her. How long she sat there, musing, debating, she did not know. When the gray dawn broke, she rose up calmly and seated herself at her writing-table. She wrote steadily for some time without erasing a single word. She addressed the envelope without a falter over the name.

"That's over," she said audibly and deliberately.

A cock crowed. It was the beginning of another day.

CHAPTER XIX

DR. KEMP tossed the reins to his man, sprang from his carriage, and hurried into his house. "Burke!" he called while closing the door, "Burke!" He walked toward the back of the house and into the kitchen, still calling. Finding it empty, he walked back again and began a still hunt about the pieces of furniture in the various rooms. Being unsuccessful, he went into his bedroom, and a few minutes later hurried again to the kitchen.

"Where have you been, Burke?" he exclaimed as that spare-looking personage turned, spoon in hand, from the range.

"Right here, General," he replied in surprise, "except when I went out."

"Well. Did any mail come here for me?"

"One little billy-do, General. I put it under your dinner-plate. And shall I serve the soup?" The last was bellowed after his master's retreating form.

"Wait till I ring," he called back.

He lifted his solitary plate, snatched up the little letter, and sat down hastily, conscious of strong excitement.

His name and address stared at him from the white envelope in a round, firm hand. There was something about the loop-letters that reminded him of her, and he passed his hand caressingly over the surface.

He did not break the seal for some minutes—anticipation is sometimes sweeter than realization. Finally it was done, but he closed his eyes for a second—a boyish trick of his that had survived, when he wished some expected pleasure to spring suddenly upon him. How would she address him? The memory of their last meeting gave him courage, and he opened his eyes.

The *dénouement* was disconcerting. Directly under the tiny white monogram she had begun, without heading of any description:

It was cruel of me to let you go as I did: you were hopeful when you left. I led you on to this impression for a purely selfish reason. After all, it saved you the anguish of knowing it was a final farewell; for even then I knew it could never be. Never! forever!—do you know the meaning of those two long words? I do. They have burned themselves irrevocably into my brain. Try to understand them—they are final.

I retract nothing that I said to my father in your presence. You know exactly how I still consider what is separating us. I am wrong. Only *I* am causing this separation; no one else could or would. Do not blame my father. If he were to see me writing this he would beg me to desist; he would think I am sacrificing my happiness for him. I have no doubt you think so now. Let me try to make you understand how different it really is. I am no Jephthah's daughter—he wants no sacrifice, and I make none. Duty, the hardest word to learn, is not leading me. You heard my father's words; but not holding him as I do, his face could not recoil upon your heart like a death's hand.

I am trying to write coherently and to the point: see what a coward I am! Let me say it now: I could never be happy with you. Do you remember Shylock—the old man who withdrew from the merry-making with a breaking heart? I could not make merry while he wept; my heart would weep also. You see how selfish I am; I am doing it for my own sake, and for no one's else.

And that is why I ask you now to forgive me—because I am not noble enough to consider you when my happiness is at stake. I suppose I am a light person, seemingly to play thus with a man's heart. If this reflection can rob you of regret, think me so. Does it sound presumptuous or ironical for me to say I shall pray you may be happy without me? Well, it is said that hearts do not break for love—that is, not quickly. If you will just think of what I have done, surely you will not regret your release; you may yet find a paradise with some other and better woman. No, I am not harsh or unreasonable; even *I* expect to be happy. Why should not you, then—you, a man; I, a woman? Forget me. In your busy, full life this should be easy. Trust me, no woman is worthy of spoiling your life for you.

My pen keeps trailing on—like summer twilight it is loath to depart. I am such a woman. I may never see your face again. Will you not forgive me?

RUTH.

He looked up with a bloodless face at Burke standing with the smoking soup.

"I—I—thought you had forgotten to ring," the man stammered, shocked at the altered face.

"Take it away," said his master, hoarsely, rising from his chair. "I don't want any dinner, Burke. I'm going to my office, and must not be disturbed."

The man looked after him with a sadly wondering shake of his head, and went back to his more comprehensible pots and pans.

Kemp walked steadily into his office, lit the gas, and sat down at his desk. He began to re-read the letter slowly from the beginning. It took a long time, for he read between the lines. A deep groan escaped him as he laid it down. It was written as she would have spoken; he could see the expression of her face in the written words, and a miserable, empty feeling of powerlessness came upon him. He did not blame her—how could he, with that sad evidence of her breaking heart before him? He got up and paced the floor unconscious of time. His head was throbbing, and a cold, sick feeling almost overpowered him.

The words of the letter repeated themselves—"Paradise with some other, better woman"—she might have left that out, he thought with a dreary smile, she knew better; she was only trying to cheat herself. "I too shall be happy." Not that, not some other man's wife!—the thought was infernal. He caught his reflection in the glass in passing. "I must get out of this," he laughed with dry, parched lips. He seized his hat and went out. The wind was

"Don't I? Why, I hardly know another girl who lives in such constant gayety as I. Aren't we going to a dinner this evening and to the ball tomorrow night?"

"Yes. But you might as well be going to a funeral for all the pleasure you seem to anticipate. If you come to a ball with such a grandly serious air, the men will just as soon think of asking a statue to dance as you. A statue may be beautiful in its niche, but people don't care to study its meaning at a ball."

"What do you want me to do, mamma? I should hate the distinction of a wall-flower as much as anyone. I'm afraid I'm too big a woman to be kittenish."

"You never were that, but you were at least a girl. People will begin to think you consider yourself above them, or else that you have some secret sorrow."

The smile of incredulity with which she answered her mother would have been heart-breaking had it been understood. No flush stained the ivory pallor of her face at these thrusts in the dark—Louis was never aesthetically annoyed by that propensity now. Her old-time excited contradictions no longer obtruded themselves into their conversations. A silent knowledge lay between them which neither, by word or look, ever alluded to. Mrs. Levice noted with delight their changed relations. Louis's sarcasms ceased to be directed at Ruth, and though the familiar sparring was missing, her mother preferred his deferential bearing when he addressed her, and Ruth's grave gentleness with him. She drew her own conclusions, and accepted Ruth's quietude with more patience with this hope at heart.

Louis understood somewhat, and in his manliness he could not hide that her suffering had cost him a new tenderness of attitude. But he could not understand as her father did. Despite her brave smile, Levice could almost read her heart-beats, and the knowledge brought a hardness and a bitter regret. He grew to scanning her face surreptitiously, looking in vain for the old, untroubled delight in things; and when the unmistakable signs of secret anguish would leave traces at times, he would turn away with a groan. Yet there was nothing to be done. He knew that her love had been no light thing, nor could her giving up be so;

but feeling that, no matter what the present cost, the result would compensate, he trusted to time to heal the wound. Meanwhile his own self-blame, in such moments of intrusion, left its mark upon him.

For Ruth lived a truly dual life. The real one was passed in her quiet chamber, in her long solitary walks, and when she sat with her book, apparently reading. Often she would unconsciously look up with blank, despairing eyes, clinched hands, and hard-set teeth when the thought of him and all her loss would steal upon her. Her father had caught many such a look upon her face. She had resolved to live without him, but accomplishment was not so easy. Besides, it was not as if she never saw him. San Francisco is not so large a city but that by the turning of a corner you may not come across a friend. Ruth grew to study the sounds the different kinds of vehicles made; and the rolling wheels of a doctor's carriage behind her would set her pulses fluttering in fright.

She was walking one day along Sutter Street toward Gough, from Octavia. The street takes a sudden down-grade midway in the block. She was approaching this declension just before the Boys' High School when a carriage drove quickly up the hill toward her. The horses gave a bound as if the reins had been jerked, there was the momentary flash of a man's stern, white face as he raised his hat, and Ruth was walking down the hill, trembling and pale. It was the first time, and for one minute her heart seemed to stop beating and then to rush wildly on. Whether she had bowed or made any sign of recognition, she did not know. It did not matter, though. If he thought her cold or strange or anything, what difference could it possibly make? For her there would be left forever only this dead emptiness. These casual meetings were inevitable, and she would come home after them worn-out and heavy-eyed. "A slight headache" became a recurrent excuse with her.

They had mutual friends, and it would not have been surprising had she met him at the different affairs to which she went, always through her mother's desire. But the dread of coming upon him slowly departed as the months rolled by and with them all token of him. Time and again she would hear allusions to him. "Dr. Kemp has developed into a real misogynist," complained Dorothy Gwynne. "He was one of the few decided eligibles on the horizon, but it needs the magnet of illness to draw him now. I really must look up the symptoms of a possible ache; the toilette and expression of an invalid are very becoming, you know."

"Dr. Kemp made a splendid donation to our kindergarten today. I hadn't seen him since we were in the country, till today, and he thought me looking very well. He inquired after the family, and I told him we had a residence—at which he smiled." This from Mrs. Levice. Ruth would have given much to have been able to ask after him with self-possession, but the muscles of her throat seemed to swell and choke her while silent.

She went now and then to see Bob Bard in his flower-shop. He would inquire without fail after "our friend," or tell her of his having passed that day. Here was her one chance of ascertaining whether he were looking well or otherwise, and the answer to her inquiry was invariably, "Splendid."

She sat one night at the opera in her wonted beauty, her soft, dusky hair rolled from her sweet, madonna face. Many a lorgnette was raised a second and a third time toward her, and Louis, seated next to her, resented with unaccountable ferocity this free admiration which she neither saw or felt.

As the curtain went down on the first act, he drew her attention to some well-known man then passing out. She raised her glass, but her hand fell nerveless in her lap. Directly following him came Dr. Kemp. His eyes met hers, and he bowed, passing on immediately. The rest of the evening passed like a nightmare; she heard nothing but her heart-throbs, saw nothing but his beloved face regarding her with simple courtesy. Louis knew that, for her, the opera was over; the telltale, bistrous shadows grew around her eyes, and she became deadly silent.

"What a big man he is," murmured Mrs. Levice, "and what a nice bow he has!" Ruth did not hear her, but when she reached her own room, she threw herself face downward on her bed in intolerable anguish. She was not a girl who cried easily. If she had been, her suffering would not have been so intense—when the floodgates are opened, the stormy river finds relief. Over and over again she wished she might die and end this eager, passionate craving for some token of love from him, or for the power of letting him know how it was with her. And it would always be thus as long as she lived. She did not deceive herself; no mere friendship would have sufficed—all or nothing, after what had been.

Physically, however, she bore no traces of this continual restraint. On the contrary, her slender figure seemed to mature to more womanly proportions. Little children, seeing her, smiled responsively at her, or clamored to be taken into her arms, there was such a tender, mother-look about her. Gradually her friends began to feel the repose and sympathy of her face, and came to regard her as the queen of confidantes. Young girls with their continual love episodes and excitements, ambitious youths with their whimsical schemes of life and aspirations of love, sought her out openly. Few of these latter dared hope for any individual thought from her, though any of the older men would have staked a good deal for the knowledge that she singled him out for her consideration. Knowing nothing, few felt the pathos of her new beauty.

Arnold viewed it all with irresistible satisfaction. He regarded memory as a sort of palimpsest, and he was patiently waiting until his own name should appear again, when the other's should have been sufficiently obliterated.

It was a severe winter, and everybody appreciated the luxury of a warm home. December came in wet and cold, and *la grippe* held the country in its disagreeable hold. The Levices were congratulating themselves one evening on their having escaped the epidemic.

"I suppose the secret of it lies in the fact that we don't coddle ourselves," observed Levice.

"If you were to coddle yourself a little more," retorted his wife, "you wouldn't cough every morning as you do. Really, Jules, if you don't see a doctor, I'll send for Kemp myself. I actually think it's making you thin."

"Nonsense!" he replied carelessly; "it's only a little irritation of the throat every morning. If the weather is clear next week, I must go to New York. Eh, Louis?"

"At this time of the year!" cried Mrs. Levice, in expostulation.

"Someone has to go, and the only one who should, is I."

"I think I could manage to go," said Louis, "if you would see about that other real estate adjustment while I am gone."

"No, you could not"—when Levice said "no," it seldom meant an ultimate "yes." "Besides, the trip will do me good."

"I shall go with you," put in Mrs. Levice, decidedly.

"No, dear; you couldn't stand the cold in New York, and I couldn't be bothered with the responsibility of your being there."

"Take Ruth, then."

"I should love to go with you, father," Ruth replied to the questioning glance of his eyes. He seemed to ponder over it for a while, but shook his head finally.

"No," he said again. "I shall be very busy, and a woman would be a nuisance to me. Besides, I want to be alone for a while."

They all looked at him in surprise; he was so unused to making testy remarks.

"Grown tired of womankind?" asked Mrs. Levice, playfully. "Well, if you must, you must; you mustn't overstay your health and fun, and—you can bring us something pretty home. How long will you be gone?"

"That depends on the speediness of the courts. Not more than three weeks at the utmost, at any rate."

So the following Wednesday, the day being bright and sunny, he set off. The family crossed the Bay with him.

"Take care of your mother, Ruth," he said at parting, "and of yourself, my pale darling."

"Don't worry about me, father," she said, pulling up his fur collar. "Indeed, I'm well and happy. If you could believe me, perhaps you'd love me as much as you used to."

"As much! My child, I never loved you better than now; remember that. I think I have forgotten everybody else in you."

"Don't, dear!—it makes me feel miserable to think I should

cause you a moment's uneasiness. Won't you believe that every-thing is as I wish it?"

"If I could, I should have to lose the memory of the last four months. Well, try your best to forgive me, child."

"Unless you hate me, don't hurt me with that thought again. I forgive you? I, who am the cause of it all?"

He kissed her tear-filled eyes tenderly, and turned with a sigh to her mother.

They watched to the last his loved face at the window, Ruth with a sad smile and a loving wave of her handkerchief.

Over at the mole is not a bad place to witness tragedies. Pathos holds the upper hand, and the welcomes are sometimes as heart-rendering as the leave-takings. A woman stood on the ferry with a blank, working face down which the tears fell heedlessly; a man, her husband, turned from her, drew his hat down over his eyes, and stalked off toward the train without a backward glance. Parting is a figure of death in this respect: that only those who are left need mourn; the others have something new, be-yond.

CHAPTER XXI

THE FIRELIGHT threw grotesque shadows on the walls. Ruth and Louis in the library made no movement to light up; it was quite cosy as it was. They had both drawn near the crackling woodblaze, Ruth's finger keeping her place within her closed book, Arnold lost in thought in Mr. Levice's broad easy-chair.

"I surely thought you intended going to the concert this evening, Louis," she said presently, looking across at him. "I fancy mamma expected you to go with her."

"What! Voluntarily put myself into the cold when there is a fire blazing right here? Hardly. At any rate, your mother is all right with the Lewises, and I am all right with you."

"I'll give you a guarantee I won't bite; you look altogether too hard for any cannibalistic designs with that look on your face."

"It is something not to be accounted soft. I think a redundancy of flesh too often overflows in trickling sentimentality. My worst enemy could not accuse me of either fault."

"But your best friend wouldn't mind a little thaw now and then. I can't complain, of course, but one of the girls confided to me today that walking on an over-waxed floor was nothing to attempting an equal footing in conversation with you."

"I'm sorry I'm such a slippery customer. Does the fire burn your face? Shall I hand you a screen?"

"No, I like to toast."

"But your complexion might not like it. Move your chair a little farther away."

"In two minutes I intend to have lights and bring my work down. Will it make you tired to watch me?"

"Exceedingly. I prefer your undivided attention. It is not often we are alone, Ruth."

She looked up slightly startled; he seldom voiced his sentiments, and his studied diction made every word doubly impressive. Her pulses began to flutter with the premonition that reference to a tacitly buried secret was going to be made.

"We've been going out and receiving a good deal lately, I know, though somehow I don't feel festive, with father away in freezing New York. Mamma would gladly have stayed at home tonight if Jennie hadn't insisted."

"You think so? I fancy she was a very willing victim. She intimated as much to me."

"She did! I didn't hear anything."

"Not in words, but her eyes were interesting reading: first, capitulation to Jennie, then, in rapid succession, inspiration, command, entreaty, a challenge, and retreat, all directed at me. Possibly this eloquence was lost upon you."

"Entirely. What was your interpretation?"

"Ah, that was confidential. Perhaps I even endowed her with these thoughts, knowing her desires were in touch with my own."

"It's wanton cruelty to arouse a woman's curiosity and leave it unsatisfied. Speak, old Tantalus!"

"It is not cruelty; it is cowardice."

She gazed at him in amazement. His apple-blossom cheeks wore a rosier glow than usual. He nervously seized a log from the box, threw it on the blaze illumining their faces, grasped the poker, and leaning forward in his chair let it grow red-hot as he held it idle in the flames. His glasses fell off, dangling from the cord, and as he adjusted them, he caught the curious, half-amused questioning in Ruth's attentive face. He gave the fire a sharp raking and addressed her, gazing into the leaping flames.

"I was wondering why, after all, you could not be happy as my wife."

A numbness as of death overspread her.

"I think I could make you happy, Ruth."

In the pregnant silence which followed he looked up, and

meeting her sad, reproachful eyes, laid down the poker softly but resolutely, as if with method in the simple action.

"In fact, I know I could make you happy."

"Louis, have you forgotten?" she cried in sharp pain.

"I have forgotten nothing," he replied incisively. "Listen to me, Ruth. It is because I remember, that I ask you. Give me the right to care for you, and you will be happier than you can ever be—in this condition."

"You don't know what you are asking, Louis. Even if I could, you would never be satisfied."

"Try me, Ruth," he entreated.

She raised herself from her easy, reclining position, and regarded him earnestly.

"What you ask," she said in a constrained manner, "would be little short of a crime to accede to. What manner of wife should I be to you when my every thought is given to another?"

His face put on the set look of one who has shut his teeth hard together.

"I anticipated this repulse," he said after a pause, "so what you have just assured me of does not affect my wish or my resolution to continue my plea."

"Would you marry a woman who feels herself as closely bound to another, or the memory of another, as if the marriage rite had been actually performed? Oh, Louis, how can you force me to these disclosures?"

"I am seeking no disclosure, but it is impossible for me to continue silent now."

"Why?"

"Why? Because I love you."

They sat so close together he might have touched her by putting out his hand, but he remained perfectly still, only the pale excitement of long repression speaking from his face. She shrank back at his words and raised her hand as if he had struck her.

"Do not be alarmed," he continued, noticing the motion. "My love cannot hurt you, or it would have killed you long ago."

"Oh, Louis," she murmured, "forgive me; I never thought you cared so much."

"How should you? I am not a man to wear my heart upon my sleeve. I think I have always loved you, but living as familiarly as we have lived, seeing you whenever I wished, the thought that some day this might end never occurred to me. It was only when the possibility of some other man's claiming your love and taking you from me presented itself, that my heart rose up in arms against it—and then I asked you to be my wife."

"Yes," she replied, raising her pale face, "and I refused. The same cause that moved me then, and to which you submitted without protest, rules me now, and you know it."

"No; I do not know it. What then might have had a possible issue, is now done with.—Or do I err?"

Her mouth trembled piteously, but no tears came as she lowered her head.

"Then listen to me. You may think me a poor sort of a fellow even to wish you to marry me when you assure me that you love another. That means that you do not love me as a husband should be loved, but it does not prove that you never could love me so."

"It proves just that."

"No, you may think so now, but let me reason you into seeing the falsity of your thought—for I do not wish to force or impel you to do a thing repugnant to your reason as well as to your feelings. To begin with, you do not dislike me?"

His face was painful in its eagerness.

"I have always loved you as a dear brother."

"Some people would consider that worse than hostility—I do not. Another question: Is there anything about my life or personality to which you object, or of which you are ashamed?"

"You know how proud we all are of you in your bearing in every relation of life."

"I was egotist enough to think as much at any rate; otherwise I could not approach you so confidently. Well, love—indifferent if you will—and respect, are not a bad foundation for something stronger. Will you, for the sake of argument, suppose, for a moment, that for some reason you have forgotten your opposition and have been led into marrying me?"

The sad indulgence of her smile was not inspiriting, but he continued:

"Now, then, say you are my wife; that means I am your husband, and—I love you. You do not return my love, you say; you think you would be wretched with me because you love another. Still, you are married to me and that gives me rights that no other man can possess, no matter how much you love him. You are bound to me, I to you and to your happiness; so I pledge myself to make you happier than you are now, because—I shall make you forget this man!"

"You could not, and I should only grow to hate you!"

"Impossible." The pallor of his face deepened. "Impossible, because I should so act that my love would wait upon your pleasure: it would never push itself into another's place, but it would, in time, overshadow the other. For, remember, I shall be your husband. I shall give you another life; I shall take you away with me. You will leave all your old friends and associations for a while, and I shall be with you always—not intrusively, but necessarily. I shall give you every pleasure and novelty the old world can afford. I shall shower my love on you, not myself. In return, I shall expect your—tolerance. In time, I will *make* you love me!"

His voice shook with the strength of his passion, while she listened in heartsick fear. Carried away by his intensity, she almost felt as if he had accomplished his object. But he quieted down after this.

"Don't you see, Ruth, that all this change must make you forget? And if you tried to put the past from you, if for no other reason than that your wifehood would be less untrue, you would be only following the instincts of the truly honorable woman you are. After that, all would be easy. In every instance you would be forced to look upon me as your husband, for you would belong to me. I should be the author of all your surroundings, and always keeping in mind how I wish you to hold me, I should woo you so tenderly that without knowing it you would finally yield. Then, and only then, when I had filled your thought to the exclusion of every other man, I should bring you home. And I think we would be happy."

"And you would be satisfied to give so much and receive so little?"

"The end would repay me."

"It's a pretty story," she said, letting her hands fall listlessly into her lap, "but the *dénouement* is a castle in Spain that we should never occupy. You think your love is strong enough to kill mine, first of all. Well, I tell you, nothing is strong enough for that. With this fact established, the rest is needless to speak of. It is only your dream, Louis; forgive me that I unwittingly intruded into it; reality would only mean disillusion. We are happy only when we dream."

"You are bitter."

"Our relations are turned, then; I have merely experienced your old theories of the uselessness of much. No; I am wrong. It is better to die than not to have loved."

"You think you have lived your life, then. I can't convince you otherwise now; but I am going to beg you to think this over—to try to imagine yourself my wife. I will not urge your decision, but in a week's time don't you think you should be able to answer me yes or no? If anything can help my cause, I don't want to overlook it; so I may tell you now that, for some unexpressed reason your mother's one wish is to see you my wife."

"And my father?" Her voice was quite hoarse.

"Your father has expressed to your mother that such a course would make him exceedingly happy."

She rose suddenly as if forced to her feet. Her face looked hard to a degree. She stood before him, tall and rigid. He stood up and faced her, reading her face so intently that he straightened himself as if about to receive a blow.

"I will consider what you have said," she said mechanically.

The reaction was so unexpected he turned giddy, and caught on to the back of a chair to steady himself.

"It won't take me a week," she went on with no change in her monotone. "I can give you an answer in a day or two. Tomorrow night, perhaps."

He made a step forward, a movement to seize her hand, but she stepped back, motioning him off.

"Don't touch me," she cried in a suppressed voice, "at least you're not my husband—yet."

She turned hastily toward the door.

"Wait!"

His vibrant voice compelled her to turn.

"I want no martyr for a wife, and no tragedy queen. If you can come to me and honestly say, 'I trust my happiness to you,' well and good. But as I told you once before, I am not a saint, and I cannot always control myself as I have forced myself to do to-night. If this admission is damaging, it is too true to be put lightly aside. I will not detain you any longer."

He looked haughty and cold regarding her from this dim distance. Her gentleness struggled to get the better of her, and she came back and held out her hand.

"I'm sorry if I offended you, Louis. Good-night. Won't you pardon my miserable selfishness?"

His eyes gleamed behind their glasses; he did not take her hand, but merely bent over the little peace-offering as over a sacrament. Seeing that he had no intention of doing more, her hand fell passively to her side, and with bent head, she left the room.

As the door closed softly, Arnold sank with a hopeless gesture into a chair and buried his face in his hands. He was not a stoic, but a man, young, a Frenchman, who loved much. And, half-blinded by his own love, he could not appreciate the depths of self-forgetfulness to which Ruth would have to succumb before she could accept the guaranty of happiness which he had offered her.

The question now presented itself to her in the light of a duty: if by this action she could undo the remorse her former offense had inflicted, had she the right to ignore the opportunity? A vision of her own sad face obtruded itself, but she put it sternly from her. If she were to do this thing, the motive alone must be considered; and she rigidly kept in view the fact that her marriage would be the only means by which her father might be relieved of the haunting knowledge of her lost peace of mind. Had she given one thought to Louis, the mere consideration of the idea would have been impossible to her. One picture alone she kept constantly before her: her father's happy eyes.

CHAPTER XXII

MRS. LEVICE's gaze strayed pensively from the violets she was embroidering to Ruth's pale face. Every time the latter stirred, her mother started expectantly, but the anxiously awaited disclosure was not forthcoming. Outside, the rain kept up a sullen downpour, deepening the sense of comfort within; but Mrs. Levice was not what one might call comfortably minded. Her frequent inventories of Ruth's face had at last led her to believe that the pallor there depicted and the heavy, dark shadows about her eyes meant something decidedly not gladsome, something decidedly serious.

"Don't you feel well, Ruth?" she asked finally, with some anxiety.

Ruth raised her heavy eyes.

"I? Oh, I feel perfectly well. Why do you ask? Do I look ill?"

"Yes, you do; your face is unusually pale, and your eyes look tired. Did you sit up over late last night?"

This was a leading move, but Ruth evaded the deeper meaning so evident to her now.

"No," she replied; "I believe it couldn't have been nine when I went upstairs."

"Why? Were you too tired to sit up, or was Louis's company unpleasant?"

"Oh, no," was the abrupt response, and her eyes fell to the open page again.

Mrs. Levice, once started on the trail, was not to be baffled by such tactics. Since Ruth was not ill, she had had some mental disturbance of which her haggard appearance was the consequence. She felt almost positive that Louis had made some advances last night judging by the flash of intelligence with which he had met her telegraphic expression. It was natural for her to be curious; it was unnatural for Ruth to be so reticent. With expectations not a little hurt she decided to know something more.

"For my part," she observed, as if continuing a discussion, "I think Louis charming in a tête-à-tête—when he feels inclined to be interesting he generally succeeds. Did he tell you anything worth repeating? It's a dull afternoon, and you might entertain me a little."

She looked up from the violet petal she had just completed and encountered Ruth's full, questioning gaze.

"What is it you would like to know, mamma?" she asked in a gentle voice.

"Nothing you do not care to tell," her mother answered proudly, but regarding her intently.

Ruth passed her hand wearily across her brow, and considered a moment before answering.

"I didn't mean to hurt you by my silence, mamma, but before I had decided I hardly thought it necessary to say anything. He asked me to—marry him."

The avowal was not made with the conventional confusion and trembling.

Mrs. Levice was startled by the dead calm of her manner.

"You say that as if it were a daily occurrence for a man like Louis Arnold to offer you his hand and name."

"I hope not."

"But you do. I confess I believe you're not one tenth as excited as I am. Why didn't you tell me before? Any other girl would have sat up to tell her mother in the night. Oh, Ruth darling, I'm so glad. I've been looking forward to this ever since you grew up. What did you mean by saying you wanted to wait till you had decided? Decided what?"

"Upon my answer."

"As if you could question it, you fortunate girl! Or were you waiting for me to help you to it? I scarcely need tell you how you have been honored."

"Honor isn't everything, mamma."

At that moment a desperate longing for her mother's sympathy seized her, but on the heel of the impulse the knowledge of the needless sorrow it would occasion came to her, and her lips remained closed.

"No," responded her mother, "and you have more than that. Surely Louis didn't neglect to tell you."

"You mean his love, I suppose.—Yes, I have that."

"Then what else do you want? You probably know that he can give you every luxury within reason—we needn't overlook honest practicality. As for Louis himself, the most fastidious could find nothing to cavil at—he will make you a perfect husband. You're familiar enough with him to know his faults, but you know that no man is faultless. I hope you're not silly enough to expect some girlish ideal—all such ideals died in the golden age, you know."

"As mine did. No; I've outgrown imagination of that description."

"Then why do you hesitate?" Her mother's eyes were shining, her face was alive with the excitement of hope fulfilled. "Is there anything else wanting?"

"No," she responded dully. "But let's not talk about it any more, please. I must see Louis again, you know."

"If your father were here, he could help you better, dear." There was no reproach in Mrs. Levice's gentle acceptance of that fact. "He will be so happy over it. There, kiss me, precious. I know you like to think things out in silence, and I won't say another word about it till you give me leave."

She kept her word. The dreary afternoon dragged on. By four o'clock it was growing dark, and Mrs. Levice grew restless.

"I'm going to my room to write to your father now—he shall have a good scolding for leaving me without a letter today," and forthwith she betook herself upstairs.

Ruth closed her book and moved restlessly about the room. She wandered over to the front window, and drawing aside the silken curtain, looked out into the storm-tossed garden. The pale heliotropes lay wet and sweet against the trellises; some loosened rose-petals fluttered noiselessly to the ground; only the gorgeous chrysanthemums looked proudly indifferent to the elements, while the beautiful, stately palm tree just at the side of the window spread its gracious arms like a protecting temple. She felt suddenly oppressed and feverish, and threw open the long French window. The rain had ceased for the time, and she stepped out upon the veranda. The fragrance of the rain-soaked flowers stole to her senses; the soft, sweet breeze caressed her temples; she stood still in the perfumed freshness and enjoyed its peace. By and by she began to walk up and down. Evening was approaching, and Louis would soon be home. She had decided to meet him upon his return and have it over with. She must school herself to some show of graciousness. The thing must not be done by halves or it must not be done at all. Her father's happiness! Over and over she repeated it. She went so far as to picture herself in his arms; she heard the old-time words of blessing; she saw his smiling eyes, and a gentleness stole over her whole face, a gentle nobility which made it strangely sweet. The soft patter of rain on the gravel roused her, and she went in, but she felt better, and wished Louis might come in while the mood was upon her.

It was nearing six when Mrs. Levice came back, humming a song.

"I thought you would still be here. Make a light, will you, Ruth; it's as pitchy as Hades, and that smoldering log looks purgatorial."

Ruth lit the gas, and as she stood with upturned eyes adjusting the burner, her mother noticed that the heaviness had departed from her face. She sank into a chair and took up the evening paper.

"What time is it, Ruth?"

"Twenty minutes to six," she answered, glancing at the clock.

"As late as that?" She meant to say, "And Louis not home yet?" but forbore to mention his name.

"It's raining heavily now," said Ruth, throwing a log upon the fire. Mrs. Levice unfolded the crackling newspaper, and Ruth moved over to the window to draw down the blinds. As she stood looking out with her hand on the back of a chair, she saw the gate swing slowly open, and a messenger-boy came dawdling up the walk as leisurely as if the sun were streaming full upon him.

Ruth stepped noiselessly out, meaning to anticipate his ring. A vague foreboding drove the blood from her lips as she stood waiting at the open hall-door. Seeing the streaming light, the boy managed to accelerate his snail's pace.

"Miss Ruth Levice live here?" he asked, stopping in the doorway.

"Yes." She took the packet he handed her. "Any charges or answer?" she asked.

"No'm," answered the boy, and, noticing her pallor and apprehension, "I'll shet the door for you," he added, laying his hand on the knob.

"Thank you. Here, take two cars if necessary; it's too wet to walk." She handed him a coin, and the boy went off, gayly whistling.

She closed the heavy door softly and sat down on a chair. She recognized Louis's handwriting on the wrapper, and her heart fluttered ominously. She tore off the damp covering, and the first thing she encountered was another wrapper on which was written in large characters:

> DEAR RUTH—Do not be alarmed; everything is all right. I had to leave town on the Overland at 6 P.M. Read the letter first, then the telegram; they will explain.
>
> LOUIS.

The solicitude which had prompted this warning was appreciated; one fear was stilled. She drew out the letter; she saw in perplexity that it was from her father. She hurriedly opened it and read:

> NEW YORK, Jan. 21, 189—.
>
> DEAR LOUIS—I am writing this from my bed, where I have been confined for the past week with pneumonia, although I managed to write a daily post-card. Have been quite ill, but am on the mend and only anxious to start home again. I really

cannot rest here, and have made arrangements to leave tomorrow. Have taken every precaution against catching cold, and apart from feeling a trifle weak and annoyed by a cough, am all right. Shall come home directly. Say nothing of this to Esther or Ruth; shall let them know by telegram of my homecoming. Had almost completed the business, and can leave the rest to Hamilton.

My love to you all.

Your loving Uncle,

JULES LEVICE.

Under this Louis had penciled,

Received this this morning at 10:30.

Ruth closed her eyes as she unfolded the telegram; then, with every nerve quivering, she read the yellow missive:

RENO, Jan. 27, 189—.

LOUIS ARNOLD, San Francisco, Cal.:

Have been delayed by my cough—feeling too weak to travel alone—come if you can.

JULES LEVICE.

Her limbs shook as she sat; her teeth chattered; for one minute she turned sick and faint. Under the telegram Arnold had written:

Am sure it is nothing. He has never been ill, and is more frightened than a more experienced person would be. There is no need to alarm your mother unnecessarily, so say nothing till you hear from me. Shall wire you as soon as I arrive, which will be tomorrow night.

LOUIS.

How could she refrain from telling her mother? She felt suddenly weak and powerless. O God, good God, her heart cried, only make him well—only make him well!

The sound of the library door closing made her spring to her feet. Her mother stood regarding her.

"What is it, Ruth?" she asked.

"Nothing," she cried, her voice breaking despite her effort to be calm—"nothing at all. Louis has just sent me word that he had to leave town this evening, and says not to wait dinner for him."

"That's very strange," mused her mother, moving slowly toward her and holding out her hand for the note. But Ruth thrust the papers behind her.

"It's to me, mamma; you wouldn't care for a second-hand love letter, would you?" she asked, assuming a desperate gayety. "There's nothing strange about it; he often leaves like this."

"Not in such weather and not after— There won't be a man in the house tonight. I wish your father were home; he wouldn't like it, if he knew." She shivered violently as they went into the dining-room.

CHAPTER XXIII

THE NEXT day passed like a nightmare. To add to the misery of her secret, her mother began to fidget over the continued lack of any communication from her husband. Had the weather been fair, Ruth would have insisted on her going out with her, but to the rain of the day before was added a heavy wind-storm which made any unnecessary expedition from home absurd.

Mrs. Levice worried herself into a headache, but would not lie down. She was sure the next delivery would bring something. Wasn't it time for the second delivery? Wouldn't Ruth please watch for the postman? By half-past one she took up her station at the window, only to see the jaunty little rubber-encased man go indifferently by. At half-past four this scene was repeated, and then she decided to act.

"Ring up the telegraph-office, Ruth; I'm going to send a dispatch."

"Why, mamma, probably the mail is delayed; it always is in winter. Besides, you'll only frighten father."

"Nonsense; two days is a long delay without the excuse of a blockade. Go to the telephone, please."

"The telephone has been out of order since yesterday, you know."

"I had forgotten. Well, one of the maids must go; I can't stand it any longer."

"You can't send any of the servants in such weather; both the maids have terrible colds, and Mary wouldn't go if you asked her. Listen! It's frightful. I promise to go in the morning if we don't get a letter, but we probably shall. Let's play checkers for a while." With a forced stoicism she essayed to distract her mother's thoughts, but with poor success. The wretched afternoon drew to a close; and immediately after a show of dining, Mrs. Levice went to bed. At Ruth's suggestion she took some headache medicine.

"It will make me sleep, perhaps, and that will be better than worrying awake and unable to do anything."

The opiate soon had its effect, and with a sign of relief Ruth heard her mother's regular breathing. It was now her turn to suffer openly her own fears. Louis had said she would hear tonight, but at what time? It was now eight o'clock, and the bell might ring at any moment. Mrs. Levice slept, and Ruth sat dry-eyed and alert, feeling her heart rise to her throat every time the windows shook or the doors rattled. It was one of the wildest nights San Francisco had ever experienced: trees groaned, gates slammed, and a terrific war of the elements was abroad. The wailing wind about the house haunted her like the desolate cry of someone begging for shelter. The ormolu clock ticked on and chimed forth nine. Still her mother slept. Ruth from her chair could see that her cheeks were unnaturally flushed and that her breathing was hurried, but any degree of oblivion was better than the impatient outlook for menacing tidings. Despite the heated room, her hands grew cold, and she wrapped them in the fleecy shawl in which she was enveloped. The action brought to mind the way her father had been wont to tuck her little hands under the coverlet when a child, after they had clung around his neck in a long good-night, and how no sooner were they there than out they would pop for "just one squeeze more, father." How long the good-nights had been with this play! She had never called him "papa" like other children, but he had always liked it best so. She brushed a few drops from her lashes as the sweet little chimes of the clock rang out ten bells. She felt heartsick with her thoughts, her limbs ached with stiffness, and she began a gentle walk up and down the room. Would it keep up all night? There! surely somebody was crunching up the gravel walk. With one look at her sleeping mother, she quickly left the room, closing the door noiselessly behind her. With a palpitating heart she leaned over the balustrade; was it a false alarm, after all? The next instant there was a violent pull at the bell, as startling in the dead of the night as a supernatural summons. Before Ruth could hurry down, Nora, looking greatly bewildered, came out of her room and rushed to the door. In a flash she was back again with the telegram and had put it into Ruth's hands.

"Fifteen cents' charges," she said.

"Pay it," returned Ruth.

As the maid turned away, she tore open the envelope. Before she could open the form, a firm hand was placed upon hers.

"Give me that," said her mother's voice.

Ruth recoiled. Mrs. Levice stood before her, unusually quiet in her white nightdress. With a strong hand she endeavored to relax Ruth's fingers from the paper.

"But, mamma, it was addressed to me."

"It was a mistake, then; I know it was meant for me. Let go instantly, or I'll tear the paper. Obey me, Ruth."

Her voice sounded harsh as a man's. At the strange tone Ruth's fingers loosened, and Mrs. Levice, taking the telegram reentered the room, Ruth following her closely.

Standing under the chandelier, Mrs. Levice read. No change came over her face. When she had finished, she handed the paper without a word to Ruth. This was the message:

RENO, JAN. 28, 189—.

MISS RUTH LEVICE, San Francisco, Cal.:

Found your father very weak and feverish and coughing continually insists on getting home immediately, says to inform Dr. Kemp, who will understand and have him at the house on our arrival at 11:30 Thursday no present danger.

LOUIS ARNOLD.

"Explain," commanded her mother, speaking in her overwrought condition as if to a stranger.

"Get into bed first, mamma, or you'll take cold."

Mrs. Levice mechanically suffered herself to be led there, and in a few words Ruth explained what she knew.

"You knew that yesterday before the train left?"

"Yes, mamma."

"And why didn't you tell me? I could have gone to him. Oh, why didn't you tell me?"

"It would have been too late, dear."

"No, it's too late now! Do you hear? I will never see him again, and it's all your fault—what do you know? Stop crying! *Will* you stop crying, or—"

"Mamma, I'm not crying, you are crying, and saying things that aren't true. It won't be too late; perhaps it's nothing but the cough. Louis says there's no danger."

"Be still!" cried her mother, her whole figure trembling. "I know there's danger now—this minute. Oh, what can I do, what can I do!" With this cry all her strength forsook her and she moaned and laughed and swayed with the hysteria of long ago. When Ruth strove to put her arms about her, she shook her off convulsively.

"Don't touch me!" she sobbed. "It's all your fault—he wants me—needs me—and, oh, look at me here! What a figure! Why do you stand there like a helpless ghost? Go away. No, come here!—I want Dr. Kemp—now, at once. He said to have him. Send for him, Ruth."

"On Thursday morning," she managed to answer.

"No, now—I must, must, must have him! You won't go? Then I will. Get out of my way!"

Ruth, summoning all her strength, strove to hold her in her arms, all to no avail.

"Lie still," she said sternly at last. "I'll go for Dr. Kemp."

"You can't; it's night and raining. Oh," she continued, distractedly, "I know I'm acting dreadfully, but he will calm me. Ruth, I want to be calm—I must be calm—don't you understand?"

The two maids, frightened by the disturbance, stood in the doorway. Both had their heads covered with shawls; both were suffering with severe colds.

"Come in, girls. Stay here with my mother. I'm going for the doctor."

"Oh, Miss Ruth, ain't you afraid? It's a awful night, and black as pitch, and you all alone?" asked Nora, with wide, frightened eyes. "Let me go with you."

"No. I'm not afraid," said the girl, a great calmness in her voice as she spoke above her mother's dreary sobbing. "Stay and try to quiet her. I won't be gone long."

She flew into her room, drew on her overshoes and mackintosh, grasped a sealskin cap, which she tied securely under her chin, and went out into the howling, raging night.

She had only a few blocks to go, but under ordinary circumstances the undertaking would have been disagreeable enough. The rain came down in heavy, wild torrents; the wind roared madly, wrapping her skirts about her limbs and making walking almost an impossibility; the darkness was impenetrable save for the sickly, quavering light shed by the few street-lamps, as far apart as angel visitants. Lowering her head and keeping her figure as erect as possible, she struggled bravely on. She met scarcely anyone, and those she did meet occasioned her little uneasiness in the flood of unusual emotions overwhelming her soul. At any other time the thought of her destination would have blotted out every other perception; now this was but one of many shuddering visions. Trouble was making her strong; life could offer her little that would find her unequal to the test. Down the broad, deserted avenue, with its dark, imposing mansions and wildly swaying trees, she hurried as if she were alone in the havocking elements. The rain beat her and lashed her in the face; she faced it unflinchingly as a small part of her trials. Without a tremor she ran up Dr. Kemp's steps. It was only when she stood with her finger on the bell-button that she realized whom she was about to encounter. Then for the first time she gave one long sob of self-recollection—and pushed the button.

Burke almost immediately opened the door. Ruth had no intention of entering. It would be sufficient to leave her message and hurry home.

"Who's there?" asked Burke, peering out into the darkness. "It's a divil of a night for anyone but—"

"Is Dr. Kemp in?" The sweet woman-voice so startled him that he opened the door wide.

"Come in, mum," he said apologetically. "Come in out of the night."

"No. Is the doctor in?"

"I don't know," he grumbled, "and I can't stand here with the door open."

"Close it, then, but see if he's in, please."

"I'll lave it open, and ye can come in or stay out according if ye're dry-humored or wet-soled." He shuffled off angrily. The door was open! Her father had assured her of that once—long ago. Inside were warmth and light; outside, in the shadow, were cold and darkness. Here she stood.—Would the man never return? Ah, here he came hurrying along. She drew nearer the door, but within a half-foot she stood still with locked jaw and swimming senses.

"My good woman," came the grave, kindly voice which calmed while it unnerved her, "come in and speak to me here. Am I wanted anywhere? Come in, please, the door must be closed."

With almost superhuman will she drew herself together, and came closer. Seeing the dark, moving figure, he opened the door wide, and she stepped in. As it closed she faced him, turning up her white, haggard face to his.

"You!"

He recoiled, but recovered himself almost instantly. "What is it?" he asked in hoarse brusqueness.

"My mother." She spoke nervously, her dark eyes sadly holding his. "She's in a frightfully hysterical condition, and only calls for you. Will you come?"

"Surely." But he did not move. He stood rigid before her, conscious only that she was there, alone with him again, his eyes enfolding her.

His arms went out to her. "Ruth," he implored.

She put out protesting hands. "Don't," she begged. "Only come. I need you so!"

The appeal steadied him. "Wait a minute. I'll ring for my carriage and—"

"No, no, please don't wait for anything. Please come at once."
She turned blindly from him to the door, and he rushed into his
office, seized a small emergency case and, throwing on overcoat
and hat, in another minute was running down the steps after
her.

At this juncture the storm seemed to reach its climax, and he
gained her side, breathless, as she ineffectually strove to hurry on
against the raging wind.

"Take my arm," he ordered, and drew her arm firmly through
his.

All along this block of Van Ness Avenue the row of heavy-
foliaged eucalyptus trees bordering the broad pavement tossed
and creaked and moaned in the fury of the tempest. One violent
broadside almost lifted the two pedestrians off their feet, and as
a heavy limb fell with a sudden crash Kemp was just quick
enough to throw her to the other side of him out of its reach.

"You're hurt," she cried above the uproar, her hands upon his
shoulders.

"No," he laughed in mad recklessness, shaking himself like a
huge mastiff while his hands pinioned hers where they had
fallen. "Only wet and leafy and terribly—"

"Oh, let go!" she begged frantically.

But the storm had taken him and he held her close within his
arms, mad as the wind roaring and raving about them, and as
inarticulate.

When his hold relaxed, penitent, he let her draw from him
but retained tight hold of her wrists. "Forgive me," he struggled
to say, "I—"

"Come now," he faintly heard, and, humbly, he drew her arm
again through his and they moved on through the steady downpour and against the abating wind.

"Dearest," he pleaded, "can't it be?"

For a space she did not answer, she was still too elementally
shaken, too uprooted from her selfless fortitude, to find her former grasp of things. When she did speak her voice was so low he

had to strain all his faculties to hear above the whimper of wind and rain, the sharp click of their hurrying feet.

"We are both—unnerved," she said. "We were unprepared—for this meeting. It must not happen again—what has just happened. Because—it is always going to be the same. He knows—better. His wisdom of experience is wiser than our wisdom of instinct. At least—I am teaching myself to believe that. Try to teach yourself too. Sometimes things—little things—have come to me. Little things in which even you showed that, subconsciously, you felt—differences."

"Differences?"

"Racial differences. As if—at root—you thought Jew and Christian were inexorably asunder—made of different clay."

"Jew and Christian! I don't know them. Men and women, yes. But you are you and I am I, and we met and loved, without prejudice. And so, individually speaking, we know there is no difference."

"Ah, individually speaking! Do you note your fine distinction? Always the *one* Jew, the *exceptional* Jew, who has found favor in your eyes! Involuntarily the Christian mind always rears its ghettoes. And in that mental ghetto, I want you to know, I belong—and proudly."

"Ghettoes! I am not a medievalist, my darling. Have you forgotten your story of the Rose of Sharon? You see, I've learned my lesson too, and it can never be unlearned again. Let your father remember that when next he brands the abstract 'Christian mind,' as you put it—with ghetto-building. Some of us can learn to build higher. And you—such as you—are our divine teachers."

Again she did not answer. Her head was bent and he saw her tears were falling.

"Am I hurting you again?" he asked miserably.

"N-no—not hurting me. Only—he doesn't see it as we—as you do. He thinks of—the general prejudice—the outside—the social distinctions that might creep in to separate—. But tonight—oh, tonight, can't we just be friends?"

"We can be anything you want us to be," he said very quietly.

"Thanks," she whispered. After a little she told him of her

father's illness and of Louis' disturbing message about his, Kemp's, "understanding."

"Yes," he said, strictly professional in response to her question, "I do understand. Your father came to me last year, probably as early as February, complaining of a cough that annoyed him nights and mornings. He told me that whenever he felt it coming on he went into another room so as not to disturb your mother. I examined him and found he was suffering from the first stages of asthma, one—you knew nothing of this?"

"Nothing. Don't try to spare me. One—?"

"Don't rush to the worst conclusion. One of his lungs I found slightly diseased, but—"

"His lung!"

"Dearest, I want you to trust me. Many a man has lived to second childhood with asthma, and the partial loss of a lung is not necessarily fatal. He knew this, and with the treatment and careful living was getting along capitally. I examined him several times and found no increase in the loss of tissue. He wasn't coughing so much, he told me."

"But just before he left he was coughing a good deal."

"Ah. I haven't seen him for several months, you know."

"No. Then you think the asthma made the pneumonia more—dangerous?" Her voice was taut and stern, but peremptory.

"In all probability—I fear so."

"Yes."

They had reached the house and went silently and quickly up the path and steps into the vestibule. He took the key from her.

"One word," he said authoritatively. "You're not to take that hopeless view. Between us—you and me—we'll keep him."

Swiftly, in a passion of gratitude, before he could grasp her intention, she had taken his face between her hands and kissed him on the eyes.

"Dedication," she whispered impetuously, and passed fleetly within as Nora opened the door.

"I heard you's coming," the maid explained. "And oh, Miss

Ruth, do hurry—she's doin' nothin' now but stare—and it's awful."

They found her indeed as the maid had described, sitting up in bed, the room in a blaze of light.

"Now, dear lady," he began in gentle firmness, but she held up a peremptory hand.

"First tell me—without reservations—what do you know about my husband's health?" She spoke in harsh intensity.

"Certainly." He lowered the blazing lights, beginning at once to tell her what, in the main, he had told Ruth, but softening the details.

"And you think—"

"That it can't be so serious, since he can travel."

Her throat moved spasmodically, her lips quivered painfully in her effort toward calmness, and he gently placed her back among the pillows, asking Ruth for water for a powder.

Together they administered it. Very slightly he used his power of hypnosis, and presently the stare in the brilliant eyes relaxed, the lids drooped, and they saw her breathing the even breath of sleep.

He turned to Ruth still in her outdoor things. "Change everything you have on," he said in a low tone. "Or, better, go to bed. I'll stay through the night."

"Is it necessary?"

"No. I want to." He smiled softly upon her.

Her eyelids fluttered. "Aren't you—aren't your feet wet?"

"No. I'm water-proof. And this splendid fire will warm me. Get out of those wet things as quickly as possible."

As he drew up a deep chair before the fire, prepared to make himself comfortable, she went without a word.

She did as he had bidden, slipping into a loose, dull-red gown against which her throat and face gleamed in spiritual softness. Then, without question, she went back to her mother's bedroom, entering noiselessly, and slipping into a corner of a remote couch.

Without turning, he knew she was there, but he made no

move to disturb the tranquillity of the situation. The sweet intimacy of the moment drove into his senses—as to hers—despite the miserable gulf separating them, and they were content to let peace hold them. The mother, the inadvertent cause of drawing them together, last as first, slept on, and he and she, the only waking mortals in the great house, kept silent vigil.

Ruth, her cheek pressed against the cushion, looked beyond with fixed gaze. She could see the crown of his dark head above the top of his chair, his knees and feet. But she looked beyond. Presently, in the utter quiet, a great weariness wrought of the storm and stress of the night overtook her, her temples throbbed painfully, and she closed her eyes. As night waxed into morning she fell into a troubled sleep. Once she gave a quivering sigh, and he turned. His gaze wandered searchingly about the room till it found a soft robe thrown over the arm of a chair. His step made no sound in the deep carpet as he came with it toward her. Tucking it lightly about her, he saw, with an inward groan, the change upon her sleeping face—the dark shadows about her eyes, not caused by the curling lashes, her close-pressed, pathetically drooping mouth, the blue veins in her temples—

He returned to his seat with stern eyes.

It was five o'clock before either mother or daughter opened her eyes, and then they started up simultaneously. Ruth noticed the warm robe about her and her eyes sped to the doctor. He, however, was speaking to her mother who, in the dim light, looked pale but calm.

"Then you'll be here tomorrow morning?" she was saying.

"I'll manage to meet him at Oakland with a closed carriage."

"You are very, very good. May I—go with you?"

"No—pardon me, but it will be best for you to receive him at home. There must be nothing whatever to disturb him. Have everything ready—especially yourself."

"I shall be ready. I don't know how to thank you." She held out both her hands. "Will you let Ruth show you to a room, and when you have rested—"

"I have rested," he said, looking at his watch. "I must hurry home now. Good-bye, and remember there may be no cause for anxiety."

Ruth followed him silently down to the door.

"Is there any preparation I can make?" she asked as he slipped into his overcoat.

"No, only have his bed and hot-water bottles ready. And—will you take care of yourself?"

She smiled, not daring to speak in the tender light of his tired eyes.

Bending his head in good-bye, he quickly opened the door and as quickly closed it behind him.

CHAPTER XXIV

THE SUN shone with its usual winter favoritism upon San Francisco this Thursday morning. After the rain the air felt as exhilarating as a day in spring. Young girls tripped forth "in their figures," as the French have it, and even the matrons unfastened their wraps under the genial wooing of sunbeams.

Everything was quiet about the Levice home. Neither Ruth nor her mother felt inclined to talk, so when Mrs. Levice took up her position in her husband's room, Ruth wandered downstairs. The silence seemed vocal with her fears.

"And I tell ye's two," remarked the cook, as her young mistress passed from the kitchen, "that darter and father is more than kin, they is soul-kin, if ye know what that manes; an' the boss's girl do love him more'n seven times seven children which such a man-angel should 'a' had." For the "boss" was to those who served him "little lower than the angels," and their prayers the night before had held an eloquent appeal for his welfare.

Ruth, her face against the window, watched in sickening anxiety. She knew they were not to be expected for some time, but it was better to stand here than in the fear-haunted background.

Suddenly, and almost miraculously it seemed to her, a carriage stood before the gate. She flew to the door, and as she opened it leaned for one second blindly against the wall.

"Tell my mother they've come," she gasped to the maid, who had entered the hall.

Then she looked out. Two men were carrying one between them up the walk. As they came nearer, she saw how it was. That bundled-up figure was her father's; that emaciated, dark, furrowed face was her father's; but, as they carefully helped him up the steps, and the loud, painful, panting breaths came to her, were they her father's too? Helpless, she stood against the wall—a picture of frustrated love.

She paused in agony at the foot of the stairs as the closing door shut out the dreadful sound. An implacable shadow fell upon her—for the first time she faced the inexorable, and burying her face in her hands, she strove to shut out the vision.

He had not seen her; his eyes had been closed as if in exhaustion as they gently helped him along, and she had understood at once that the only thing to be thought of was, by some manner of means, to remove the choking obstacle from his lungs. Oh, to be able in her young strength to hold the weak, loved form in her arms and breathe into him her overflowing life-breath! She walked upstairs presently; he would be expecting her. As she reached the upper landing, Kemp came from the room, closing the door behind him. His bearing revealed a gravity she had never witnessed before. In his tightly buttoned morning-suit he might have been officiating at some solemn ceremonial. He stood still as Ruth confronted him at the head of the stairs, and met her lovely, miserable eyes with grave sympathy. She essayed to speak, but succeeded only in gazing at him in speechless entreaty.

"Yes, I know," he responded to her silent appeal; "you were shocked at what you heard: it was the asthma—it has completely overpowered him. The pneumonia has made him extremely weak."

"And you think—"

"We must wait till he has rested; the trip was severe for him in his condition."

"Tell me the truth, please, with no reservations. Is there danger?"

Her eager, abrupt questions told clearly what she was suffering.

"He has never had any serious illness; if the asthma has not overleaped itself, we have much to hope for."

The intended consolation conveyed a contrary admission which she immediately grasped.

"That means—the worst," she said, her clasped fingers speaking the language of despair. "Oh, you, you who know so much, can't you help him? Think, think of everything; there must be something! Do something—dear—for my sake!"

His grave, tender eyes answered her silently as he took both her little clasped hands in his one strong one, saying simply—

"Trust me, but only so far as lies within my human power. He is somewhat eased already, and asks for you. Look at your mother: she is surpassing herself. If your love for him can achieve one-half such a conquest, you'll only be making good your inheritance. I'll be in again at one, and will send some medicines up at once." He ended in his usual matter-of-fact tone, and went hurriedly down the stairs.

There was perfect quiet in the room when Ruth entered. Propped high by many pillows, Jules Levice lay in his bed, his wife's arm about him. His head rested on her bosom; with her one disengaged hand she smoothed his white hair. Never was the difference between them more marked than now, when her beautiful face shone above his with the touch of the destroyer already upon it; never was the love between them more marked than now, when he leaned in his weakness upon her who had never failed him in all their wedded years.

His eyes were half closed as if in rest; but he heard the opening door, and Mrs. Levice felt the tremor that passed over him as Ruth approached.

"My child."

The softly whispered love-name of old made her tremble; she smiled through her tears, but when his feeble arms strove to draw her to him, she stooped, and laying them about her neck, placed her cheek upon his. For some minutes these three remained knit in a close embrace. Love, strong and tender, spoke and answered in that silence.

"It's—good—to be at home," he said, speaking with difficulty.

"It wasn't home without you, dear," murmured his wife, laying her lips softly on his brow. Ruth, kneeling beside the bed, noticed how loosely the signet-ring he wore hung on his slender finger.

"You look ill, my Ruth," he said, after a pause. "Lay my head down, Esther—you must be tired. Sit before me, dear, I want to see your two faces together."

His gaunt eyes flitted from one to the other.

"It's a fair picture to—take with one," he whispered, his eyes wistfully smiling upon them.

"To keep with one," softly trembled his wife's voice. His eyes met hers in a commiserating smile.

Suddenly he started up.

"Ruth," he gasped, "will you go to Louis? He must be worn out."

She left the room hurriedly. Her faint knock was not immediately answered, and she called softly. Receiving no reply, she turned the knob and it yielded to her hand. Sunbeams danced merrily about the room of the young man, who sat in their light in a hopeless attitude. He evidently had made no change in his dress, and as Ruth stood unnoticed beside him her eyes wandered over his gray, unshaven face, travel-stained and weary to a sad degree. She laid her hand upon his shoulder.

"Louis," she whispered gently.

He shook under her touch, but made no further sign that he knew of her presence.

"You must be so tired, Louis," she continued sympathetically.

It may have been the words, it may have been the tone, it may have been that she touched some hidden thought, for suddenly, without premonition, his breast heaved, and he sobbed heavily, as only a man can sob, without a tear.

She started back in pain. That emotion could so unstring Louis Arnold was a revelation. It did not last long, and as he rose from his chair he spoke in his accustomed, quiet tone.

"Forgive my unmanliness," he said. "It was kind of you to come to me."

"You look very ill, Louis. Can't I bring you something to eat or drink—or will you lie down? You so need rest."

"We shall see. Is there anything you would like to ask me?"

"Nothing."

After a pause, he said:

"You must not be hopeless; he is in good hands, and every-thing that can be done will be done. Is he resting now?"

"Yes; if to breathe like that is to rest. Oh, Louis, when I think how for months he has suffered alone, it almost drives me crazy."

"Why think of it, then? Or, if you must, remember that in his surpassing unselfishness he saved you much anxiety; for you could not have helped him."

"Not with our sympathy?"

"Not him, Ruth; to know that you suffered for him was—would have been his crowning sorrow. Is there anything I can do now?"

"No, only think of yourself for a moment; perhaps you can rest a little—you need it, dear."

A flame of color burned in his cheek at the unusual endearment.

"I'll bring you a cup of tea presently," she said as she left him.

The morning passed into afternoon. Silence hung upon the house. A card had been pinned under the door-bell, and the many friends who, in the short time since the sick man's arrival, had heard of his illness, dropped in quietly, and left as they came.

Kemp came in after luncheon. Mr. Levice was sleeping—in all truth, one could not say easily, but the doctor counted much from the rest. He expected Dr. Harvey for a consultation. This he had done upon his own initiative, as a voucher, and a com-forting assurance to Mrs. Levice that nothing would be left un-done. Dr. Harvey came in blandly; he went out gravely. There was little to be said.

Kemp walked thoughtfully upstairs after his colleague had left, and went straight to Arnold's room. The freedom of the house was his; he had established himself as one of the family without explanation or ado.

"Mr. Arnold," he said to the Frenchman, who quickly rose from his desk, "I want you to prepare your aunt and cousin for the worst. You know that; but if he should have a spell of cough-ing, the end might be sudden."

A cold pallor overspread Louis's face at the confirmation of his unquestioning fears.

He bowed slightly and cleared his throat before answering. "There will be no necessity," he said; "my uncle intends doing so himself."

"He mustn't hasten it by excitement," said Kemp, moving toward the door.

"That is unavoidable," returned Arnold. "You must know he had an object in hurrying home."

"I did not know; but we must try to prevent any unnecessary effort to speak. You can do that, I think."

"I cannot."

"You know that he has something important to say?"

"I do."

"Then for his sake—"

"And for the others, he must be allowed to speak."

Kemp regarded him steadily, wondering wherein lay the impression of concealed power which emanated from this delicate-visaged man. He left the room without further parley.

"Dr. Harvey must have gone to school with you," panted Levice, as Kemp entered; "even his eyes have been educated to express the same secrecy—except for a little—"

"There, there," quieted Kemp; "don't exhaust yourself. Miss Levice, that fan, please. A little higher? How's that?"

"Don't go, doctor," said Levice, feebly. "I have something to say, to do, and you—I want you—give me something—I must say it now. Esther, where are you?"

"Here, love."

"Mr. Levice, you must not talk now," put in Kemp, authoritatively. "Whatever you have to say will last till morning."

"And I?"

"And you. Now try to go to sleep."

Mrs. Levice followed him to the door.

"You spoke just now of a nurse," she said through pale lips; "I won't need one: I alone can nurse him."

"There is much required; I doubt if you are strong enough."

"I am strong."

He clasped her hand close. "I know. But it will be best—while I'm away. I'll come in and stay with you tonight," he said simply.

"You! Why should you?"

"Because I too love him."

Her mouth trembled and the lines of her face quivered, but she drew her hand quickly over it.

Kemp gave one sharp glance over to the bed. Ruth had laid her head beside her father's and held his hand. In such a house, in most Jewish houses, nursing is of a calling that needs little training.

CHAPTER XXV

SHAFTS OF pale sunlight darted into the room and rested on Mr. Levice's hair, covering it with a silver glory. They trailed along the silken coverlet, but stopped there, one little beam straying slowly, and almost as if with intention, toward Arnold, seated near the foot of the bed. Ruth, lovely in her pallor, sat near him; Mrs. Levice, on the farther side of the bed, leaned back in her chair placed close to her husband's pillow. More remote, though inadvertently so, sat Dr. Kemp. It was by Mr. Levice's desire that these four had assembled here.

He was sitting up, supported by many pillows; his face shone hollow and colorless; his hands lay listlessly upon the counterpane. No one touched him; bathed in sunlight, as he was, the others seemed in shadow. When he spoke his voice was almost a whisper, but it was distinctly audible to the four intent listeners; only the clock seemed to accompany his staccato speech, running a race, as it were, with his failing strength.

"It's a beautiful world," he said dreamily, "a very beautiful world." The sunbeams kissed his pale hands as if thanking him. No one stirred—who were they to arrest his climbing soul? Finally he realized that all were waiting for him, and thought sprang, strong and powerful, to his face.

"Dr. Kemp," he began very laboredly, but clearly, "I have something to say to you—to you in particular, and to my daughter Ruth. My wife and nephew know, in brief, what I have to say; therefore I need not dwell on the painful event that happened here last September. You will pardon me, when you see the necessity, for my reverting to it at all."

Everyone's eyes rested upon him—that is, all but Arnold's, which seemed holding some secret communion with the cupids on the ceiling—and the look of convulsive agony sweeping across Ruth's face was unnoticed.

"In all my long, diversified life," he went on, "I had never suffered as I did after she told me her decision—for in all those years no one had ever been made to suffer through me; that is, so far as I knew. Unconsciously, or in anger, I may have hurt many, but never, as in this case, with knowledge aforethought— when the blow fell upon my own child. You will understand, and perhaps forgive, when I say I gave no thought to you. She came to me with her sweet, renunciating hands held out, and with a smile of self-forgetfulness, said, 'Father, you are right; I could not be happy with this man.' At the moment I believed her, thinking she had adopted my views; but, with all her bravery, her real feelings conquered her, and I saw. Not that she had spoken untruly, but she had implied the truth only in part. I knew my child loved me, and she meant honestly that my pain would rob her of perfect happiness with you—my pain would form an eclipse strong enough to darken every joy. Do you think this knowledge made me glad or proud? Do you know how love, that, in withholding, justifies itself, suffers from the pain inflicted? But I said, 'After all, it is as I think; she will thank me for it some day.' I was not altogether selfish, please remember. Then, when I saw her silent wrestling, came distrust of myself; I remembered I was pitted against two, younger and no more fallible than myself. As soon as doubt of myself attacked me, I strove to look on the other side. I strove to rid myself of the old prejudices, the old superstitions, the old narrowness of traditions. It was useless—I was too old, and my prejudices had become part of me. It was in this state of perturbation that I had gone one day up to the top floor of the Palace Hotel. Thank you, doctor."

The latter had quietly risen and administered a stimulant. As he resumed his seat, Levice continued:

"I was seated at a window overlooking Market Street. Below me surged a black mass of crowding, jostling, hurrying beings, so far removed they seemed like little dots, each as large and no larger than his fellows. Above them stretched the same blue arch

of heaven, they breathed the same air, trod in each other's footsteps; and yet I knew they were all so different—ignorance
walked with enlightenment, vice with virtue, rich with poor, low
with high. But I felt, poised thus above them, that they were all
merely—humans. Go once thus, and you will understand the
feeling. And so I judged these alien brothers. Which was greater;
which was less? This one, who from birth and inheritance is able
to stand the equal of anyone, or this one, who through birth and
inheritance blinks equally blindly at the good and the beautiful?
Character and circumstance are not altogether of our own making. They are, to a great degree, results of inherited tendencies
over which we have no control—accidents of birth, in the choosing of which we had no voice. The high in the world do not
always shine by their own light, nor do the lowly always grovel
through their own debasement. I felt the *excuse* for humanity. I
was overwhelmed with one idea: only Infinity can weigh such
circumstantial evidence. We, in our little biased knowledge of
time and place, pronounce sentence, but final judgment is reserved for a higher court, that sees the cross-purposes in which
we all are blindly caught. We shall never know that final judgment, but glimpsing it, here a little, there a little, shall we, as
men and women, not strive toward it?

"Below me prayed Christian and Jew, Mohammedan and Bud-
dhist, pagan and atheist. Why was man thus separated from man?
Because he was born so, because he was bred so, because his
parents were so—because, in nine cases out of ten, it seemed
natural and convenient to remain so. The tenth case? Ah, we
shall speak of that—but, for all the others, chance and environment and custom had given them their religion.

"Race? We know that, in the case of the Jew, a peculiar adapt-
ability to environment has, with the progress of the generations,
obliterated all differences except one—the historical. And shall
that—in all its ugliness—endure forever?

"Because, nearly two thousand years ago—according to the
gospels—Jesus Christ, a Jew himself, attacked the threatening
weaknesses of his own people: their fall from the loftiest spirituality down to the blind materialism of the day—the Jews, then

powerful, first reviled, then feared, then slew him. Because, then, the Jew could not honestly say, 'I believe this man to be God—or the son of God,' according to their meaning of the term God—because they, emerging from their ghettoes—ghettoes of preservation as well as of deprivation—continue to say, 'I need no intermediary between my God and myself,' are they so widely different from other men that they need be dragged in the dust? Not so. Shall we Jews never forgive—shall you non-Jews never forget? Will prejudice and hate be forever?—will the mind of man remain closed forever upon this question?—But God forgives, and God forgets. For what is God? Justice is God—'it comes with lame foot, but it comes!'—and Light is God—and Light travels from man to man, and shall penetrate even into the darkest pale—I know not how—insidiously perhaps—through some great cataclysm perhaps, but it will penetrate! For Love is God, and the Voice of Love is never wholly hushed—and everything that is beautiful and good is God—and so God's in the world—And so, I hope!"

The visionary looked beyond them; almost in his frail casement, he seemed to have slipped beyond them, his voice a thin spirit of sound. They leaned closer to hear.

"All this passed vaguely through me up there upon my worldly height. But only when I came down upon the street did it take form. A little raggedy child touched me, and as I laid my hand upon her curly head, the beam fell from my eyes—the eyes of my humanity—and I knew anew, as Abraham of old knew anew, that there is one God for all humans—though 'man has sought out many inventions.'

"But it was not until I went to New York that the emotions I had so deeply experienced took on practical shape. There, removed from my old haunts and associates, I wandered alone where I would. Then I thought of you, my friend, of you, my child—I had always, subconsciously, been thinking of you! And beside you I was pitiful—pitiful, because, in my narrowness, I had thought it right to uphold an outworn restriction. I resolved to be practical; I have been accused of being a dreamer. I grasped your two images before me and drew parallels: Socially—in my opinion society is a mutual drawing together of resemblances—socially, each was as fair as the other. Mentally, the woman was of the same stratum as the man. Physically, both were perfect types of pure, healthy blood. Morally, both were irreproachable. Religiously, both held a broad, abiding love for man and God. I stood convicted. I was in the position of a blind reactionary who, with a beautiful picture before him, fastens his critical, condemning gaze upon a rusting nail in the wall behind—a nail even now loosened, and which, some day, please God, shall fall. Yet what was I to do? Come back and tell you that I had been needlessly cruel? What would that avail? True, I might make you believe that I no longer thought marriage between you wrong. But that would not remove the fact that the world which has so powerful a voice in our happiness or unhappiness, does not yet see as I see—that, because of the rest of the world, marriage between you two must still be a grave experiment.

"In this vortex I was stricken ill. All the while I wanted to hurry to you, to tell you how it was with me, and it seemed as though I would never be able to get to you. 'Is this Nemesis,' I thought, 'or divine interposition?' So I struggled, till Louis came. Then all was easier. I told him everything and said, 'Louis, what shall I do?' 'Only this,' he answered simply: 'tell them that their happy marriage will be your happiness, and the rest of the world will be as nothing to these two who love each other.' "

The old man paused; the little sunbeam had reached the end of the coverlet and gave a leap upon Louis's shoulder as if with intent, but his gaze remained fixed upon the cupids on the ceiling. Ruth had covered her face with her hands. Mrs. Levice was softly weeping, her eyes on Louis. Dr. Kemp had risen and stood, tall and pale, meeting Levice's eyes.

"I believe, and my wife believes," said Levice, heavily, as if the words were so many burdens, "that our child will be happy only as your wife, and that nothing should stand in the way of the consummation of this happiness. Dr. Kemp, you have assured me you still love my daughter. Ruth!"

She sprang to her feet, looking only at her father.

"My little one," he faltered, "I have been very cruel—in my ignorance."

"Never, never, father," she whispered.

"Yes," he said, and took her hand in his. "Kemp, your hand, please."

He grasped his hand and drew the two together, and as Kemp's strong hand closed firmly over her slender one, Levice stooped his head, kissed them thus clasped, and laid his hand upon them.

"There is one thing more," he said. "At the utmost I have but a few days to live. I shall not see your happiness: I shall not see you, my Ruth, as I have often pictured you. Ah, well, darling, a father may be permitted sweet dreams of his only child. You have always been a good girl, and now I am going to ask you to do one thing more—you also, doctor. Will you be married now, this day, here, so that I may yet bless your new life? Will you let me see this? And listen: will you let the world know that you were married with my sanction, and did not have to wait till the old man was dead? Will you do this for me, my dear ones?"

"Will you, Ruth?" asked Kemp, softly, his fingers pressing hers gently.

Ruth stifled a sob as she met her father's eager eyes.

"I will," she answered so low that only the intense silence in the room made it audible.

Levice separated their hands and held one on each of his cheeks.

"Always doing things for her ugly old father," he murmured; "this time giving up a pretty wedding-day that all girls so love!"

"Oh, hush, my darling."

"You will have no guests—unless, doctor, there is someone you would like to have."

"I think not," he decided, noting professionally the pale, weary face. "We will have it all as quiet as possible. You must rest now, and leave everything to me. Would you prefer Dr. Stephens—or a Justice?"

"Either. Dr. Stephens is a good man, whom I know, however,

and one good man with the legal right is as good as another to marry you."

There was little more said then. Kemp turned to Mrs. Levice and raised her hand to his lips. Arnold confronted him with a pale, smiling face; the two men wrung each other's hands, passing out together immediately after.

CHAPTER XXVI

ERBERT KEMP and Dr. Stephens stood quietly talking to Mr. Levice. The latter seemed weaker since his exertion of the morning, and his head lay back among the pillows as if the support were necessary. Still, his eager eyes were keenly fastened upon the close-lipped mouth and broad, speaking brow of the minister who spoke so quietly and pleasantly. Kemp, pale and handsome, answered fitfully when appealed to, and kept an expectant eye upon the door. When Ruth entered, he went forward to meet her, his hand closing over hers. They had had no word together, no meeting of any kind but right here in the morning, and now, as she walked toward the bed, the gentle smile that came as far as her eyes was all for her father. Thought could hold no rival for him that day.

"This is Miss Levice, Dr. Stephens," said Kemp, presenting them. A swift look of wonderment passed under the reverend gentleman's beetle-brows as he bent over her hand. Could this tall, beautiful girl be the daughter of little Jules Levice? Where did she get that regal bearing, that mobile and expressive mouth? The explanation was sufficient when Mrs. Levice entered.

They stood talking, not much, but in that wandering, obligatory way that precedes any undertaking. They were waiting for Arnold; he came in presently with a bunch of pale heliotropes. He always looked well and in character when dressed for some social event; it was as if he were made for this style of dress, not the style for him. The delicate pink of his cheeks was more like the damask skin of a young girl than ever; his eyes, however, behind their glasses, looked old. As he handed Ruth the flowers, he said—

"I asked the doctor to allow me to give you these. Will you hold them—with my love?"

"They are both very dear to me," she replied, raising the flowers to her lips.

Their fragrance filled the room while the simple ceremony was being performed. It was a striking picture, and one not likely to be forgotten. Levice's eyes filled with proud, pardonable tears as he looked upon his daughter—for never had she looked as today in her simple white gown, her face like a magnolia bud, sadly dreamy. Standing next to Kemp, they made a striking-looking couple. Even Arnold, with his heart like a crushed ball of lead, acknowledged it in bitter resignation. For him the scene was one of those silent, purgatorial moments that are approached with senses steeled and thought held in a vice. To the others it passed as if it were happening in a dream. Even when Kemp stooped and pressed his lips for the first time upon his wife's, the real significance of what had taken place was far away to Ruth; the present held but one thing in prominence—the shadowy face upon the pillow. She felt her mother's arms around her; she knew that Louis had raised her hand to his lips, that she had drawn his head down and kissed him, that Kemp was standing silently beside her, that the minister had spoken some gravely pleasant words; but all the while she wanted to tear herself away from it all and fold that eager, loving, dying face close to hers. She was allowed to do so finally; and when she was drawn into the weak, outstretched arms, there was only the long silence of love.

Kemp had left the room with Dr. Stephens, having a further favor to intrust to him. The short announcement of this marriage, which Dr. Stephens gave for insertion in the evening papers, created a world of comment.

When Kemp reentered, Levice called him to him, holding out his hand. The doctor grasped it in the firm clasp which was always a tonic.

"Will you kneel?" asked Levice; Kemp knelt beside his wife, and the old father falteringly spoke the beautiful words that held a double solemnity now:

" 'The Lord—bless thee—and keep thee.

" 'The Lord—make his face to shine upon thee—and be gracious unto thee.

" 'The Lord lift up his countenance—upon thee—and give thee peace—and—give—thee—peace—' "

The words trailed off into space, holding them in echoing benediction.

In the sweet echoes of it they arose and stood silent beside him, while Ruth, with full eyes, laid her hand in his.

"I think, dear," he murmured smiling wistfully up at her, "I'll close my eyes now. I am—very—tired."

She moved to draw down the shades.

"Don't close out all the sun," the faint voice said. "I love it—it's an old friend—. After all, I don't think I'll sleep. Let me lie here and look at you all awhile. Louis, my boy, must you go?"

"Oh, no," he replied, and, turning from the door, went back to his chair.

"Thank you; and now don't think of me. Go on talking—it will be a foretaste of something—better—to lie here and listen. Esther, are you cold? I felt a shudder go through your hand, love. Ruth, give your mother a shawl—don't forget that—sometimes—someone should see that your mother is not—cold. Just talk, will you?"

So they talked—that is, the men did. Their grave, deep voices and the heavy breathing of the invalid were the only sounds in the room. Finally, as the twilight stole in, it was quite still. Levice had dropped into a sort of stupor. Kemp arose then.

"I'll be back presently," he said, addressing Mrs. Levice, who started sharply as he spoke. "I have some few directions to give to my man that I entirely forgot."

"Couldn't we send someone? You mustn't stay away now."

"I'll return immediately. Mr. Levice doesn't need me while he sleeps, and the instructions are important. Don't stir, Arnold; I know my way out."

Nevertheless Arnold accompanied him to the door. Ruth gave little heed to their movements. Her agitated heart had grasped the fact that the lines upon her father's face had grown weaker and paler, his breathing shorter and more rasping; when she passed him and touched his hand, it seemed cold and lifeless.

At nine the doctor came in again—the only appreciable dif- ference in his going or coming being that no one rose or made any formal remarks. He went up to the bed and placed his hand on the sleeping head. Mrs. Levice moved her chair slightly as he seated himself on the edge of the bed and took Levice's hand. Ruth, watching him with wide, distended eyes, thought he would never drop it. Her senses, sharpened by suffering, read every change on his face. As he withdrew his hand, she gave one long, involuntary moan. He turned quickly to her.

"What is it?" he asked, his grave eyes scanning her anxiously.

"Nothing," she responded. It was the first word she had spo- ken to him since the afternoon ceremony. He turned back to Levice, lowering his ear to his chest. After a faint, almost imper- ceptible pause he rose.

"I think you had all better lie down," he said softly. "I will sit with him, and you all need rest."

"I couldn't rest," said Mrs. Levice; "this chair is all I need."

"If you would lie on the couch here," he urged, "you would find the position easier."

"No, no! I couldn't."

He looked at Ruth.

"I'll go by and by," she answered.

Arnold had long since gone out.

Ruth's "by and by" stretched on interminably. Kemp took up the *Argonaut* which lay folded on the table. He did not read much, his eyes straying from the printed page before him to the "finis" slowly writing itself upon Jules Levice's face, and thence to Ruth's pale profile. She was crying—so quietly, however, that, but for the visible tears, an onlooker might not have known it; she herself did not—her heart was silently overflowing.

Toward morning Levice suddenly sprang up in bed and made as if to leap upon the floor. Kemp's quick, strong hand held him back.

"Where are you going?" he asked. Mrs. Levice stood instantly beside him.

"Oh," gasped Levice, his eyes falling upon her, "I wanted to get home—but it's all right now. Is the child in bed, Esther?"

"Here she is. Lie still, Jules; you are ill."

"But not now. Ah, Kemp, I can get up now; I am quite well, you know."

"Wait till morning," he resisted, humoring the familiar symptom.

"But it's morning now, and I feel so light and well. Let in the light, Ruth. See, Esther—a beautiful day!"

It was quite dark with the darkness that immediately precedes dawn; the windows were bespangled with the distillations of the night, which gleamed as the light fell on them.

Mrs. Levice seated herself beside him.

"It is very early, Jules," she said, smiling with hope, not knowing that this deceptive flash was but the rose-flush of the sinking sun, "but if you feel well, when day breaks, you can get up. Can't he, doctor?"

"Yes."

Levice lay back with closed eyes for some minutes. A quivering smile crossed his face and his eyes opened. "Were you singing that song just now, Ruth, my angel?"

"What song, father dear?"

"That—Adieu—adieu—pays—amours—we sang it—you know—when we left home together—my mother said—I was too small—too small—and—too—"

Ruth looked around wildly for Kemp. He had left the room; she must go for him. As she came into the hall, she saw him and Louis hurriedly advancing up the corridor. Seeing her, they reached her side in a breath.

"Go," she whispered through pale lips. "He can't breathe—he can't—"

Kemp laid his hand upon her shoulder.

"Stay here a second. It will be quite peaceful."

She looked at him in agony, and walked blindly in after Louis.

He was lying as they had left him, with Mrs. Levice's hand in his.

"Keep tight hold, darling," the rattling voice was saying.

"Don't take it off till—another takes it—it will—not be hard then." Suddenly he saw Louis standing pale and straight at the foot of the bed.

"My good boy," he faltered, "my good boy, God will bless—" His eyes closed again; paler and paler grew his face.

"Father!" cried Ruth in agony.

He looked toward her, smiling.

"The sweetest word," he murmured, "it was—my glory."

Silence. A soul is passing, a simple, loving soul, giving no trouble in its passage—dropping the toils, expanding into spirit. Not utterly gone: immortality is assured us in the hearts that have touched ours—in the heaven of beautiful memories.

Silence. A shadow falls, and Jules Levice's work is done. And the first sunbeams crept about him, lay at his feet a moment, touched the quiet hands, fell on the head in benediction, and rested there.

CHAPTER XXVII

Rose delano seated herself opposite her friend in the library the Thursday evening after the funeral. They looked so different in the waning light—Ruth in soft black, her white face shining like a lily above her somber gown, Rose, like a bright fire-fly, perched on a cricket, her cheeks rosy, her eyes sparkling from walking against the sharp, cold wind. "I thought you would be quiet at this hour," she said.

"We are always quiet now," Ruth answered softly. "Friends come and go, but we are very quiet. It does me good to see you, Rosebud."

"Does it?" her sweet eyes smiled happily. "I was longing to drop in if only to hold your hand for a minute, but I didn't know exactly where to find you."

"Why, where could I be but here?"

"I thought possibly you had gone to your husband's home."

For a second Ruth looked at her wonderingly; then the slow rich color mounted, inch by inch, back to her little ears till her face was one rosy, bewildered cloud.

"No; I've stayed right on."

"I saw the doctor today," Rose chatted. "He looks pale. Is he too busy?"

"I don't know—that is, I suppose so. How are the lessons, Rose?"

"Everything is improving wonderfully. I am so happy, dear Mrs. Kemp, and what I longed to say was that every happiness and every blessing would, I pray, fall on you two who have been so much to me. Miss Gwynne told me that to do good was your birthright. She said that the funeral, with its vast gathering of friends, rich, poor, old, young, strong, and crippled, of all grades of society, was a revelation of his life—even to those who thought they knew him best. You should feel very proud."

"Yes," assented Ruth, her eyes quickly suffused with tears.

They sat quietly thus for some time, till Rose, rising from her cricket, kissed her friend silently and went away.

The waning light fell softly through the lace curtains, printing quaint arabesques on the walls and furniture and bathing the room in a rich yellow light. A carriage rolled up in front of the house. Dr. Kemp handed the reins to his man and alighted. He walked slowly up to the door. It was very still about the house in the evening twilight. He pushed his hat back on his head and looked up at the clear blue sky, as if the keen breeze were pleasant to his temples. Then with a quick motion, as though overruling a hesitation, he turned and rang the bell. The latchkey of the householder was not his.

Ruth, sitting in the shadows, had scarcely heard the ring. She was absorbed in a new train of thought. Rose Delano was the first one who had clearly recalled to her the fact that she was really married. She had been very quiet with her other friends, and everyone, looking at her grief-stricken face, had shrunk from mentioning what would have called for congratulations. Rose, who knew only these two, naturally dwelt on their changed relations.—Her husband! Her dormant love gave an exultant bound. Wave upon wave of emotion beat upon her heart; she sprang to her feet—the door opened, and he came in. He saw her standing faintly outlined in the dark.

"Good-evening," he said, coming slowly toward her with extended hand. He felt her fingers tremble in his close clasp, and let them fall slowly. "Bob sent you these early violets. Shall I light the gas?"

"If you will."

He turned from her and rapidly filled the room with light.

"Where is your mother?" he asked, turning toward her again. Her face was hidden in the violets.

"Upstairs with Louis. They had something to arrange. Would you like to see her?" Judging from her manner, he might have been any chance visitor.

"No," he replied. "If you will sit down, we can talk quietly till they come in."

As she resumed her high-backed chair and he seated himself in another before her, he was instantly struck by some new change in her face. The far-away, impersonal look with which she had met him in these sad days had been what he had expected, and he had curbed with a strong will every impulse for any closer recognition. But this new look—what did it mean? In the effort to appear unconcerned the quick color had risen to his own cheeks.

"I had quite a pleasant little encounter today," he observed. "Shall I tell it to you?"

"If it won't tire you."

Keeping his eyes fixed on the picture over her head, he did not see the look of anxious love flooding into her eyes as they swept over him.

"Oh, no," he responded, slightly smiling over the recollection. "I was coming down my office steps this afternoon, and had just reached the foot, when a bright-faced, bright-haired boy stood before me with an eager light in his eyes. 'Aren't you Dr. Kemp?' he asked breathlessly, like one who had been running. I recollected him the instant he raised his hat from his nimbus of golden hair. 'Yes; and you are Will Tyrrell,' I answered promptly. 'Why, how did you remember?' he asked in surprise. 'You only saw me once.' 'Never mind; I remember that night,' I assured him. 'How is that baby sister of yours?' 'Oh, she's all right,' he replied, dismissing the subject with the royalty brotherhood confers. 'I say, do you ever see Miss Levice nowadays?' I looked at him with a half-smile, not knowing whether to set him right or not, when he finally blurted out, 'She's the finest girl I ever met. Do you know her well, doctor?' 'Well,' I answered, 'I know her slightly—she's my wife.' "

He told the little incident brightly, but as he came to the end, his voice gradually lowered, and as he pronounced the last word, his eyes sought hers. Her eyelids fluttered; her breath seemed suspended.

"I said—you were my wife," he repeated softly, leaning forward, his hands grasping the chair-arms.

"And what," asked Ruth, an excited little ring in her voice—"what did Will say?"

"Who cares?" he asked unsteadily. "Ruth, have you completely forgotten what we are to each other?"

She arose, moving with beautiful swiftness to him as he stood up with outheld arms. "No, I haven't forgotten," she said simply, laying her hands upon his shoulders, but holding him from her while her eyes gazed gravely into his. "We are everything to each other. We are—all the world to each other. We are—the past, present, and future to each other—we are husband and wife."

Reverently he drew her to him in all her loveliness.

A little later Mrs. Levice and Arnold came in. Mrs. Levice, entering first, stood still, and Arnold, following, saw too, and the sight drained every drop of blood from his face. For a moment they were unseen, but when Ruth, the first to feel their presence, started from Kemp, Arnold came forward with his accustomed ease.

"We are intruding," he said, smiling.

"Oh, no," laughed Ruth, absently watching Kemp draw her mother into a comfortable chair. "We were only—we were thinking, mother dear, that it will do you good to come out of this great house to our little one—till we find something more suited to our needs—that is, if Louis can spare you."

Sorrow had laid its quieting hand upon Mrs. Levice, ageing her, perhaps, but touching her with a twilight beauty. Yearning for a lost love, wistfully she sought to find it by giving love to others. Now she looked across to Louis, who stood beside a table, turning the pages of a book.

"It is very sweet to be wanted by you all now," she said, her voice trembling slightly. "But I never could leave this house to strangers—every room is too full of associations, too full of his presence. At least, not yet, my dear ones. Presently—in a few weeks, I am going for a short trip south, with Louis. That's settled, isn't it, Louis?"

He looked up then.

"Yes," he said, smiling quietly into Ruth's questing eyes. "We have settled that. You don't need her—now. And I do."

And so the future took them.

THE END

NOTES

88. **heliotrope**   Wolf's use of flowers throughout the novel reflects the popular associations reflected by "the language of flowers." Heliotrope was commonly associated with "faithfulness" and "devotion" as noted in Nugent Robinson's *Collier's Cyclopedia of Commercial and Social Information and Treasury of Useful and Entertaining Knowledge* (1882).

102. **Maréchal Niel**   A rose meaning "yours, heart and soul," as noted in *Collier's Cyclopedia.* Also, refers to an alternative title to Childe Hassam's 1893 painting, "The Sonata." The on-line site, "The Nelson-Atkins Museum of Art Collections—American Art before 1945" at <http://www.nelson.atkins.org/collections/american/detail/sonata.htm>, suggests that

> the meaning of the painting depends on the relationship between the woman, her music and the rose in a bowl on the piano. The figure of a woman in white was often used by 19th-century painters to symbolize such qualities as innocence, purity, and the nobility of art. One of Hassam's alternate titles . . . [is] "The Maréchal Niel Rose," [which] identifies the specific flower that is portrayed—a kind of climbing rose with a stem too weak to support its large bloom.

103. **Fruit and Flower Mission**   The on-line site, "Museum of the City of San Francisco" at <http://www.sfmuseum.org/

hist10/equality.html>, re-presents an 1891 essay, "Snap Shots," from the *San Francisco News Letter and California Advertiser* (31 October 1891) by Di Vernon who was "a member of a social organization called the 'Flower Mission,' with a goal to uplift the spirits of San Francisco working women." Vernon's description of the activities of the "Fruit and Flower Mission" suggests that the efforts of women of leisure to beautify the workplace and lift the spirits of the factory women by bringing bouquets of flowers and baskets of fruit to the factories was viewed with skepticism by the workers.

111. **Baldwin Theater**   The Baldwin Theater, designed by J. A. Remer, was part of the magnificent Baldwin's Hotel and Theatre at Market and Powell Streets, owned by "Lucky" Baldwin, "who had won his name on the race-track. With a certain 1880 elegance of crimson plush and gilded trimmings, the Baldwin had an attractive, intimate warmth. The dress circle was raised about the orchestra circle, and in its long first row people 'dressed' as they did in the boxes, which gave brightness to the house" (Amelia Fansome Neville, *The Fantastic City*. Cambridge: 1932), on-line at "San Francisco History" <http://www.zpub.com/sf20/sf/hbtfc8.htm>.

111. **Booth**   Refers to Edwin Booth. Amelia Fansome Neville explains that "Edwin Booth played his last San Francisco engagement at the Baldwin, and I found his Hamlet as thrilling as in younger years. The poetry of his acting has a deathless quality. By that time San Francisco recalled that the great actor had once lived in a cottage out on the Mission Dolores Road, back in the eighteen-fifties when he came as a boy to California with his father; and he was welcomed with proprietary affection" (Amelia Fansome Neville, *The Fantastic City*. Cambridge: 1932 on-line at "San Francisco History" <http://www.zpub.com/sf20/sf/hbtfc8.htm>.

125. **cabbage-rose**   Meaning "ambassador of love" in *Collier's Cyclopedia*.

143. **Santa Filomena**   Reference most likely from Henry Wadsworth Longfellow's 1857 poem of that name:

> Whene'er a noble deed is wrought,
> Whene'er is spoken a noble thought,
> Our hearts, in glad surprise,
> To higher levels rise.
> The tidal wave of deeper souls
> Into our inmost being rolls,
> And lifts us unawares
> Out of all meaner cares.
> Honor to those whose deeds
> Thus help us in our daily needs,
> And by their overflow
> Raise us from what is low!
>
> .   .   .   .
>
> A lady with a lamp shall stand
> In the great history of the land,
> A noble type of good,
> Heroic womanhood.
> Nor even shall be wanting here
> The palm, the lily, and the spear,
> The symbols that of yore
> Santa Filomena bore.

The poem was published in *The Atlantic Monthly* I, 1 (November 1857): 22–23; an on-line version can be found at <http://www.theatlantic.com/unbound/poetry/nov1857/filomena.htm)

146. **Recamier**   May refer to the painting by Jacques-Louis David, "Madame Recamier" (1800); see <http://www.artchive.com/artchive/D/david/recamier.jpg.html>.

148. **The Bugle**   Refers to a section of Tennyson's poem, "The Princess," known as "The Bugle Song":

> The splendor falls on castle walls
> And snowy summits old in story;

The long light shakes across the lakes,
And the wild cataract leaps in glory.
Blow, bugle, blow, set the wild echoes flying,
Blow, bugle; answer, echoes, dying, dying, dying.
O, hark, O, hear! how thin and clear,
And thinner, clearer, farther going!
O, sweet and far from cliff and scar
The horns of Elfland faintly blowing!
Blow, let us hear the purple glens replying,
Blow, bugle; answer, echoes, dying, dying, dying.
O love, they die in yon rich sky,
They faint on hill or field or river;
Our echoes roll from soul to soul,
And grow for ever and for ever.
Blow, bugle, blow, set the wild echoes flying,
And answer, echoes, answer, dying, dying, dying.

156. **Yahrzeit**   A special candle lit four times a year in Jewish homes in memory of loved ones who have died: on the first night of Yom Kippur, the eighth night of Sukkot, the second night of Shavuot, and the last night of Passover.

159. **niphetos rose**   A pure white rose introduced in 1843; a white rose means "I am worthy of you" (1885/1892; Greenaway and *Collier's*).

161. **Coronado**   Refers to the Hotel Del Coronado, a lush resort near San Diego, California built in 1888 and owned by Elisha Babcock and H. L. Story, "who dreamed of building a hotel which they envisioned would be 'the talk of the western world'" as described at the on-line site, <http://www.hoteldel.com/history/ history_babcock_story.html>.

161. **Del Monte**   Refers to the Hotel Del Monte in Monterey owned by Charles Crocker.

> [Crocker was] one of the four rail barons who owned Southern Pacific Railroad. Crocker envisioned Monterey as a resort and lost no time in erecting a magnificent Victorian castle . . . [spending] $1 million [and]

building the Hotel Del Monte in a mere 100 days.
When the doors opened in 1880, the hotel was an immediate success. It was built in a park-like setting, and
no expense was spared . . . each room had a telephone,
and the bath was equipped with hot and cold running
water, both rarities in the late 1800s. . . . [T]he hotel
was completely destroyed by fire on March 31,
1887. . . . The following year the Hotel Del Monte was
rebuilt in a Gothic-Victorian architectural style and
was even more sumptuous. It covered 16 acres and
could lodge 700 guests. . . . The hotel grounds boasted
a 15–acre lake, lawn tennis courts, archery ranges, ex-
otic gardens and miles of walking paths. . . . A second
fire in 1924 again destroyed the hotel, and it was rebuilt
in a Spanish-or Mediterranean-style.

Description from the on-line site, "Insiders' Guide to
Monterey Peninsula, 2nd Edition" at <http://www.
insiders.com/monterey/main-history2.htm>.

162. **White Wings**   *White Wings: A Yachting Romance* was a
popular novel written by William Black (New York:
Harper, 1892). In the early 1900s, a musical comedy,
White Wings, book and lyrics by Alexander Stewart, music
by Manlio de Veroli, was performed. An on-line source
attributes a 1912 song, "White Wings," to Banks Winter
and reproduces the lyrics; see <http://www.contemplator.
com/folk2/wwings.html>.

162. **Nancy Lee**   A popular song by this name was written by
German baritone and composer Michael Maybrick (who
published under the name Stephen Adams) with lyrics by
Frederick E. Weatherly most likely in the 1870s. The
lyrics can be found on-line at <http://www.contemplator.
com/folk5/nancylee.html>.

166. **Doré's mystic work**   Refers to Gustav Doré's illustrations
of Dante's *The Divine Comedy*.

177. **stanch**   Archaic spelling of "staunch."

202. **'Behüt' dich Gott! es wär zu schön gewesen'** This German folk song's lyrics are by Josepf Viktor von Scheffel
(1853), and the melody is from Victor Ernst Nessler's
opera, "Trompeter von Saeckingen" (1884). The German lyrics are on-line at <http://ingeb.org/Lieder/
behutdic.html>.

May God Be With You! It Would Have Been Too Good!
In life we find the ugly:
Next to the rose stands its thorns.
And whatever the poor heart might long for,
In the end, we say good-bye.
In your eyes I thought I read
A flash of love and bliss.
May God be with you! It would have been too good!
May God be with you! It was not meant to be!"
Suffering, envy and hatred, I felt them, too.
A storm-tossed, tired wanderer,
I dreamt of peace and silent hours
When the path would lead to you.
In your arms I would heal completely,
And from gratitude, dedicate my young life to you.
May God be with you! It would have been too good!
May God be with you! It was not meant to be!"
Clouds fly by, wind rushes through the leaves,
Sheets of rain fall in woods and fields—
Just the right weather to say good-bye.
As world stands before me, gray as the sky,
It doesn't really matter if things turn out good or bad.
Slender maiden, steadfastly I will think of you.
May God be with you! It would have been too good!
May God be with you! It was not meant to be!"

Transposed from literal translations from the German by
Holger Koch and Robert Monk.

260. **Argonaut** A San Francisco weekly newspaper published
between 25 March 1877 and 1958 by the Argonaut publishing company.